Alfred Lewis Castleman

The Army of the Potomac: Behind the scenes

A diary of unwritten history

Alfred Lewis Castleman

The Army of the Potomac: Behind the scenes
A diary of unwritten history

ISBN/EAN: 9783337197100

Printed in Europe, USA, Canada, Australia, Japan

Cover: Foto ©Andreas Hilbeck / pixelio.de

More available books at **www.hansebooks.com**

THE ARMY OF THE POTOMAC.

BEHIND THE SCENES.

A DIARY OF UNWRITTEN HISTORY;

FROM THE ORGANIZATION OF THE ARMY, BY
GENERAL GEORGE B. McCLELLAN,
TO THE CLOSE OF THE CAMPAIGN IN VIRGINIA, ABOUT THE
FIRST DAY OF JANUARY, 1863.

BY ALFRED L. CASTLEMAN,

Surgeon of the Fifth Regiment of Wisconsin Volunteers.

"Oh that mine enemy would write a Book."

MILWAUKEE:
PUBLISHED BY STRICKLAND & CO.
BOOKSELLERS, STATIONERS, PRINTERS AND BINDERS.
1863.

THE ARMY OF THE POTOMAC—BEHIND THE SCENES.

[From the Milwaukee Sentinel, July 27.]

We have seen and had the chance to peruse the greater portion of the work in sheets, and can speak of it understandingly. In his preface, the author says: "The record having been made for the writer, is, for the most part, confined to a statement of such things as are not written in histories;" and also as will be noticed by the title page, it purports to be a look "behind the scenes." These statements truly indicate its character, and insure its interest to the reader. The current partial history of the war all readers are familiar with, and for a perfect accurate history, of course, the time has not yet come. This work furnishes what the newspapers have never given, and what no history of the war will ever pick up.

It is a dash at all the salient, interesting points of a military life, through the most interesting and eventful period of the history of the Potomac army, written in a style, easy, flowing, and in itself attractive. And, besides its reference to passing events, the opinions of the author, touching the men, McClellan among the chief, who have led and figured prominently in the Potomac army, given evidently without "fear, favor, affection or the hope of reward," are valuable as the candid views of an intelligent observing man, with the data on which to form an opinion.

The book, besides its general interest, has a local interest to all Wisconsin readers, and especially those particularly interested in the 5th Wisconsin. We can most cheerfully recommend it as a book of much more than ordinary interest and value of the present time.

PREFACE.

In offering this journal to the public, my own inclinations and my ideas of expediency are overruled by the wishes of my friends. It is offered, except the introductory chapter, just in the style in which it was written, without correction of even its grammatical errors. The charitable reader will not lose sight of the fact, that it was written, not for the public, but for myself, whilst performing the most arduous duties—in the confusion of camp life—sometimes amidst the depressing scenes of the hospital, sometimes in the tumult of battle, and amid the groans of the dying—much of it on horseback, whilst witnessing the scenes described, but none of it with the slightest idea that it would be subjected to the ordeal of public criticism.

The hyper-critical reader may be disposed to smile sometimes at my quotations, and to exclaim "with just enough of learning to misquote." To this I plead guilty, in advance; and in extenuation offer only the fact, that in every case I quoted just as the author should have written to make his language accord with my feelings.

If a pronoun of the first person, singular number, should seem obtrusive in the pages, bear in mind that the journal was written by it, for it, and that whatever, or whoever else appears in the narrative, does so by sufferance of that perpendicular part of speech.

The record, having been made for the writer, is for the most part confined to a statement of such things as are not written in histories. Histories of the war will be always accessible. This was intended to perpetuate, in the mind of the author, such thoughts and scenes as are not elsewhere written.

With this explanation, but without apology, the book is offered to the public.

CONTENTS.

CHAPTER I.

Introductory.

CHAPTER II.

Regiment Leaves Baltimore for Washington—Sick Left at Baltimore—Fort McHenry—Hospitality Extraordinary.

CHAPTER III.

At Washington—Across Chain Bridge—Capt. Strong's Adventure and Fight with six Rebels—He shoots four of them and escapes—"Paid Off"—Our First Fight—Alone—As it was, and as it is.

CHAPTER IV

Move Camp—Lewinsville—Commodore Ap' Catsby Jones—An Incident—Our Generals—A Review—Arlington—"The Grand Review."

CONTENTS.

CHAPTER V.

CHAPTER VI.

CHAPTER VII.

CHAPTER VIII.

CHAPTER IX.

CHAPTER X.

CHAPTER XI.

CHAPTER XII.

CHAPTER XIII.

CHAPTER XIV

CHAPTER XV

CHAPTER XVI.

CONTENTS.

CHAPTER XVII.

CHAPTER XVIII.

CHAPTER XIX.

APPENDIX.

CHAPTER I

1861, *July* 31.—On the 19th of June, 1861, the 5th Regiment of Wisconsin Vols., being partially organized, went into camp at Madison, Wis.   Here it remained for a time, perfecting its organization, drilling and preparing itself for the hardships, the dangers, and the responsibilities to be encountered in the battle-field, against a people warlike and chivalric ; a people who are taught to regard physical courage, and recklessness of physical danger, as the noblest qualities of the human race, and a people whose chief pride was to win in fight, whether with individuals or in masses; but a people, who, having entrusted their politics to professed politicians, were misled to believe that, by their brothers of the Northern States of this Union, their rights of property were invaded, and their homes were coveted as a prize for distribution amongst the overgrown population of the North.   But to enter into a discussion of the merits of this rebellion, now devastating the most beautiful country known to man, carrying in its march a passover of beggary, of destitution, and of death, is not in accordance with the object of this little book.   It is therefore passed over, that the reader may at once be permitted to enter into a detail of the subjects indicated in our preface.

From the time of the commencement of the rebellion, by

actual war on Fort Sumter, in April of this year, its settlement by rapid and decisive victories over the rebels was subject of merriment, and looked on as matter of course. We were going to war with a people of not half our numbers, without money, without munitions of war, without navy, without anything in fine of those elements which go to make up the *ensemble* of a people powerful in war, and we were entering into the strife as a short interlude to the hum-drum vocations of life. "How could a people thus situated hope to compete with the parent Government, rich in every element which makes a great people?" This was the reasoning. In vain were our people told of the character of the Southerners. In vain were they referred to the results of our own rebellion and successful revolutionary war with England. "Oh!" was the reply, "Steamships were not known in those days, and England had to cross the ocean to fight us." "But Hungary, with its population of only 3,000,000, and without revenue, withstood the whole power of Austria, till the hordes of Russia had to be called in to aid in their subjugation." "But Austria had become a superannuated and feeble people." No reasoning would answer. The subjugation of the revolted States was to be a pastime, and could be nothing but a pastime. Thus went on matters, drilling as an amusement, preparatory to the enjoyment of a war, all the results of which were to be on our side, and obtained without sacrifice or uffering.

*　　*　　*　　*　　*　　*

On the afternoon of the 21st July, 1861, the electric wires brought us the intelligence from Bull Run that our army was whipped, was routed, was scattered in flight. The heart of the whole North received a shock of sadness and of disappointment. Soldiers in camp began to realize that war meant work and danger, and the Regiment of which I was a member at once received orders to be in readiness to march at the earliest possible moment, to hurry to the aid of its companions in arms. It was in sad plight for the exposures of camp life. 'Twas in the heat of summer, when fevers and diarrhœa prevail in their worst forms. The measles had broken out in camp, and one-third of the soldiers were suffering from disease of some kind. Nevertheless, active preparation went on, and on the fourth day after the receipt of the sad news the Regiment was on its way to battle.

On the 27th of July we reached Harrisburg, Pennsylvania, and went into Camp Curtin. For months this had been a rendezvous for regiment after regiment. The grounds had not been cleaned—the weather was intensely hot, without a leaf to intercept the scorching rays of the sun. The stench of the camp was intolerable, and the sickness of the troops rapidly increased.*

On the 29th of July, at night, we received orders to be ready to march at 3 o'clock next morning. Our destination was supposed to be Harper's Ferry, where we were at once to engage the enemy and to " wind up the war." So great was the excitement (these things were all new then) that very few laid down for rest during the night. At 3 A. M., of the 30th, all tents were struck and rolled up ; mess chests were

---

*I made it my business to visit every tent twice a day, to see that they were thoroughly cleaned, and that the sides of the tent were raised so as freely to admit a current of air. But here the air without was so foul as to improve the condition inside but little. I will here say, however, that the Surgeon of a Regiment who does not visit every tent in his encampment at least once a day, to satisfy himself by personal inspection that it is thoroughly cleaned and ventilated, and that at least once a week the tents are all struck, and the sun admitted for several hours to the ground on which they stand, is not deserving of the position which he holds.

packed, and everyone ready for the order to move.   But sunrise came and found us sitting on our packages.   The day wore on, I think the hottest I ever experienced.   The troops remained exposed to the broiling sun till 2 o'clock P. M., when we embarked on open platform cars, without seats, and without covering.   We ran down through the city, crossed the Susquehannah Bridge, halted, and remained sitting or standing in the sun till evening.   The heat of the day, determining the circulation to the skin, had brought out the eruption in many cases of measles, and the poor fellows had to sit and suffer, without a place to lie down, or even a back to lean against.   At dusk we found ourselves again under way; ran down to York, Pa., about forty miles.   It had now commenced raining, and the cars were run out from the depot, and the suffering men who had been all day washed with their own perspiration, were compelled to sit all night in the rain.   Sick or well, 'twas all the same.   None were permitted to leave the open cars and go back into the depot. Towards morning the rain stopped; the wind shifted suddenly to the Northwest, and it was cold as November.   After the long tedious night of suffering, the morning came, and we ran down to Baltimore, arriving there at 8 o'clock on the morning of July 31st.

We had anticipated trouble here.   We disembarked, marched with muskets loaded, and bayonets fixed, from north to south through the entire length of the city, without molestation, except from the scowls of secessionists, and the welcoming hurrahs of friends.*   At the Camden Street depot we remained in the most uncomfortable condition

---

*Only two companies were armed.   They were placed one in front, the other in the rear of the Regiment, and so marched through the city.

which it is possible to conceive till sunset, when we were ordered for the twentieth time during the day to "fall in." We disembarked, marched about two and a half miles, and camped on an elevated ground to the north of, and overlooking a large part of the city and bay. The regiment did not get settled till midnight, and many were so exhausted that they threw themselves on the ground, with their clothes still wet from the previous night's rain. The medical department, however, succeeded by 10 o'clock in getting up tents to protect the sick, and they were made as comfortable as the circumstances would permit.

Here the regiment remained till the 8th of August, without any occurrences worthy of note, except that sickness continued to increase, and the knowledge I gained as to how little *some* military commanders cared for the comfort of their sick men. After we had been here five or six days, the Colonel was positively ignorant of the fact that we had a hospital on the ground, though there were three within fifty feet of his quarters, filled to their utmost capacity with the sick and suffering. I was now receiving but little support in my efforts for their health and comfort.

CHAPTER II.

August, 8th.—"I am monarch of all I survey." Last night, intelligence being received that an attack was expected on Washington ; we were ordered to move there instanter, and at once the regiment was in motion. It got off in the course of the night, leaving me here in charge of about forty men who were too sick to be moved. I am left without provisions or money, except a few pounds of flour with which to feed and care for the sick, and the ten well ones left with me, to aid me and to look up deserters who have been left here. How *am* I to do it ? I find a strong secession element here, and at times it is very bold. The hurrahs for Jeff. Davis are frequent, and all day the children are flaunting secession flags in our faces, and flying secession kites in our camp ground

9*th.*—What a wonderful effect the hardships of camp life, with the troubles and cares which they entail on a surgeon, have had on my health. For many years I have been dyspeptic. Now I can eat what I please, and go without sleep almost entirely, and suffer no inconvenience. Last night, at 11 o'clock, after having ate a piece of hard salt beef for my supper, I "cared for" a pint of rich ice cream, and feel no inconvenience from it to-day. This would kill an ordinary *civil man*. I have to work very hard, but feel it a great comfort to work amongst the sick without suffering from fatigue, as I have been accustomed to.

Having received an order this morning from Gen. Dix to put all my sick into general hospital, and finding them bitterly opposed, I visited Fort McHenry, saw Gen. D., and prevailed on him to rescind the order.

I was highly gratified with what I saw at Fort McHenry. It, being the first equipped fort I ever saw, was an object of much interest; its numerous cannon, large enough for a small soldier to sleep in, pointing in all directions overlooking Baltimore and guarding all the approaches to it. No matter from what direction you come, you find these monster guns looking right in your face. Low down behind the walls lie almost innumerable ugly bull-dog-looking mortars, not over two and a half feet long, loaded with a 20 to 40-pound shells filling them to the very muzzle, and ready to be vomited forth at the first approach of trouble. There, too, is the great Dahlgren, stretching its long black neck away beyond the embrasures, as if looking for an object into which to pour its monster shot and shell, or its shower of grape and cannister. Its howitzers are there, and its great Columbiads, into some of which I was strongly tempted to crawl and take a nap, but a sudden recollection of the history of Jonah reminded me that its stomach, too, might sicken, and that I might awake in a trip across the mighty deep on the wings of the wind. I didn't go in. The bright little brass 6, 8, and 10-pounders, on the greater number of which Napoleon said God always smiled in battles, were conspicuous amongst these great leviathans, and above all, the newly invented rifle cannon, ready to demolish ships or houses at two to five miles distance.

Have lost no man yet from sickness, but I have one who, I fear, will not recover. He is supposed to be poisoned by a glass of lemonade, bought of a man suspected of being a rebel.

I have succeeded, by selling a half barrel of flour, and by the approval of a small requisition made on the commissary, in getting provisions of all kinds to make my little detachment comfortable.

10th.—The poisoned soldier is very sick to-day, but I have hopes of his recovery. In a city where we have received so much kindness and attention as in Baltimore, it is painful to have to suspect anyone of so devilish an act as that of poisoning a man.

11th.—I was sick yesterday. Last night took an opiate. This morning, when I awoke, I turned over and looked upon a dirty tin cup, and a greasy tin plate, sitting on a chair beside my bed. It required quite a rubbing of the eyes to recall my faculties, so as to realize where, and what I was. But at last I awoke fairly to the contrast between what I looked on, and the little waiter with its spotless napkin, its cup of beautiful drab-colored coffee, and its nicely browned toast, presented to me by loving ones who had sometimes watched over my restless slumbers in sickness, and waited at early morn with these delicious antidotes to the prostrating effects of opiates. Had there have been "music in my soul" I should have sung, "Carry me back, oh! carry me back." But I arose, went to work, and am better to-night. I think, however, that it will be some time before I hunger for another meal from a tin cup and tin plate.

Received to-day, from Miss M. H. C., a draft on New York for fifty dollars, to be used for the relief of the sick under my care. This is a bright spot in the darkness around me.

"How far that little candle throws its beams!"
*   *   *   *   *   *

12*th.*—Sixteen of my sick have so far recovered that I sent them to-day to join their regiment at Kalorama Heights, near Washington. I have quite recovered from my attack, which was rubeolous fever. I had been so much mixed up with measles that, notwithstanding I had passed through the disease in childhood, the system in some degree yielded to its contagious influence, and I have had all the symptoms of measles, except the eruption. I have termed this rubeoloid, or rubeolous fever. It is common in camp.

13*th.*—H. S. S. arrived at my hospital to-day, with orders, as I was sick, to take charge of and bring forward all the men left here. From the tenor of our Colonel's letter of instructions to his messenger, I should take him to be a little "miffed" at the men's not being sent forward earlier. What in the name of heaven can he wish to do with sick men in camp? However, I have no discretion, but shall turn over the men to S., and see how he will carry out instructions. I had already sent forward to-day, before his arrival, quite a number, leaving me only ten here.

14*th.*—I left the camp to-day, and have determined to make my headquarters at Barnum's Hotel, for a few days, till I recover some of the strength lost by my sickness and over-exertion. My ward master, on whom I have mainly to rely for assistance as a nurse, has been drunk every night, which has made me much extra trouble. Oh the misery resulting from whisky!

15*th.*—I wish to record, what I have omitted, an acknowledgment to many of the people of Baltimore during our stay here, for such kindness as I never expected to meet with amongst strangers. On the morning of our arrival, at the depot, in this city, I was detained some time in looking after the sick who were brought forward, and in getting them into conveyances to the depot where we were to re-embark. The regiment marched forward and left me, so that I must pass through the city alone. I armed myself well, expecting to be insulted at every corner, and, perhaps, to meet with personal violence. My dress showed me to be a member of the regiment which had just passed. Scarcely a rod did I walk without being accosted with kind greetings and "God-speeds;" scarcely a corner did I pass without being stopped by gentlemen, inviting me to their houses to partake of their hospitality, in the shape of a cup of coffee, a breakfast, a little rest. Ladies, as I passed, would come to the door, or send out their servants to know if they could do anything for the comfort of myself or regiment.

Since I have been left here with the sick of the regiment, their kindness and attention have, if possible, been even more marked. The house which I use for both hospital and head-quarters, is constantly crowded by ladies, gentlemen, children, pressing in to see what they can do for the relief of the sufferers. The tables groan under the delicacies brought in, and citizens beg for permission to take my sick and care for them at their houses. Nor is this done from the novelty of seeing a regiment pass through. There are always from ten to twenty thousand volunteer troops here, and from one to twenty new regiments pass through daily.

I confess to myself that this is a discouraging feature in the war. This is a Southern city, and this is a type of Southern character. They become interested, and their whole heart is wrapped up in the subject. It is a representation of the character of the people against whom we fight, and on this earnestness for what they believe to be right, is based much of their opinion that the Southerner will prove himself so far superior to the Northern man in battle. I fear there is more truth in it than we of the North are willing to admit. Whatever may be the result of the struggle now going on, to the people of Baltimore I shall ever remember that I am under deep obligations for their kindness to me personally, as well as to the sufferers under my care, and for their interest in the cause which I believe to be not only right, but sacred. I leave Baltimore with much regret, and beg its kind citizens to remember that at least one soldier, a recipient of their kindness, will ever treasure in his heart a grateful remembrance of them.

16*th.*—I am still at Barnum's, and having transferred my sick to the charge of Mr. S., I have a little more time to think, and to journalize my thoughts. I have looked around a little to-day, and my observations have almost made me wish I had no country. When every right which freemen hold dear is at stake, to see men calculating the pecuniary cost of preserving them, sickens the heart, and shakes our confidence in human nature. When the poorer classes are laboring day and night, and exposing their lives in the cause of that government on which the rich lean for protection in the possession of their wealth, to see these *loud mouthed* patriotic capitalists cheating them in the very clothes they wear to battle, the soul revolts at the idea of human nature *civilized* into a great mass of money-makers. May we not expect, ere long, that these same *patriots* will be found opposing the war because it will require a tax on the riches which they shall have amassed from it, to defray its expenses? We shall see.

There must be great imbecility too, somewhere, in the management of our affairs. We are 20,000,000 of people fighting against 6,000,000.* We boast that we are united as one man, whilst our enemies are divided. Congress has voted men and money *ad libitum*. We boast of our hundreds of thousands of soldiers in the field, whilst the rebel army is far inferior. Yet Sumter yielded to the superiority of numbers. Pickens dares not venture out of her gates, on account of the hosts surrounding her. At Big Bethel we fought against great odds in numbers. At Martinsburg we were as one to three. At Bull Run the united forces of Beauregard and Johnston bore down on and almost annihilated our *little* force; whilst even in the west we see the brave Lyon sacrificed, and Sigel retreating before superior numbers. And yet we seem insecure even in the defences of our great cities. We are in daily apprehension of an attack on Washington. Baltimore is without an army. St. Louis is in danger, and even Cairo defended by a handful of men compared to the number threatening to attack her. Surely the god of battles cannot have made himself familiar to our leaders.

---

*I assume that the slave population are not of those against whom we fight.

CHAPTER III.

19th.—To-day came from Baltimore and joined my regiment at Meridian Hill, where I find the whole country a vast city of camps.

20th.—Reported to-day (according to requirements of army regulations) to the Medical Director for instructions. I was astonished and shocked to be met by the reply that "your assistant has been here, and reports that you have never been commissioned." How pleasant to be associated in business with *gentlemen.* I had no difficulty in removing the complaint, and think I have lost nothing by the motion.

21st.—I sit down to-night, journal on my knee, to write by the light of a tallow candle, stuck into the mouth of a whisky bottle, (whisky all out), that "I have nothing of importance to note to-day."

22nd.—I do not know but that I have the blues to-day. However that may be, it is sad to contemplate the selfishness of our officers. When I witness the political manœuvreing here, the conducting affairs for political effect at home, I am almost inclined to believe our war a humbug, and our Government a failure.   I must not *talk* this, but I must not forget it.

23*d*.—Colonel ——— to-day complains that I have too much force employed in the hospital, and says that he will cut it down.   The regulations allow ten nurses and two cooks to the regiment, besides Surgeons, and Hospital Steward. All I have, are three nurses and two cooks.   Will he dare to cut that down?   Should he do so I will "try conclusions" as to his authority to do it.   Three nurses, for one hundred sick, and that must be cut down'   Nor is this all.   The Quartermaster, taking his cue from the Colonel, refuses to acknowledge our right to a hospital fund, and I therefore get but few comforts for the sick, except through charity or a fight for it.   It is to be hoped that these officers will, by a little more experience, become better posted in their duties, and that the sick will not then be considered interlopers, or intruders on the comforts of the regiment.   I forgot to say, in the proper place, that we are brigaded, forming a part of Gen. Rufus King's brigade, composed of four regiments.

I have not yet donned the full uniform of my rank, and there is scarcely a day passes that I do not get a reproving hint on the subject from our Colonel.   A few days ago, whilst in Baltimore, he came to me almost railing at certain army officers for appearing in citizens' dress.   "There," said he, "is Major B., Major K., Gen. D., Doct. N. P., all of the regular army, and not one of whom can be distinguished from a private citizen."   "Colonel," I replied, "they probably fear being mistaken for *volunteer* officers.   He did not feel flattered, but dropped the subject.   Since I came here, I think I can tell a man's calibre by his shoulder-straps.   The amount of brain is generally in inverse proportion to the size of his straps.

26th.—I was visited by my Colonel to-day. He introduced the subject of reducing my hospital force. I was extra-polite, and replied that I had not the slightest objection, provided it was done with the understanding that it would shift the responsibility of the care of the sick from my shoulders to those of others. The subject was dropped, and will hardly be renewed. The jealousy existing in the military towards the medical department of the army astounds me. The military commanders claiming that the medical have *no* authority except through them, has driven the medical officers to assume the other extreme, and claim that they are the only officers in the army who are really independent of command. This quarrel is often bitter, and makes not only themselves uncomfortably captious, but subjects the sick and wounded to suffering whilst these settle their unnecessary quarrels.

27th.—On my arrival here, I found our tents pitched on ploughed ground, in a swale. The bottoms of the tents were very damp, and the mud in the streets over shoe-top. I at once set to work to correct this. I had the streets all ditched on either side, the dirt thrown into the middle, and already, instead of the mud and water streets and tents, we have them so firm, smooth and dry that they are swept every day. I hope by this, and by constant care in ventilating the tents, to arrest the rapidly increasing sickness.

Having finished the above note for the day, I have, on the point of retiring, just received an order from Gen. King to be ready to move at a minute's notice. The enemy is probably again threatening Washington. I must prepare.

30th.—It is now between two and three months since our regiment went into camp. We have had nearly three hundred cases of measles, with about as many of diarrhœa, dysentery and fever. Not one quarter of the regiment but has been sick in some way, and yet last night every man who left home with the regiment slept in camp—not one death by sickness or accident, none left behind, not one lost by desertion! May we not challenge the armies of the world for a parallel? We are sleeping on our arms every night, in anticipation of an attack on Washington, and it seems to be the general belief that we shall be attacked here. I am no military man, and my opinion here is of no account to the world, but to me, for whose especial benefit it is written, it is worth as much as would be the opinion of a Napoleon. That opinion is, that we shall have no fight here—that the enemy is out-generaling us by feints to induce us to concentrate our forces here, whilst he makes a strike and overpowers us elsewhere.

September, 1st.—I cannot but feel depressed at what seems to be great imbecility in the management of our military affairs. By whose fault, I know not. Here we are with one hundred and fifty thousand troops, and we can stand on our National Capitol and see the rebels fortifying on Munson's Hill. I wonder if Gen. McClellan does not need a rest to hold his glass steady whilst he looks at them.

We have just received news of Dupont's having got a foothold in North Carolina. This places us in rear of the enemy, and brightens our prospects wonderfully, if our army there will only press their advantage.

2nd.—The following extract from a letter which I have just written to a friend, is the sum and substance of my thoughts, journalized for to-day. "Major ———— will not write his mother whether an attack on Washington is expected. I will tell you what I think : From the dome of the Capitol we can see the rebels throwing up works just beyond Arlington. Every day or two we have picket skirmishing.

On Wednesday night we had, within a short distance of Washington, seven men set as picket guards. The next day I saw one of the seven wounded in the side by a musket ball. The other six were killed. Almost everybody here is looking for an attack, but I do not believe we shall have one. I have no doubt that Beauregard would like to draw *us* out to attack him; that he would then retreat, with the hope of drawing us into his nets as he did at Bull Run. *But he will not attack us here.*

6th.—I introduce the following letter to a friend, as sufficiently explicit as to the occurrences since the last date:

CHAIN BRIDGE, VA., Sept. 6, 1861.

I commence this letter with the reiteration, Poor Virginia! That State, which for forty years has stood as the guiding star of our galaxy of States,—that State, which *alone* could, six months ago, have assumed the position of umpire to the belligerents, and which *only* would have been respected in the assumption—now stands at the very foot of the list. In the commencement of this contest she degraded herself by offering to become the cat's paw for South Carolina, and was still farther degraded by South Carolina rejecting the proposition to become her menial. By her officious subservience, however, she got her paw into the fire, and how dreadfully it is burned only those who are on her soil can form any idea. Everywhere is the destruction going on. Her soil is the battle-field, and, so far as the destruction of property is concerned, it matters but little which party is successful. Armies *must* have room to move and manœuvre, soldiers *will* have the fruits and vegetables which grow around their encampment, and camp life is a poor fertilizer of that moral growth which marks the line of " *meum et tuum.*"

This letter is written on sheets taken from the former residence of Hon. W W Slade, once a member of Congress from Virginia. I rode around with a foraging party. We entered his fine old mansion, and I could not but weep over the sad changes which I could see had taken place within a few hours, Within no living soul was left. The soldiers entered; for a time I stood back, but when I did go in what a sight presented itself! Already the floors were covered knee-deep with books and papers, which it must have required a long life of toil and trouble to amass, fine swinging-mirrors shivered into thousands of pieces—a fit emblem of the condition to which efforts are being made to reduce this glorious government—each piece reflecting miniature images of what the whole had shown, but never again to reflect those pigmy images in one vast whole. In the large and spacious drawing-room stood the ruins of one of those old-fashioned sideboards, around which had grown so much of the reputation of Southern high life and hospitality; its doors, wrenched from their hinges, lay scattered on the floor; large mahogany sofas, with their covers torn off, marble-top tables, stationery, china, stoves and spittoons, were there in one promiscuous heap of ruins. I stepped into the library, hoping to bring away some relic that had been untouched by the soldiers, but I was too late—all here was ruin. In a corner I picked up a few yellow pamphlets, and read "Constitution and By-Laws of the National Democratic Association." Sadly enough I left the house, and seated myself, to rest and think, on the spacious verandah. For a moment I looked on the vast orchards, the beautiful flower garden, the long rows of laden grape vines, the broad acres of corn and clover, and thought, "What a place and what a condition to pass old age in comfort and quiet," and my heart began to lighten. How momentary the lightning, for just then company after company from the different regiments came up; gates were thrown open, fences thrown down, and horses, cattle and mules were destroying all these evidences of prosperity and comfort. And this is but one feature in the great haggard countenance of war which stares at us whenever we look at Virginia's "sacred soil." Alas, poor Virginia! This subject alone would give interest to a whole volume, but I must leave it.

On Tuesday night, at half-past ten o'clock, the "long roll" brought our brigade, of five regiments, to their feet, when we found ourselves under orders to march at once for the Virginia side of the river, where, it was said, a large body of rebels had been collecting just at night. We had had slight skirmishing in that neighborhood for several days, and now the crisis was expected, and our regiment was to have a chance. All was excitement, and in half an hour from the alarm we were ready to start. By the time we arrived here it had commenced raining—we found no enemy—bivouaced for the night, and slept in the rain to the music of the tramp, tramp of infantry, and the rattling, roaring *tear* of artillery wagons over the roughly macademized road which passed by our encampment. Yesterday it rained all day, as if every plug had been pulled out; still we kept on our arms and ready for action—our general and brigade officers dashing about all the time, and warning us to be ready for an attack.

Day before yesterday a scouting party of our brigade went in pursuit of a party of cavalry who had been seen hovering about us. When they came in sight the cavalry took to their heels, leaving to us only three large contrabands, who "tink massa oughten to run away from poor nigga so, heah! heah! They just run and leab us to de mercy of de darn abolishuns, heah! heah!" They report that around Fairfax and Centreville there are sixty or seventy regiments, who are well provisioned, but that there is a great deal of sickness among them, measles being the prevailing disease. We had, when we left Kalarama, about twenty-five in the hospital, whom we left there under the charge of Dr. ———. There are three or four here who have sickened in consequence of exposure to the two days and two night's rain, but they will be out in a day or two. We have not yet lost a man by disease or acci- dent, though I hear that one man yesterday received a musket ball through his cap, but as it did not hit his head it is thought he will recover. The musket was carelessly fired by some soldier in our camp.

A little occurrence to-day has caused quite a stir in our camps, and I deem it worthy to be noted here for my remem- brance. Capt. Strong, of the Second Regiment of Wisconsin Volunteers, was with a small party on picket guard. He strolled away from his company, and suddenly found himself surrounded by six of the rebel pickets. Being out of reach of help from his men, he surrendered himself a prisoner. After a short consultation as to whether they should kill the "d——d Yankee" on the spot, they concluded that they would first take him into camp. They demanded his pistols, which he took from his belt and presented. But at the moment when the rebels were receiving them, they both *went off*, killing two of his captors on the spot. But there were four left, two on foot, two on horse- back. He dashed into a pine thicket, they discharging their pieces after him and immediately giving chase. He struck into a deep hollow or ravine leading down to the Potomac. It was so precipitous that the horsemen could not follow. But when he emerged from it near the river, he found himself confronted by the two horsemen who had ridden around and reached the spot in time to head him off. He had received a shot through his canteen. Immediately on seeing his pursuers he fired again, killing one more of them, and simultaneously he received another shot through his cheek. He continued firing with his revolvers till he had made in all eleven shots. By this time the fourth man had been unhorsed. The footmen did not pursue, and he made his way into camp. This is the story, though some are so uncharitable as to discredit it, notwithstanding one hole through his canteen and another through his cheek.

7th.—On the high land overlooking the Potomac, about six or seven miles above the Navy Yard at Washington, we have, since our arrival here, thrown up a small fort, formed extensive abattis, and made redoubts and fortifications to command the turnpike leading down the river, and the bridge over which any enemy must pass from any direction above here to reach Washington. This looks like business. The earthwork fort is small, but very strong, and its large siege guns, from twelve to eighteen feet long, with their sullen faces watching up and down the road in every direction, give it a most formidable appearance. A brigade (I have not learned what one) has just advanced beyond us to commence another fort, about two miles to the southwest of us. Neither fort has yet been officially named, but the one just finished is called by the soldiers Fort Mott; the one about to be built they will for the present distinguish by the name of Fort Ethan Allen. In this manner we are closing on the enemy by slow approaches, or parallels. Let Dupont and Butler, from North Carolina, advance to meet us, whilst Fremont takes care of the Mississippi, and we shall have an early closing up of the war. Every day's observation more and more satisfies me that the enemy will not fight us here.

9 P. M.—Our fort is completed, and we have just received

orders to cook three days rations, and be ready to move at a moment's notice.

I will here note, once for all, the manner of the soldiers taking care of themselves in a storm, when they have no tents. They all have "rubber blankets." Two forks are set, and a pole laid from one to the other, some four or five feet from the ground. A kind of lean-to roof is made by placing brush or poles against this, one end resting on the ground, the other end resting on the pole. To make this roof water-proof, the rubber blankets are stretched, like tiles on a roof, and no water gets through. In moderate weather the men cuddle together under this, and are reasonably comfortable. In cold weather they make large log fires in front of these "bivouacs," and pass the nights without freezing.

An order was received to-day from the War Department, that in future no labor shall be required of soldiers on the Sabbath, except what is absolutely necessary for our defence.

*   *   *   *   *   *

10th.—Our regiment has received two months pay to-day, and to-night all are boisterously happy. We had been notified to have our muster-rolls ready, and we should be paid off on the first day of this month. The rolls were ready but the pay was not. We had received no pay since we entered Uncle Sam's service. We had had to use all our little private means to buy uniforms and outfit for the war, and there was not money enough in the whole regiment to pay for washing one shirt. We were all in debt, and momentarily expecting orders to march into the deserted parts of Virginia. What were we to do? We could not think of leaving so. Day before yesterday we had intimations from our commanding officers that we should remain a day or two longer where we are, and our troops who heretofore had been constantly impatient to advance, were now overjoyed at the delay, not doubting but that it was to receive our pay, and oh how many dreams of little presents to be sent home before we should be plunged into the wilderness. Perhaps some thought of photographs for sweethearts and wives. But scarcely had the joyous echoes from the rocky hills around us died away, when we were officially informed that there was no money in the treasury. It was a damper. I at once made business to the city; saw the paymaster; through him and my friends got audience of the Secretary of the Treasury; told a story of our penury (and *such* a story). I got the money which the paymaster had failed to procure. To-day we have been paid off, and to-night I ride a high horse in the affections of the regiment. If they do not dismount me before their money is all expended, their constancy will be greater than my knowledge of human nature generally warrants me in expecting. We are all joyous to-night.

11*th.*—Had some skirmishing to-day. Took some prisoners, who state that within twelve miles of us is the center of operations of about one hundred thousand rebels, who are preparing to attack us and march on Washington. This, if true, falsifies all the predictions of this journal, that there is no considerable force of the enemy in front of us, and that we shall have no general engagement here. Nevertheless, my opinion is unchanged.

This morning quite a body of troops, infantry, cavalry and artillery, passed us, on the road going in the direction of where the enemy are supposed to be. By twelve o'clock artillery firing was distinctly heard some four miles in the direction which they took. In the afternoon we were hurriedly called to march to the support of our retreating men.

We met them about two miles this side of where the fight was. They claim to have gained a great victory, but they brought in no prisoners; no guns captured. Why was that. These reports of victories are very unreliable affairs. All kinds of stories are going through the camp, but I shall record none of them till they have assumed a shape worthy to be remembered.

12th.—Part of the truth relating to the story of yesterday's fight has come to light. The fact is, these "great fights," "great victories," "great number of prisoners," "great numbers killed," are the greatest humbugs of the times, and as a specimen I put on record here the stories with the facts of yesterday. At 8 o'clock A. M. a body of soldiers passed up the turnpike. They were followed by batteries of artillery, and a few companies of cavalry. What does all this mean? was asked. And everyone wishing to be wise, an answer was soon manufactured satisfactory "to all concerned." "Four thousand infantry and artillery had passed (Lie No. 1, there were only 2,000), to take a fort about seven miles off." (Lie No. 2, there was no fort near.) About 12 o'clock we began to hear frequent reports of artillery, and by 2 P. M. the firing was brisk, and we could see the smoke of the shells exploding in the air from four to five miles away. About 3 o'clock we got orders to march on double-quick to the support of our troops, who were said to be retreating. (Truth No. 1.) Off we went on a full run, all vieing to see who could get there first. We had gone about a mile, when we were told to push forward, that one of our regiments was surrounded and being cut to pieces. (Lie No. 3.) On we went for another half mile, when "Halt, the rebels are retreating," (lie No. 4,) and in a few minutes, "We must change our position, for the rebels were flanking us." (Lie No. 5.) A few minutes later, our officers ordered us back to camp; we had gained a great victory. (Lie No. 6.)

Now these are the generalities of statements of the "great victory" of yesterday, which are being proclaimed to-day loud-mouthed. Let me put here the particulars, that in future when I hear of our great victories, I may refer to these, and draw some conclusion as to the probability of their truth.

In the morning, about two thousand men from Gen. Smith's division, with a few pieces of artillery, passed up the pike to reconnoitre, in other words to examine the country and to ascertain what they could of the whereabouts of the enemy. They made their reconnoissance and started for camp. When they had marched about a quarter of a mile on their return, the rebels opened fire on them from a masked battery. Our artillery replied quickly and with spirit, our shot and shell mowing down hazels, oak grubs and saplings. These were all the enemy they saw. But above the heavy brush, in which the enemy's batteries were masked, the smoke from their guns could be distinctly seen, and into this brush we fired without knowing the effects of our shot, though it is said that we silenced their battery. After about an hour thus spent our force retired, with the loss of some twenty or thirty men in killed and wounded, without capturing the battery which they had silenced, or without taking time to bring away *even our own killed and wounded!* What a "glorious victory!" So glorious that we must rush back to camp to announce it, leaving the enemy to look after our killed and wounded! A few "such victories would ruin us." Gen. McClellan visited us to-day; made a speech, and promised us the luxury of a fight soon unless the rebels run. The appreciation of his kind promise was manifested by most unmistakable signs of joy.

15th.—I am alone to-night, and tired enough to lie and sleep for twenty-four hours, did not the scenes around call up associations which banish repose, and yet invite it. In the deep, deep woods, in a deep, deeper valley, with a mountain rising high on either side of me, and the semi-roaring babble of a large mountain brook, leaping over stones and precipices just in front of my lonely tent; the night speaks of the wildness of nature, and carries back my imagination to the times when the red man revelled here in the luxury of his mountain hunt. The song of the catydid talks to me of the rural home of my childhood, while the scream of the screech-owl right over my head awakens mingled feelings of aboriginal wildness, and of the ruins of civilization. The night is still, and over the mountain comes the strain of vocal music, with the accompaniment of a martial band, from more than a mile away, where with a regiment of Vermonters our chaplain is holding religious exercises, and "Dundee's sacred strain," mellowed by the distance, is in harmony with all around me. These are my nearest settled neighbors to-night, and so far away that I am outside of all their guards, yet near enough to hear the " Halt ! who comes there ?" of the picket, as he hails the rock, loosened from above, as it comes rushing down the mountain side. The tattoo of the night drums, too, as it comes rumbling over the mountains, and calls the soldier to his hard, but welcomed bed, awakens in the reflecting mind sad stories of the passions of men; of happy homes, deserted; of families, once united, now separated, perhaps forever; of the once freeman, to whom the dungeon now denies all hope of liberty again; of a country, once a unit, which held the world at bay, now an object of the ridicule or pity of nations which but a few short months before trembled at her power; of reflections which, I fear, must convince that "war is the normal condition of man." There were threats of an attack on us yesterday and to-day. My hospital was in an exposed position, and my sick must be moved. At dark I commenced moving to a more secure place; selected this beautiful ravine; got my tents here, but not deeming it best to disturb the sick by moving them in the night, am here alone to take care of my tents and stores. And how beautifully the moon sheds its reflections over this quiet little valley, and brightens, as with myriads of diamonds, the ripplings of the little mountain streams! How deliciously sweet the fresh odor of the clean grass, untainted by the stench of the camp. But hark! I hear at this moment, from Fort Corcoran, "the three guns," a signal of approaching danger, and in another moment the "long roll" may summon us to scenes of trouble. I am still stubborn in the belief that the enemy is only making a feint, and that we shall have no fight here. The long roll does not call me. The "three guns" must have made a false alarm, and so I will retire and "bid the world good-night."

23*d.*—As a description of the appearance of the country in which we were settled, I here introduce a letter written at this date to a friend:

CAMP ADVANCE, Sept. 23, 1861.

A short time since I undertook, from a single feature in the marred and distorted face of this country, to give you some idea of the effects of the war on Virginia, and of how dearly she is paying for her privilege of being shamefully servile to South Carolina. It may not be uninteresting for you, now, to know, to know something of its *general* appearance as it *is,* and as it *was;* and yet when I tell you that my attempt to describe one scene fell far short of the reality, you may imagine something of the difficulty of undertaking, in a single letter, to convey any adequate idea of the whole. When Gov. Pickens said last spring to the Carolinians: "*You may plant your seeds in peace, for Virginia will have to bear the brunt of the war,*" he cast a shadow of the events which were coming on the head of this superannuated "mother of States and of statesmen."

Chain Bridge is about seven miles from the Capitol in Washington, and crosses the Potomac at the head of all navigation; even skiffs and canoes cannot pass for any distance above it, though a small steam tug runs up to the bridge, towing scows loaded, principally, with stone for the city. The river runs through a gorge in a mountainous region, and from here to Georgetown, a suburb of Washington, is unapproachable on the Virginia side. There are very few places where even a single footman can, with safety, get down the precipitous banks to the water. The river then is a perfect barrier to any advance by the enemy from this side, except at Georgetown, Chain Bridge, and Long Bridge, at the lower end of Washington City. On the Columbia side is a narrow plateau of land, along which runs the Ohio and Chesapeake Canal, and a public road. These occupy the entire plateau till you come near Georgetown, where the country opens out, making room for fine rolling farms of exceeding fertility, with here and there a stately mansion overlooking road, city, canal and river, making some of the most beautiful residences I ever beheld. On Meridian Hill, a little north of the road from Washington to Georgetown, stands the old Porter Mansion, from which one of the most aristocratic families in America were wont to overlook the social, political, and *physical* movements of our National Capital; from which, too, they habitually dispensed those hospitalities which made it the resort, not only of the citizens of Columbia and Maryland, but also of the F. F. V 's, for whom it had especial attractions. All around it speaks in unmistakable language of the social and pecuniary condition of those who occupied the grounds. Even the evidences of death there speak of the wealth of the family. The tombstone which marks the place of repose of one of its members, and on which is *summed up* the short historical record of her who sleeps within, tells of former affluence and comfort.

A little further on we pass the Kalorama House—the name of the owner or the former occupant I have not learned, but it is one of the most magnificent places that imagination can picture. You enter the large gate, guarded by a beautiful white cottage for the the janitor, and by a circuitous route through a dense grove of deciduous and evergreen forest, you rise, rise, rise, by easy and gradual ascent, the great swell of ground on which stands the beautiful mansion, shut out from the view of the visitor till he is almost on the threshold, but overlooking even its whole growth of forest, and the whole country for miles around.

You next pass Georgetown. The plateau begins to narrow, and the dimensions of the houses grow correspondingly less, but they are distributed at shorter intervals till you reach the bridge.

This is what it *was*. What is it? In passing the Porter mansion, the stately building, with its large piazza shaded by the badly damaged evergreens, and covered more closely by the intermingling branches of every variety of climbing rose, of the clamatis and the honeysuckle, invite you to enter, but the seedy hat and thread-bare coat appearance of the old mansion, give notice that the day of its prosperity is passing away. You would cool yourself in the shade of its clumps of evergreens, but at every tree stands tied a war horse, ready caparisoned for the "long roll" to call him into action at any moment, and, lest you be trampled, you withdraw, and seek shelter in the arbor or summer house. Here, too, "grim-visaged war presents his wrinkled front," and under those beautiful vines where fashion once held her levees, the commissary and the soldiers now parley over the distribution of pork and beef and beans. In the sadness, inspired by scenes like these, you naturally withdraw, to a small enclosure of white palings, over the top of which is seen rising a square marble column. As you approach, large letters tell you that ELIZABETH PORTER lies there, and the same engraving also tells you that she is deaf to the surrounding turmoil, and has ceased to know of the passions which caused it. That marble rises from a broad pedestal, on one side of which are two soldiers with a pack of cards, and the little pile of money which they received a few days ago, is rapidly changing hands. On the opposite side are two others busily engaged in writing. perhaps of the glories and laurels they are to win in this war; but I venture the opinion, never once to express an idea of the misery and despair of the widows and orphans at whose expense their glories are to be won! On the third side of the pedestal stand a tin canteen, two tin cups, and a black bottle! The fourth awaits a tenant. Again, for quiet, you approach the mansion. As you step on the threshold, half lost, no doubt, in musing over what you have witnessed, instead of the hospitable hand extended with a cordial "Walk in, sir," you are startled by the presented bayonet, and the stern command to "halt; who are you and your busines?" A good account of yourself will admit you to spacious rooms with black and broken walls, soiled floors, window sills, sash and moulding, all disfigured or destroyed by the busy knife of the universal Yankee. This room is occupied by the staff of some regiment or brigade. The next is a store room for corn, oats, hay, and various kinds of forage. The house has been left unoccupied by its owners, and is now taken possession of by any regiment or detachment which happens to be stationed near.

Tired of this desolation in the midst of a crowd, you pass through long rows of white tents, across the little valley which separates you from the hill of Kalorama. Your stop here will be short, for after having climbed the long ascent and reached the house, you find the windows all raised, and anxious lookers-out at every opening. From the first is presented to your view a face of singular appearance, thickly studded with large, roundish, ash-colored postules, slightly sunken in the center. The next presents one of different aspect—a bloody redness, covered here and there with with scaly excrescences, ready to be rubbed off, and show the same blood redness underneath. In the next, you find another change—the redness paling, the scales dropping, and revealing deep, dotted pits, and you at once discover that the beautiful house of Kalorama is converted into a *pest house* for soldiers. Shrinking away from this, you pass through a corner of Georgetown, and then enter the narrow valley between the high bluffs and the Potomac. Onward you travel towards the bridge, never out of the sight of houses, the fences unbroken, the crops but little molested, the country in the peace and quietness of death almost; for the houses, farms, crops, are all deserted, in consequence of the war which is raging on the opposite side of that unapproachable river; and you travel from our National Capital through seven miles of fine country, inviting, by its location and surroundings, civilization and refinement in the highest tone, without passing a house —save in Georgetown—in which the traveler would find it safe to pass a night—indeed I can recall but one which is inhabited by whites. On all these farms scarcely a living thing is to be seen, except the few miserably-ragged and woe-begone-looking negroes, or some more miserable-looking white dispensers of bad whisky, who seem to have taken possession of them because they had been abandoned by their proper occupants. The lowing of herds is no longer heard here; the bleating of flocks has ceased, and even Chanticleer has yielded his right of morning call to the bugle's reveille. "If such things are done in the green tree, what may we expect in the dry?" Cross the bridge into Virginia, and you will see.

Gloomy as is the prospect just passed, it saddens immeasurably from the moment you cross the Virginia line. In addition to the abandonment and desolation of the other side, *destruction* here stares you in the face. Save in the soldier and his appendants, no sign of life in animal larger than the cricket or katy-did, greets you as you pass. Herds, flocks, swine, and even fowls, both wild and domestic, have abandoned this country, in which scenes of civil life are no longer known. Houses are torn down, fences no longer impede the progress of the cavalier, and where, two months ago, were flourishing growths of grain and grass, the surface is now bare and trodden as the highway. Even the fine growths of timber do not escape, but are literally mowed down before the march of the armies, lest they impede the messengers of death from man to man. And this is in the nineteenth century of Christianity—and these the results of the unchristian passions of fathers, sons and brothers, striving against the lives and happiness of each other. Alas! Poor Virginia! Your revenues are cut off, your *industry paralysed, your soil desecrated, your families in exile, your prestige gone forever.

But as so many others are writing of exciting scenes, I fear you will grow impatient for *my* description of the last battles— for *my* account of anthropophagi—of men who have their heads beneath their shoulders—but I have no tact for describing unfought battles, or for proclaiming imperishable glories won to-day, never to be heard of after to-morrow. When we have a fight worth describing, I shall tell you of it. In the meantime I am "taking notes," and "faith I'll print 'em." If the rebels will not give us a fight to make a letter of, I will, at my first leisure, for fear my men forget their Hardee and Scott, have a *graphic* dress parade. in which our different regiments shall contribute at least a battalion, to pass review before you. Then let him who loses laugh, for he who wins is sure to. Till then good night. ———.

25th.—We had a great time to-day, having sent out this morning some six thousand troops, with about one hundred wagons, on a foraging expedition. This evening they returned, loaded with hay, oats, corn, cows, sheep, hogs, and one Irishman—all captured from the enemy. In this deserted and desolated country, where we have for weeks been enjoying (?) rural life without a sign of pig or poultry, without even those indispensable concomitants of civil life—the cries of babies, or the flapping in the wind of confidential garments from clothes lines in the back yard*—the sight of the woolly bleaters called back reminiscences of savory mutton and warm under-dresses, with whispered wishes for the time when we may return to the pleasures of *civil* life.

---

*A something whispers to me that if this should ever be read by housekeepers, it may call up unpleasant reminiscences of "ironing days." I hope not.

30 *h.*—(I shall not, in this book, feel obliged to give the proceedings and doings of every day. Whilst in camp, sometimes for whole weeks, one day was so like the others that to state the occurrences of each would be but a repetition of words. As most of this fall and winter were spent in one place—Camp Griffin—I shall refer only occasionally to occurrences or events, without feeling the necessity of confining myself accurately to dates.)

During the past week I have been much shocked by the growing tendency to drunkenness amongst the officers of the army. I do not doubt but that if the soldiers could procure spirituous liquors, they would follow the example set them by their much loved officers.

I have been somwhat amused for a few days by the antics of an officer of high rank, who has been shut up by sickness in his tent, and under my supervision. He entered the army about the time I did, and had for some time been a much esteemed member in good standing of the Good Templars. He had been from camp a few days—I think to Washington—and returned sick. He had been with me but a short time when his vivid imagination began to convert the stains on his tent into "all manner of artistic beauties— figures of beasts and men, and of women walking on the walls of his tent, feet upwards." Fie, fie! Colonel; if I did not know that you were a Good Templar and a married man, I should think such fancies were unbecoming. 'Tis a good thing to be a Templar and a married man, but still "All is not gold that glitters."

CHAPTER IV.

October, 1st and 2nd.—During these two days the regiment has been busily engaged in moving its camp about four miles. The new camp is to be called Camp Vanderwerken, from the name of a man owning a large property in the immediate neighborhood.

Very shortly after crossing Chain Bridge, our regiment was transferred from Gen. King's to Gen. Smith's brigade, to which we remained attached till about the 28th of September, when Gen. Smith was promoted to the command of a division, and we transferred to a new brigade under command of Brigadier General Winfield Scott Hancock, an officer of fine appearance, but with rather a narrow forehead, and from what little I have seen of him, I should presume him to be at least excitable, if not irritable. We have been between three and four months organized, and have not yet lost a man by either disease or accident. So after all, the life of a soldier, if his health is properly looked after, is not more exposed to sickness than that of a civilian. I am fast coming to the conclusion that the great mortality of camp life is owing much more to neglect of the proper means within our reach of preserving health, than to any exposures to which the soldier is peculiarly liable.

8th.—To-day our division made a "recognizance in force." Marched to Prospect Hill, on the river turnpike, about four miles, and after settling into bivouac two or three times during the day, brought up about 11 o'clock at night at Lewinsville. Having crawled into my ambulance to rest. I note this before dropping asleep.

9th.—We have remained bivouaced all day, and there is talk of our moving our camp to this place to-morrow. This will advance us another three miles in the direction of Richmond. On the 8th of August we arrived in Washington—two months ago yesterday. We are now eight miles nearer Richmond than then. At this rate when shall we reach that famous city? If we do not go faster. I fear Mr. President Lincoln will never dine there at the head of his armies. But these delays are doubtless necessary on the start. War is new to us. Our armies had to be organized and educated to war. Munitions had to be procured, and as most of those belonging to the nation had been appropriated by the South, much of them had to be manufactured. Our navy had to be called home from the four quarters of the world, and innumerable other preparations had to be made, of which we uninitiated are wholly ignorant. Gen. McClellan seems to be active, and we doubt not that under the counsels of the veteran General Scott, matters will be pushed forward as rapidly as circumstances will permit. True, many of us think that Gen. McClellan's "Stand by me and I'll stand by you" speech was not in refined taste—in about as good taste as Pope's proclamation—but as we do not expect or desire exhibitions of delicate taste on the battle-field with an unscrupulous enemy, we overlook the departure from it in our General, and accord to him full confidence, as to both his will and ability to lead us to victory.

We are at present within half a mile of the splendid mansion of the late Commodore Thos. Ap' Catesby Jones. I visited that and his splendid grounds, found them deserted by the whites; a few of the old and almost helpless negroes being left on the place. The soldiers had entered, and made some havoc amongst books and papers. The fine furniture stood in every room in the house, and the walls were covered by the finest paintings, including the family pictures. But the strictest orders, denouncing severe punishment to depredators, were posted about the house, and a strong guard placed to enforce them. I picked up a few articles of little value, except as relics from the home of this once happy and popular family, now in rebellion against the Government to which they were indebted for the favors and protection to which they owed their prosperity I was strongly inclined to take down the family pictures, and to remove them to where they could be taken care of till happier times befall us, that they might then be returned to the family, by whom they must be held in high estimation, but I feared that the motive would be misconstrued, and that it would lead to trouble.

10th.—We have commenced moving our camp equipage from Camp Vanderwerken to this place, to be named Camp Griffin—I suppose for Capt. Griffin, of one of the batteries of the regular army. Capt. G., with his battery, has been one of us and with us since we crossed the Potomac. We have had much trouble and vexation to-day in establishing medical headquarters for the regiments of our brigade, but after much ordering of us and changing of orders, we are at last to take charge of the stone house of Mr. Jno. N. Johnson, in which.

and in the tents we are able to pitch, we hope to make comfortable all the sick of our brigade.

11th.—Sent off ambulances to-day to commence bringing forward the sick of my regiment, and whilst they were gone, after having put my hospital in good order for their reception, I stepped over again to Commodore Jones' house to see how the guards stationed there had succeeded in carrying out their orders. Till I entered the house, I thought I had seen evidences of extreme vandalism, but the wanton destruction here beggars everything I have before witnessed. Furniture broken; feather beds opened, and their contents emptied over house and yard; even those beautiful family pictures were ground to atoms and thrown to the winds. But I need not describe here, for the impression is deeply stamped in memory, more durable and more accurate than words and letters can ever make. Everything destructable was destroyed.*

In handling over the papers I picked up the Commodore's "Journal of a cruise in the U. S. ship Relief—bearing the broad pennant of Commodore Jones—Thos. A. Downer, Esq., Commander," which I have preserved, and also a letter from a son of Commodore Tatnall (late of the rebel Merrimac) to Commodore Jones, written from the Meditterranean, asking to be relieved from duty there, and to be permitted to return to America.†

*It is worthy of remark here, that thus whilst this wanton destruction was going on, a half a mile away, everything on the place of Mr. Johnson, (a loyalist, whose house and garden were in the very midst of the encampments,) though unguarded was unmolested ; every article he had to dispose of was bought and paid for, at high prices, by the soldiers. Even thus early could we read the soldier's aversion to guarding, or having guarded the property of rebels.

†This letter I handed to a lady connection of the Tatnall family, who was with me at the time, and she found means of restoring it to them.

As it will be a matter of interest to me, in future, to study my predictions as to the course and conduct of this war—to rejoice and be vain over those which prove correct, and to laugh at or be ashamed of those which prove false, I shall continue to record them as I have begun; and here I enter one in which I hope to take interest a long time hence. As I have constantly predicted, we have had no fight here nor shall we have; and I now very much doubt whether we shall have a fight even at Manassas, and for this reason: "After all the feints of the enemy here to draw Gen. Banks from Harper's Ferry had failed, they, seeing that we have got foot-hold in North Carolina, will fall back on their fortifications at Centerville and Manassas, and then presenting a bold front with a small body, will cover the withdrawal of the larger part of their force, which they will distribute in Kentucky, Missouri, Tennessee and Western Virginia, and I very much doubt whether they will retain enough at Manassas to make a respectable fight. Kentucky and Tennessee are to become the theatre of war; and if I am not greatly mistaken, Kentucky will have trying times between this and the first of January. I hope that Gen. McClellan is taking the same view of things, and is preparing to meet it." What I have here marked as a quotation is a copied from a letter this day written to a friend on the prospects of the war.

12*th*.—I find vast trouble in doing justice to the sick, in consequence of the unwarrantable interference of military officers in matters of which they are about as well qualified to judge as would be so many of their mules. The two forts which we built near Chain Bridge, and have left some three miles in our rear, have been officially named Fort Marcy and Fort Ethan Allen. The former encloses about one, the latter about five acres of land, and are both very strong.

Our division now holds the post of honor, the advanced center in the Army of the Potomac. Nobody ahead of us, but in the rear, and the right and left, for miles it is but a city of tents. By night the views over these camps are beautiful; by day the stench and noise is abominable.

Surgeon Owen, of Chester, Penn., to-day enters on the duties of Surgeon of our brigade, and I entertain strong hopes that he will be able to stop the pernicious interference of military officers with matters purely medical.

21st.—Our camp here was made without consulting the the Surgeons. It was laid out without order, and the tents are so close together that teams cannot pass through to remove its rubbish, its offal, and its filth. My Colonel, too, has interfered much with my sanitary orders, particularly those in reference to ventilation. The result is the largest sick list we have had. I have succeeded, however, in getting consent to move the camp to other ground, high and dry, where I am now engaged in ditching the streets, and staking out the ground preparatory to a move, where I hope we shall be able to reduce the list of sick. I believe I omitted in the proper place the record of the first death in our regiment. It occurred on the 3d of this month. The poor fellow died of Nostalgia (home--sickness), raving to the last breath about wife and children. It seems strange that such an affection of the mind should kill strong, healthy men; but deaths from this cause are very frequent in the army; the sufferer, towards the last showing evidences of broken down nervous system, accompanied by most of the symptoms of typhoid fever.

Oct. 21st.—A little incident to-day. A reconnoitering party went out this morning towards Vienna and Flint Hill. At noon, a courier came in with a report that they were fighting. I was ordered to take an ambulance and join my regiment "in the direction of Vienna" immediately. On starting, I met with Surgeon Thompson, of the 43d N. York Vols., told him I was going in search of an adventure, and invited him to go with me. He accepted. We reached our outer lines "in the direction of Vienna," but had not found my regiment. To Surgeon T.'s question, "What now!" I replied that my orders were to "go till I found my regiment." "But are you going to cross the lines into the enemy's country?" "My orders are unconditional; will you go with me further?" "Certainly," said the Doctor. Shortly after leaving head-quarters, we met the 1st Regt. Regular Cavalry, who told us they had left one man badly wounded between Flint Hill and Vienna. This man we determined to rescue, if possible. We found him in a house in Vienna. I had now obeyed my order, though I had not found my regiment, and I determined to take this man back with me, though the enemy were all around us. One ball had passed between his ear and skull, a second had passed through the leg, a third had entered the back, just below the shoulder blade, but had made no exit. He was suffering severely from pain and difficult respiration. He could not ride in an ambulance, so Doctor T. volunteered to return to our lines for litter-bearers and an escort, whilst I should remain with our newly made friend. I confess that as I caught the last glimpse of the Doctor's fine black horse dashing over the hill, there was at the ends of my fingers and toes a sensation very much akin to the "oozing out of courage." I was alone in the enemy's country. But there was no other way now, so I dressed the wounds, and waited his return, with what patience I could. He soon returned. We started the man in the direction of our lines, under an escort of eight

men. We mounted our horses, and paying but little attention, got some mile ahead of our escort, when suddenly, eight
horsemen, well mounted and armed, came bearing down
on us, evidently intending to surround us. They were about
a quarter of a mile off when first discovered. "We are in for a
trip to Richmond," said Doctor T. "Is it not safer," replied I, "to fight than to be taken prisoners by these fellows ?"
"I'm in," said the Doctor. We drew our revolvers and
waited, one of us, I am certain, in considerable trepidation.
By this time they were in hailing distance. We called
them to halt, when, to our mutual disgust, we found that
we were friends—they were cheated of the capture of two
"very fine looking rebel officers," and we of a short road to
"that borne whence no traveller returns." A little after
dark we reached camp with our man. In civil life, it will
hardly be credited that the commanding officer of this regiment, when he found his man so badly wounded, ordered
him to be taken from his horse and left, whilst the horse was
to be taken away; yet the man states that such is the fact,
and that he saved himself from such a fate by drawing his re-
volver and threatening to shoot the first man who should approach him for that purpose. After the regiment left him, he
managed to sit on his horse till he reached Vienna, about
three miles from where he was shot.

Since last date, we have had an opportunity of learning
something of the military qualities of our brigade officers.
We have not been before on ground where we could have
our brigade drills ; but here we have them.

General Smith, who commands the Division, is a stout,
short man, rather under size, from Vermont, I think. He
is taciturn, but exceedingly courteous and gentlemanly, and
firm and decided. Of his mental calibre, we have not yet had

an opportunity to judge. It is a strange paradox of human nature, that whilst we acknowledge that a vast majority of our mentally big men are quiet and reserved, yet when we meet a stranger, if he says little, we fall at once into the opinion that he knows little. How this is with General Smith, I do not know. I am much disposed to construe his quiet and courteous manner favorably; but I confess that whispers from the grove have rather prejudiced me against him.

Brigadier General Winfield Scott Hancock is the very antipode of General Smith. He is fully as long as his name, with title perfixed, and as for quiet and courtesy—Oh, fie! I saw him come on to the field one morning this week, to brigade drill. He was perfectly sober. He is one of those paradoxes who believe that *one* man, at least, is to be known by his much talking. He became excited, or wished to appear so, at some little mistake in the manœuvering of his Brigade, and the volleys of oaths that rolled and thundered down the line, startled the men with suspicion that they were under command of some Quarter Master lately made General, who mistook the men for mules, and their officers for drivers. He must be a facetious chap, that General, to wish to excite such suspicions. I think he hails from Pennsylvania, but nobody seems to know much about him, except from his statement that he has "been seventeen years in the service, and knows all about it." Wherever he has been, he has certainly acquired a perfect intimacy with the whole gamut of profanity.

22d.—Went to Washington to see off a friend who has been spending a few weeks with me, as mess-mate. I felt sadly at the parting, and being lonely to-night, I cannot help thinking of home, of home! Where is it? One child in Connecticut, the other in Wisconsin, my wife in New York, and I in Virginia. This separation—disintegration of my family saddens me, and I wish it were otherwise. But the maintenance of government demands war, and war demands sacrifices, to which all patriots must yield. The whisperings of yesterday that we were repulsed at Ball's Bluff, or Edward's Ferry, are more than confirmed, and another good man is sacrificed on the altar of his country. General Baker fell in the battle. The particulars have not reached us, but I fear that we have been sorely defeated, notwithstanding General McClellan's promise, a short time since, that we should meet with no more defeats. Shall we have this proclaimed through telegraph and press, as another "Great Victory?" I regret that McClellan made that foolish speech. It has lost him the confidence of many of his friends.

24th.—A little skirmish to-day, amounting to almost nothing. A party of four or five hundred went out in the morning, came upon the enemy's pickets, and firing on them, drove them in. Then, on returning, our four or five hundred found five men in the field, drawing manure, and well armed with shovels and dung-forks. We took them all prisoners, *without losing a man!* Wonder, if by to-morrow, this cannot be magnified into another "Great Victory," to offset the terrible disaster at Edward's Ferry. This "Grand Army of the Potomac" is a great field in which to win glory. Victories make glory, and victories with us are very cheap.

25th.—We have moved our camp about one hundred rods, are out of the mud, on high dry ground, where the tents can be ventilated and the streets kept clean. I look for a great improvement in the health of the regiment from this.

29th.—A little occurrence of a very unpleasant nature, to-day. I have, for a long time, felt that my Colonel was interfering with the Medical Department of the Regiment, to an extent not warranted by the rules of war, and greatly to the prejudice of the health of the men. Seeing so many sick around me, I became excited, and said to him that his interference must stop; that I would submit to it no longer. He considered this insubordination, or something worse, and used language which I construed into a threat of Court-Martial. This was not very soothing to my excitement, or my excitability, and I wrote him a defiant note, inviting him to put his threat in execution. I know it is an offence against military law to use either insulting or disrespectful language to superior officers; and I felt that it was against the law of self-respect to submit to be forever trampled on, so as one of these laws had to be violated, I took my choice. Perhaps I did wrong. The result will show.

5th.—I have for some time had as mess-mates Surgeon J—V—— and his two sons. I find him a most estimable Quaker gentleman, and he is by his courteous and affable manner, doing very much to smooth down the asperities of the rough road over which I am now traveling. Since the removal of camp, the sickness is abating rapidly. The list, which two weeks ago numbered over two hundred, is now less than sixty, and every day diminishing. I have much trouble in getting my assistant to perform his duties, which, with the constant interference of military officers, greatly embarrasses me in my course. We have to pass some trying scenes. Last week a private in our regiment, a lawyer from ————, heard of the sickness of his daughter. He asked a furlough of thirty days to visit her. The officers here granted it, but when it reached General McClellan he cut it down to fifteen days, which would but give him time to go and return. He declined to go on it, and yesterday intelligence of his daughter's death reached him. Oh, how much I thought of this, and thought if it were my case! 'Tis very sad to think of.

7th.—On the third of September we stopped at Camp Advance, near Chain Bridge, on our way to Richmond. That was nearly ten weeks ago. We are now about four miles nearer to Richmond than we were then. Three weeks to a mile! When shall we close this war? Could we only move once a week, even though it were but a mile at a time, it would keep up an excitement, and contribute largely to the preservation of both health and subordination. There is much talk amongst the soldiers of going into winter quarters here. but I do not believe it. McClellan will hardly dare risk his popularity on such a stake. He must go forward.

8th.—Night before last was made hideous by the yells and drunken orgies of officers. who, in obedience to the order that no work should be done on the Sabbath, omitted all duty. but to make amends. employed the day in getting beastly drunk, and the night in howling themselves sober. It is with deep regret that I notice the rapid increase of drunkenness in the army.

One day last week Colonel ————, of the ———— Regiment ———— Volunteers, appeared on drill, took Hardee's tactics from his pocket, and *read aloud*, in commanding voice, his drill orders. I took a little stroll the day after, and came upon a squad of the 43d New York Regiment, armed with sticks and corn stalks, with a quasi Colonel, reading orders from an old almanac. To my question what they were at, they replied "only playing ———— ————."

9th.—This morning, as I passed through the camp giving directions about cleaning and ventilating tents, whilst the regiment was on parade, my Colonel, seeing me so engaged, gave orders that no directions of mine need be obeyed till he sanctioned them. A very strange order; but as it releases me from responsibility for the health of the regiment, I shall henceforward leave the police regulations of the camp to him, and stay at the hospital. I think it will take but a short time to convince him of his mistake, and that he knows nothing of the sanitary wants of a camp.

13th.—The Regiment received two months' pay to-day, and to-night are all busy as bees making up express packages, to be sent to fathers, mothers, sisters, sweethearts and wives. To-morrow, all who can get passes to go, will be in Washington buying presents and sitting before a camera to "stain the glass" with reflections from their faces, all to be sent to friends at home. As man, in the mass, can be, in no condition, however bright, which will exempt him from cares, fears and apprehensions, so there is none so dark as to exclude hopes and anticipations of better things. Even here we have our joys and our aspirations, and these are of them. We preach that man should study to be contented. What! man in his imperfect condition, contented, that he, as an individual, or as a part of a great whole, should remain forever, as he is! It is opposed to all God's plans. Discontent is the only stairway to progress. Through the discontent of Israel, Egyptian bondage was broken. The discontent of Russia brought war, which more than compensated for its ravages and its horrors, by the introduction of her people to a knowledge of liberal ideas. Czarism was shaken, and already the Goddess of Liberty waves her cap over the downfall of serfdom. The seceder's discontent in England was the Genesis of a mighty nation. Elijah cast off the cloak, too small for his growing aspirations, whilst his followers eagerly grasped its folds to aid their progression. The discontent of an Almighty God substituted Noah for Adam—Christ for Diana—Eternity for Time. And is the discontent which occasioned this great war, with all its horrors, its butcheries, its temporary demoralization, to have no great result? Is it a bare interlude of the parties engaged, taking advantage of the time when "God sleepeth;" or is it a spark emitted from the great restless spirit of Jehovah, destined to ignite into a "pillar of fire," and to light us on in the journey of universal progress?"

"Hope springs eternal—"

I have to-day seen a "speck of war," with another touch of Vandalism. I have, for the first time, seen *an army* in drill. Fifteen to twenty thousand men, a thousand horses, and one hundred artillery wagons, on parade. To me, who had never seen anything of the kind, it was grand, and looked like war. I note here an extract of a letter written to a friend to-day, attempting a description of part of it: "It was, indeed, a magnificent sight, to see six hundred horses harnessed to a hundred wagons, in full run, in line, like a regiment of infantry, and at a word of command, to become so instantly and inconcievably mixed that you would think a universal smash inevitable, appear in another instant dashing across the vast plain without a wagon attached. Turn your eyes to see the wrecks, and you will be surprised to see the carriages in four *straight* lines, forming a hollow square, with the mouth of every gun pointing outwardly, and a laughing expression of "Surround me if you dare!" An - other look will show you that the carriages are so close together that the horses can not pass between them, yet the wagon poles to which the horses had been hitched are all *inside* of the square. How *did* the six hundred horses get out? The cannon at once open their hundred mouths and are enveloped in smoke. The horses return, disappear for a moment in the dense smoke, and seemingly without their stopping long enough to be hitched to, the four lines straighten out into column, and the cavalcade is again dashing across the plain. In less than forty rods, the jumble is repeated, the square formed, the horses gone, and the hundred cannons again open. When *did* they reload?" The vandalism : The finest orchard I have seen in Virginia, was cut down to-day, and in one hour converted into a brush-heap ; and for no other purpose than to give the infantry a chance to "show off" in an hour's parade. The fruit trees were in the way, and were cut down ! It will take forty years to replace that orchard.

14th.—This morning our Brigade Surgeon ordered me to leave the hospital for a few days, on account of my fatigue and prostration. He said that a regard for my health demanded it, and I must go where I pleased. I rode to Arlington, the headquarters of General King. The Arlington house, I believe, is (unless confiscated) the property of Gen. Lee. It is a magnificent mansion, overlooking Georgetown, Washington, Alexandria, and miles of the beautiful Potomac. In a room of this house, said to have been a favorite room of General Washington, I found my old friend Surgeon ———, badly broken by the fatigue and excitement of the campaign. I called on him, in company with Doctor A——, and after talking of his illness for half an hour, Doctor A. proposed to him to have my advice, to which he replied "Yes ! if he will not medicate me too much." I said, "Doctor, I will prescribe for you, and with a single dose will medicate every fibre of your body, and by a healthy shock, restore you to health at once." With a look as if he thought me a hyena, he asked: "What do you mean to do with me?" "To take you out of this place and put you for thirty days under the care of your wife and family." The poor suffering man grasped my hand, burst into tears and sobbed aloud, "My *Colonel* won't consent to it." For a moment, forgetting his religion, and not having the fear of military commanders before my eyes, "Your Colonel may go to the d–vil, and you shall have a furlough." I rode immediately to medical headquarters in Washington, procured him the promise of a furlough as soon as his papers could be sent in, returned, informed him of it, and had the pleasure on my long night ride back to camp, of feeling that I had contributed something to the happines, and, perhaps, had saved the life of a good and worthy man. How easy for any man, however humble his position, to find opportunities of doing good, if he will only wear the "spectacles of benevolence."

After the vandalism I have witnessed in the destruction of property, in and about the houses of rebels and elsewhere, it was a pleasurable relief to find here, that General King, in the goodness of his always good heart, had enforced respect for the property and furniture. The garden, with its fences, is preserved, and the walls of almost every room in this immense old building, are covered with the rich paintings and old family pictures, left hanging when this favorite of rebeldom left his home. The garden is fine, but I think does not compare with that of Kalorama. The antique bureaus and ide-boards calling up impressions of generations long passed away, are still tenants of the building; and the halls recall Scott's fine description of the Halls of the Douglass, where the arms of the hunters, and the trophies of the hunt, mingled with the trappings of the warrior, constituted the attractive features of the chieftain's forest home. Over the halls, and at every angle in the stairs, were the antlers of the elk and the red-deer fastened to the walls and nearly interlocking their branches over my head as I walked through. They were hung, too, with the arms of the hunter and the warrior. So perfectly does this position command Washington, that had the rebels there secretly collected a dozen mortars, they might have fired the city before a gun could have been brought to bear on them. Everybody is talking of a prospect of a move within three days, but the origin of the reports I know not; perhaps in the impatience of the army to be led forward.

19*th*.—It is blustering weather, and my cat is beside me, *lying on her head*, by the fire in my little tent. Everybody says that is "a sign" of cold weather. Let it come, if it will only drive us forward.

The Surgeon General and the Brigade Surgeon have both been urging me, to-day, to accept a Brigade Surgeonship. I decline, for two reasons: 1st. It would retain me as a Surgeon, whilst it would exclude me from the immediate care of the sick. 'Twould be to me like Hamlet, with Hamlet left out; and, 2d. It would greatly add to my responsibilities, without advance in rank or increase in pay. I shall remain where I am.

Glorious news just received: the morning paper is just here. Mason and Slidell both prisoners. They should be hung.

20*th*.—This morning we received marching orders to Bailey's, to have a grand review of the whole army. Very few had any confidence in that part of the order announcing the purpose—a review. All believed it was to take Fairfax, and then perhaps to move forward on Centreville and Manassas; but all were disappointed. It was a "Grand review," —a very grand one—such as I doubt whether this continent ever witnessed before. It may never witness the like again.

There were about one hundred thousand men in battle array; not in one long line stretching far beyond the reach of vision, and leaving the imagination to picture what we could not see, but all in sight at once, on an immense plain, in squares and columns, marching and countermarching, charging and retreating. The President was there; General McClellan and the Prince de Joinville were there; all the elite were there. But to the poor soldiers it was a very hard day. They marched heavy, with knapsacks and all the equipments of a soldier. They started early, marched ten miles, were then several hours under review, and then marched back to camp. Many gave out, and were left by the way side, to come up when they can; the rest of us are back in camp to-night, worn out and heartily tired of grand reviews. I hope that the crowding of my hospital is not to be one of the result of the overwork.

29th.—Since the order of the early part of this month, that my directions in reference to the sanitary measures could be disregarded. I have not visited the camp, or given any directions in regard to cleaning, ventilating, &c., and though it is now but three weeks since that order was made, the sick list, which had decreased in two weeks from about two hundred to thirty-nine, has suddenly run up again to one hundred and sixty, and the diseases are assuming a low typhoid type. So foul are the tents that if a soldier, with simple intermittent, remains three days in his quarters, he is sent to hospital in a condition approximating ship-fever. The seeds of disease are now sown in our regiment, which, in despite of the greatest care, will not fail to yield rich harvests of sickness all winter. Our Governor has been in camp to-day. He has no doubt seen the effect of this military interference, for he has called on me to know if something cannot be done to arrest the trouble. I have laid the whole matter fully before him, and I have no doubt that what is in his power to do, will be done to avert the evil.

30*th* —It is a great relief to my feelings that the difficulties heretofore existing between the Military and Medical Departments in our Regiment are to-day adjusted, and I hope removed by the rescinding the order of the 9th inst., that my directions about the sanitary police of the camps need not be obeyed, and by a substitution of a public order from which this is an extract: "The condition of the health of the regiment requires more than ordinary care. The sanitary regulations of the camp must be entrusted to the Surgeon of the regiment." I have good reason to hope, too, that all personal feelings of an unpleasant character, which have grown out of this unhappy difference of opinion as to official rights, are removed, and that in future the relations of the two departments may be pleasant to the parties, and beneficial to the sick. I now determined that more than ever will I devote my energies to the removal of the causes of the recent severe sickness, and to counteract their results.

CHAPTER V

December, 3d.—There is a rumor here to-day that our troops are in possession of both Savannah and Pensacola. I do not believe it.

What do our leaders mean to do with us this winter? Here we are, the 3d December, a cold, freezing, windy day, in our open tents, without intimation of what we are going to do—with no more preparation for winter quarters than we had a month ago. Are we to be kept in this condition all winter? We are getting tired of McClellan's want of vim. How long is he going to be "getting ready?" All is conjecture, except that the wind howls dreadfully around our tents this cold night.

This morning the three divisions of the army here sent out five hundred to a thousand men each, to beat the bush. This moment comes the statement that they woke up about four hundred rebel cavalry, surrounded them, and that they are even now endeavoring to fight their way out; that they have killed about fifteen of our men; that we have taken about two hundred prisoners, and are fishing in the dark for the rest. All this may be true, but I am getting to be a great doubter of the truth of anything I hear in camp. We shall know all about it to-morrow.

4th.—The story of yesterday's fight is all *bosh*. There were no two hundred prisoners taken—no fifteen killed—no fight—not a rebel seen! Munchausen must have been the legitimate son of a camp, or rather, the camp must be the legitimate progenitor of the whole race of Munchausen.

But it is surprising how camp life enhances the *capacities* of some men. I left home in July a dyspeptic. I came to Camp Griffin, in October, weighing one hundred and thirty-nine pounds. I record here, as something worth my remembering, an extract of a letter written to-day to a friend inquiring how camp life affected my health:

"   *   *   *   I weigh now one hundred and fifty pounds. I have *almost* recovered my appetite. With other things in proportion, I now take three cups of coffee for breakfast, three cups tea at dinner, two cups at tea, and eat five meals a day, or suffer from hunger. My last meal is usually taken at 11 to 12 o'clock at night, and consists of one or two chickens, or a can of oysters, with a pot of English pickled cauliflower. With that I contrive to get through the night.

> "But with the morrow's rising sun
> The same dull round begins again."

"Last night, however, I was so unfortunate as to have no chickens. My can of oysters was sour, and I had to put up with a single head of boiled cabbage, half a dozen cold potatoes, and some cold boiled beef. I wonder what I shall do when we get away from the neighborhood of Washington to where there is no market, no oysters, no chickens, no cabbage, no cauliflower, ' no nothin' ' I shall be compelled to settle back to dyspepsia, and have no appetite."

5th.—It is now six days since I resumed the charge of the hygiene of the camp. My first work was to have my tent struck and removed from the ground, that the spot on which it stood might be thoroughly sunned and cleaned. I then had the whole sprinkled with disinfectants. Have daily visited every tent since, to see that it was ventilated, by having the bottoms turned up for an hour or two, and that it was well cleaned. The result has been most striking. The sick list has already, in only six days, decreased fifty in number, though the seeds of typhus, sown some time since, still sprout, and occasionally give us serious trouble. Another trouble is off of my hands to-day. I have got a settlement with our Quartermaster, the first I have been able to get since the organization of the regiment. On settlement, I find my hospital fund to amount to one hundred and forty dollars. This sum, above the regular rations, will buy all the comforts my sick need, and will relieve the Sanitary Commission and our friends at home from the expense and trouble of providing those things for us. Nor will this be only temporary, for I find that I can, by good economy, after providing well for all the wants of the sick, still have a surplus of from fifteen to fifty dollars a month, to spare to general hospitals, or to the new regiments who have been less fortunate in providing a fund for this purpose.

6th.—Have received to-day a box of delicacies from the good people of Middletown, Connecticut, for my hospital. It is a great comfort to us to feel that the ——— Regiment is remembered in so many places and by so many good people. The contents are generally in fine order, except that a few of the eatables became saturated by some brandy—the corks in some manner having got out of place. This, however, has not injured them. Indeed, many of the sick boys think that the contact of the "spiritual essence" has rather improved them.

All the talk now is of moving, and if we should not be "put forward" next week, I fear our General will lose prestige with this part of the army.

I have had to forbid one of the female nurses admission to the hospital on account of her improper interference with matters under my supervision. I regret this. She is a capable good nurse, but sometimes some things are just as contagious as others, and she meddled and made trouble. I begin to doubt very much the expediency of having female nurses in *fie'd* hospitals. They are absolutely necessary in the general hospital, but in the field they are out of place.

We have had time to read and deliberate on the President's Message. It is not what the soldiers expected, or wished. They had prepared their minds for a real sharp-shooter message, but they think this is a "smooth bore," and carries neither powder nor ball. They like Secretary Cameron's talk much better, But new beginners are always impatient to be at it. We may become sobered down before long.

7th.—Eight days ago to-day, the sick list was 144. To-day it is 72! I begin to think that a Surgeon may be as indispensable to an army as a Colonel,—that

> " A doctor skilled our deadly wounds to heal,
> Is more than armies to the common weal."

Another "speck of war" yesterday. About ten thousand men from the three divisions here having seen a " track" of the enemy, started in pursuit. After four or five miles march, we came on them in line of battle. Our army looked at t'other army and t'other army looked at our army, when our army came to the conclusion that the "touch" had become "too fresh," and so they turned around and came home! Oh, but we are a great people. For four months we have been coaxing them to "come out," and when at last they came out we ran off and left, and the report to.day is that we shall now go into winter quarters *here*, at a safe distance from the enemy we came to whip! Wonder if we may not soon expect a consignment of petticoats. Hope the ladies association will not send any. I have too much respect for the garment to see it disgraced by being worn by such officers. *The honor of the day* is divided between Captain ———, of ———'s Battery, and Colonel ———, of the ——— regiment of ——— Volunteers.* Yesterday, on the field, they disputed, each claiming the honor of command. To-day they dispute, each claiming that this honor attaches to the other. "Par nobile fratrum."

11th.—I have just received a letter from a lady friend of mine aye, and of the soldiers, too, in which she says she "cannot but think of the suffering patriot-soldier, with nothing but a tent above his head, with no covering but a single blanket, and but so little care when sick." This induces me to put on record here, the following description for reference, a long time hence, when, if this war continues, I may wish to read it and compare it with the hospitals then existing, with the improvements which experience shall have causes to be adopted:

My hospital at present consists of five large tents, fourteen feet long by fifteen feet wide. They open into each other at

---

*Were I publishing a history of the war, I should feel it my duty to fill these blanks; but as it is only a journal or record of events, AS THEY APPEARED, AT THE TIME, I feel that it is more proper, as a general thing, to turn over persons to the care of the historian.

the ends, so as to make of the whole one continuous tent, seventy feet long. This will accommodate forty patients comfortably. On an emergency, I can crowd in fifty-five. In the center of the first tent is dug a hole about three feet in circumference and two and a half deep. From this hole there passes through the middle of the tents a trench or ditch two feet wide and of the same depth, which terminates in a large chimney just outside of the fifth tent. It is covered for about ten feet of its length, at the beginning with broad stones, the next fifteen feet with sheet iron, thence to the chimney with stones and earth. A fire is made in the hole at the beginning of this ditch, which, through its large chimneys, has a great draught. The blaze sweeps through its whole length, and by means of this fire, no matter what the weather, or how changeable, the temperature in the hospitals need not vary three degrees in a month, and at all times, night and day, have full ventilation without varying the temperature. Since the adjustment of the difficulties, I have my full quota (10) of nurses, and these are never, night or day, less than two on watch. The cots for the sick are ranged side by side, with their heads to the wall and feet to the center of the tent, leaving just room between their sides for the nurses to move freely, and for the patients to get up and down, and between their ends for the ditch, on which, over the covering already described, is a ladder or rack, with slats so close as not to admit the feet between them when the nurses and patients are walking on them.

So long as there is room in the hospital, no patient of my regiment is permitted to be confined to his tent by sickness. The moment he is sick enough to be confined to bed, he is brought to hospital, where he remains constantly under the eye of the Surgeon and nurses till he recovers. There are, to-day, thirty-six in hospital, each, instead of lying with "nothing but a tent above his head, and with no covering but a single blanket," is on a comfortable bed of straw, the tick emptied and refilled once in four weeks, with all the covering they want. I have plenty of good sheets, and not less than two blankets for each, besides what they bring with them. They are never without fresh meat, rarely without rice, potatoes, jellies in abundance, tea, coffee, sugar, milk, and I am now purchasing for them two dozen chickens a week; and I have this day a hospital fund of not less than one hundred and seventy-five dollars, which is increasing every day, from from which I can replenish or add to the comforts now allowed.* This is a description of my own hospital. I regret to learn from the U. S. Medical Inspector who has visited me to-day, that other hospitals are not so well provided or so comfortable. I regret it, because there is no reason why all may not be provided just as well, so long as we remain near a good market; and if they are not, there is blame either in medical or military departments, which ought to be corrected.

From ninth of November to this date, the time I was shut

---

*It may be a matter of some interest to the reader to know how this hospital fund is realized. It is thus: The soldier is entitled to certain rations every day, and these continue, whether he is sick or well. When well, they are drawn by the captains of companies and distributed to the men. When sick and in hospital, the Surgeon notifies the Commissary of the fact, and they are not issued to the Captain, but credited to the hospital. The Surgeon draws them in whole, in part, or not at all. The days' rations are worth from 17 to 20 cents per man. Now, any economical and honest Surgeon can feed his sick men well when near a market, and save to the hospital fund at least one third of this amount, for the purchase of delicacies. Give him thirty in hospital, he can realize two dollars per month on each man, ($60 per month.) In a neighborhood where markets are very high, this will be proportionally reduced. Where he cannot buy at all, it will be increased.

out from the medical supervision of the camp, there have been more deaths in the regiment than during the whole five months before, including the sickly season of August, September and October. The health of the regiment now, however, is good, and I hope it will remain so during the winter.

17*th* —This is the anniversary of my advent to this noisy, scheming world of vanity and trouble. What wonderful changes have taken place on this continent, in the life time of a little man like me. I will not attempt to write them here; the changes in myself, are sufficient to keep me constantly in remembrance (without a written journal) of the changes going on around me. I hope those of the world are more palpably for the better, than those which I experience. Some malicious representations have been made in camp, to-day, as to the condition of my hospital, and as to my proper disposal of its funds. I have written to the Brigade Commander, demanding an immediate and thorough investigation. In consequence of the long time that I could get no settlement with the Commissary, I advanced for the sick, and the hospital is considerably my debtor. I hope I shall succeed in getting a thorough examination.

18*th*.—I am disappointed to-night, and feel sadly. I had almost no letters from home lately. None yesterday, to-day none. To-morrow I hope I shall hear from home, and get news of the returning health of my family, and then feel better. It is very hard to be shut up here, hundreds of miles from those we love most dearly, and during their sickness, can have no hope of getting to see them. I suppose the "necessities of war" demands the sacrifice, and we must submit.

19th.—To-day I have received the expected letter ; but it relieves no part of my sadness. My dear child at home is no better. I may never meet her again. This in another of the trials of this unholy war ; but I am selfish. How many have so much more reason to complain than I ?

Boxes of luxuries and comforts for the sick received from home to-day. Many of the days which we have spent in this army have been days of gloom and darkness ; and, oh ! how these stars of kindness do sparkle in the gloom and lighten the darkness around us' The luxuries contained in the boxes are a comfort to the sick, but these are not THE comforts which we derive from them. *They come from friends at home.* They tell of the interest felt by them in the cause for which we suffer, of their interest in us as the defenders of that cause, and that we are not forgotten ' Names of many of those who are engaged in this work of kindness are known to us, and whenever heard will call up a thrill of grateful affection so long as memory holds a place among us.

21st.—Did ever husband and father need the comforting aid of the help-meets of home as I need them this evening ? See my table. Six *full* foolscap sheets of letters from home —read, re-read, studied, *spelled*, and now to be answered. I wonder if any body ever imagines the value of a letter to a soldier His power of estimating must be large indeed, if he can appreciate it. Were it not for this value I should never have the courage to attempt answering all this pile. But then, I have no *room* to arrange all these with a view to replies, for my whole tent is as crowded as my table, full of evidences of the kindness—I will dare to say, of the affection of so many of my kind lady-friends. The dictates of kindness and benevolence may crowd upon you articles of comfort and utility, but it requires the affections to indicate the numerous little tokens which peep from the packages of useful things now piled around my tent. They strengthen and they cheer me. I shall endeavor, right here, to make mysel worthy of all this confidence. What a field this is for the exercise of the "unseen heroism" of life!

But how in the name of Legerdemain do our friends contrive to get so many things into a little box? Why, my 10x10 tent is absolutely full. It is well, too, that the box was opened just to-day, for things in it were getting considerably "mixed." Two or three preserve and jelly jars, and a bottle of pickles had been broken. The contents had escaped, and to make amends for their long confinement, like colts let loose, they *ran* considerably. The pickles had "pitched into" the sugar. The jelly had made a dash at the tea. The nutmegs were luxuriating in a mixture of preserves and coffee. There seemed to be an inclination amongst these belligerents to get into "a muss" generally; but I "offered mediation." After two or three hours of back-ache work, I got the conglomerates restored to their original elements, and gave the men a look at them. They were gratified and thankful. I do not think one man looked on one of these evidences of home rememberance but felt strengthened in his resolves to perform manfully the duties which he had undertaken.

Yesterday we had the first fight worthy the name, since we joined the army. General McCall sent out a Brigade (about 4,000 men) to reconnoitre. They came upon an equal number of the enemy, and after taking a good look at each other, concluded to " go in." In this fight we gained a decided victory. No mistake this time. We fought and won.

We lost a few men—about ten killed and some thirty wounded. Amongst the latter is Lieutenant Colonel Kane of the Pennsylvania "Buck Tails." He is a brother of the late Doctor Kane, of the Arctic Expedition.*

Yesterday a few Surgeons met in my tent and gave expressions to their feelings against a self-constituted organization calling itself the "U. S. Sanitary Commission." I have had very little acquaintance with its members, or with its mode of doing business. From the almost universal prejudice which the Surgeons have against it, I infer that it must possess many bad or troublesome traits of character. I have naturally enough imbibed impressions which are anything but favorable in regard to it. At our little talk, yesterday, it was determined amongst us that the Commission must be " written down." I am selected to do the writing, my professional brothers to furnish the data. This morning I commenced my first article, but before it was finished, the roar of cannon and the bursting of shells arrested my attention, and I left my writing to watch the progress of the battle of Drainesville. In a little while, the wounded began to be brought in, and the whole being new to us, the Surgeons, now, for the first, began to examine their stores and appliances for wounded men. We had very few things which we needed, and whilst mourning over the delay necessary to procure them from Washington (some 9 miles distant) the agents of this Commission, having got wind of the progressing fight, had loaded up light wagons with their sanitary stores and rushed to the scene of suffering with the very things most needed. I confess that I feel a little

---

*Battle of Drainesville.

ashamed to have been caught in the act of writing such an article, under such circumstances. Something good may come out of Nazareth yet. I think I shall wait and see, rather than be induced by the prejudices or opinions of others, to commit an act, perhaps a wrong, which I may be sorry for.

CHAPTER VI.

A great day of sport to usher in the new year. Amongst other amusements in our army, Hancock's Brigade " got up a time on its own hook." At twelve o'clock I went into the parade ground, and found about 10,000 people, soldiers and civilians, collected to witness the sport. Hancock's Brigade is composed of the 5th Wisconsin, 6th Maine, 43d New York, and 49th Pennsylvania Volunteers. The sport commenced by a foot race of one thousand yards, purse $20 for the first out, $10 for second. About twenty started. The 5th Wisconsin took both prizes. Then jumping three jumps, prize $15, won by a member of the 5th Wisconsin. Next, climbing a greased pole, first prize won by a member of 6th Maine. Second, by 5th Wisconsin. Next, a greased pig (a two hundred-pounder) with a face as long as the moral law, or as a speech in Congress, shorn of his hair, the knot which had been tied in his tail to prevent his crawling through fence cracks, was untied, and his whole skin thoroughly " greased " with soft soap, was turned loose, with the announcement, " get what you can, and *hold* what you get." The holder was to have the pig and ten dollars. For this prize, there were about four thousand competitors. The word was given, and the " Grand Army of the Potomac " was at last on the move. This chase commenced a little before sun-set. Pig had one hundred yards the start. One fellow far outran all the rest, and as he drew close on to his game, piggy suddenly turned on him with a "booh," and the fellow ran t'other way as if he had seen a rebel. The whole crowd came rushing on piggy, expecting him to run; but piggy stood his ground and said " booh !" " The front line" suddenly brought a halt. But the rear, not prepared for so sudden a check, pressed forward, and the whole came down in a heap. A scream of "murder." Piggy answered "booh." At every "booh" a "line was swept away." The pile of humanity became impassable. Those in the rear, filed to right and left, and by a " flank movement " took piggy in the rear. And now came a hand to hand encounter. As the last streak of the expiring day shed its light upon the excited combatants, it revealed a living mass of four thousand people—and a pig ; the pig crowning the heap at the moment when the ray withdrew its light. Night was then made hideous by the screams of murder and replies of "booh." Neither party could distinguish friend from foe; and as I retire for rest, the combat still rages. I I do not permit myself to doubt, however, that the morning will bring us the news of "another great victory by the grand army of the Potomac."*

At twelve o'clock last night, just as the old year was being crowded out of existence to make room for the new, I was

---

* Notice that in this athletic contest for prizes, three Eastern and one Northwestern Regiment engaged ; all the prizes save one (climbing the pole, which was taken by a Maine sailor) were carried off by the one Western Regiment.

awoke by a gentle thumbing of a guitar. 'Twas right at the door of my tent. In a moment commenced at the other end of the tent, the soft, sweet notes of a violin; then, from all sides came up, low, soft, sweet sounds, as ever a band of *small* instruments poured forth. The music stopped for awhile, and a voice asked, "Shall we now strike up with the band?" "No! no! No drum, nor fife, nor horn;—they will disturb the sick, and he will not like that!!" Could a more delicate compliment than was conveyed in this remark have been devised by a soldiery whose business is pomp and noisy war? "*He won't like it—it will disturb his patients.*" I appreciated this. It struck a cord which vibrated in unison with my pride, my vanity, my ambition. I of course acknowledged it; and so deeply felt the compliment that I record it, as worthy of my remembrance. "The hospital boys" got up a handsome supper to-night, at which the Surgeons were guests. It was a very pretty supper, and to me a pleasant affair.

2nd.—I think my hospital can boast, just now, the happiest set of sick men I ever saw. I have now twenty-seven of them. This morning, as I was prescribing for them, (all sitting up) some reading the morning papers, and talking loudly over war news, some playing whist, some checkers, some chess, some dominoes—all laughing and merry, Gen. H—— walked in, and, looking for a moment along the line of sick, exclaimed, "What the h—ll have you got here?" "My hospital, General." "A Brigade," replied he in his roughest manner, "of a d——d sight better men than you have left me. Where are your sick, sir?" "All here, sir." "Well, this beats anything I have seen in the army, and if you give your men such beds and such comforts as this, you will have every man of your regiment in hospital before a month." They have had a glorious holiday. The boxes, and other presents received within the last eight days, have awakened vivid recollections of home, and of "the girls they left behind them." They are all the better for these things, and when I return them to their quarters, they take hold of their work with a will, and with a feeling that if taken sick, they have a pleasant hospital to go to.

I make here a record of some observations in relation to "hospital fevers," "hospital sores," "foul air of hospitals," and such clap-trap. I have lately visited many tent hospitals, in the open field, where I have witnessed cases of "hospital gangrene," low typhoid fevers, with gangrenous toes or fingers dropping off, and heard scientific men, in scientific discussions, attributing it all to the foul air of the hospital! And this, too, in the open field, where not more than thirty or forty were together, and where the wind swept past them, free as the fresh breezes on the top of the Alleghanies!! 'Twas a gangrene of the mind, for want of free ventilation of the brain. There is no disease so contagious, or so depressing to vital energy when taken, as inactivity and gloominess of mind. Introduce one such temperament into your hospital, *without an accompanying antidote*, and the condition will be communicated to all others in the hospital, with as much certainty, and with greater rapidity, than would the infection of small-pox or measles. Let the admission of such a patient be accompanied by the presence of a long, sour-faced hospital steward, who keeps in the hospital tent a table covered with cups, and spoons, and vials, and pill-boxes, and syringes, and who mingles with every potion he gives a homily on hospital sickness, on fatality in the army, on the number of deaths from typhoid in the next tent, and my word and observation for it, though the breezes of that hospital come fresh "from

D

Greenland's icy mountains," they will be freighted with the mephitic vapors of hospital fever and gangrene.

Instead of the above, let the Surgeon pass frequently through his hospital, making it a rule never to leave till he has elicited a hearty laugh from every one in it. For his Steward's table of mirth-repelling instruments, introduce light reading, chess-men, checkers, dominoes, cards, puzzles, their use to be regulated by a corps of jolly, mirth loving, but judicious nurses. Then let him throw up the bottoms of his tent walls, giving everything around an air of cheerfulness, and if he does not find the diseases of the field hospital milder and more tractable than at home, my word for it, it will be in consequence of the officious over-dosing by the doctor. I do not mean that cleanliness is not an essential; but I must bear in mind that a pile of nasty, out-of-place rubbish, is as incompatible with cheerfulness, as it is with purity of surrounding air. A clean bed, even, exhilarates the mind, as promptly as it corrects the foul odors of a soiled one. Since I have been in the army, I have lost all dread of the much-talked-of foul air of hospitals, *only so far as it is diffi-cult to correct the mental atmosphere about it.* This is in reference to its influence on diseases. I have not yet had an opportunity of observing the effects of crowds *in surgical* wards—that will come before long, and I shall be greatly relieved if I find the same records applicable there.

5th.—I am very hard worked just now. The Brigade Surgeon is sick, and I being the ranking Surgeon in the Brigade, have his duties to perform. In addition, I have charge, at present, of a large share of the Hospital of the 49th Regiment Penn. Vols., the Surgeon being very ill. That regiment is in dreadful condition. Very many of them are sick, and of very grave diseases. Then, my assistant is off of duty, being suspended on account of charges pending against him, in court martial. From altogether I am much worn down, and need rest.

In my own Regiment, I have none who can be properly called *sick*. I excuse 75 to 100 from duty almost every day, but it is chiefly on account of bad colds, chaffed feet, or some minor trouble. I have not one man confined *to bed*, from sickness.

There are many dark clouds hanging over the country now. Amongst them, there are evident signs of loss of confidence in Gen. McClellan. I hope he will make haste to give good account of himself, and thus regain the confidence he has lost.

7th.—This has been a cold, blustry day, and the Regiment has been out skirmishing. They found no enemy ; bought a little corn, and came home.

All is conjecture here as to the intention of our leaders. My conjecture is that outside pressure will compel us to do something within the next fifteen days, or lose still more confidence. But what can we do? Nothing, here. The roads are impracticable for artillery—the weather too bad to fight. If we do anything we must go south. I am getting very tired of this, and wish I could feel that it would be proper for me to resign.

18th.—I visited Washington to-day, through such rain and such mud, as no civilized country, save this, can sustain, and preserve its character for purity. Am back to-night. On my return, I find on my table the following :

" General Order No. 11.

" HEADQUARTERS, &c.

" When the time arrives for the troops of this Brigade to

move, the following will be the allowance of the means of transportation:

"Five wagons to the companies of a Regiment (two wagons to each company); one wagon to the Regimental Hospital.

"Each wagon will carry the forage for its horses. The sixty rounds of reserved ammunition will be carried in extra wagons. In the company, wagons will be carried rations for two or three days, company mess equipage, and officers' baggage, which will in no case exceed the amount by regulations for baggage in the field. The forage for horses of regimental and field officers will have to be carried in their wagons. This notice is given so that soldiers and officers may be aware, that all property not above mentioned, to be preserved, had better be removed, for if the troops march, it is probable the first notice given will be the presence of wagons for loading.

"By order of Brig. Gen. ————."

Now that begins to look like business, and if our General means to put us in the way of doing something—if it will only not prove another counterfeit cry of "wolf"—we shall be pleased. Gen. McClellan has already grown several inches in the estimation of those whose confidence began to get shaky. I do not like that expression of "for if the troops march." It looks a little wolfy. But I shall try to think it means "go in."

19*th.*—I confess to myself to-night, that deeply as I am interested in the cause for which we fight—the question of government against anarchy—what I have witnessed to-day has cooled much of the enthusiasm with which I entered the service of this government, which I find so tardy in doing justice to those who are fighting for its preservation: This is a stormy day in mid-winter. Whilst going my rounds of camp to see what was needed for the health and comfort of the men, I passed the guard house of the regiment, and stepped in to see the condition of things. I there found soldiers—formerly my neighbors—sons of my friends, imprisoned in a *pen* where pigs could not have lived a fortnight without scalding the hair off them, (this is not figurative language) and in which these men had been kept for three months, awaiting the decision of a court martial which had tried them for some trivial offence, the extremest penalty of which would have amounted to some three to six days' confinement! at all events, under the extremest limit of the law, its punishment could not have exceeded in severity a sentence of three days' imprisonment in this vile hole of filth and water! Yes, they had been tried, and for three months had been kept, not only in this vile hole, but under indignity and disgrace, awaiting the convenience of gentlemanly officers, to send them word whether they were honorably acquitted, or that they must be imprisoned for two or three days. When these men, who, perhaps, have never been guilty of offence besides being suspected of it, are released from this disgraceful punishment, will they not feel indignant at hearing the justice of their government questioned, and be ready to rush to arms again to defend it? If scenes like this are *necessary* to the preservation of a government for my protection, then in God's name let *me* be untrammelled by conventional forms, and left dependent on my own powers for my protection. I assumed a prerogative; I pronounced most of these men sick, and ordered them sent to my hospital. They will hardly be pronounced well before the gentlemanly members of the court get ready to inform them of their sentence.

From this last scene I passed on to look up a party of our Regiment, who had been detailed to guard the General's Headquarters. I found them; and, my God! what a sight!—Around the house occupied by the General was a large ditch, some five feet deep, and some ten or twelve feet wide, dug as the commencement of a fort. In this ditch, over which a few evergreen boughs had been thrown as a covering, stood a well dressed Lieutenant, (from my own county) with a squad of soldiers guarding the General's house—the Lieutenant trying to infuse into the men a little warmth of patriotic feeling, whilst the winter torrents poured through the evergreen branches, and their whole frames shook with cold in this *sentry house*, charitably built for them by orders of the General, who at that moment was being joyful over his wine, and with his friends'' And is this the REPUBLIC, the government of equality for which I am fighting? If we were *men*, this would be pitiable, but we are only soldiers, volunteer soldiers at that; and what right have we to be cold, when our services are wanted for the comfort of a General? But these are only *thoughts*; should I write or speak them, it would amount to shameful insubordination, and I should be disgracefully dismissed from the service of the country which tolerates it. I am too honorable a man to permit myself to be disgraced, even for the privilege of uttering a truth. I therefore decline to say, or even to write, what I have seen.

This afternoon I received an order to be ready to move at a moment's notice, and to give no more certificates for furloughs, as the applications would not be entertained. I have lost faith in the idea that the authorities have the slightest intention to move. They have seen our impatience to do something, and this order is a mere dumb-watch thrown us children to amuse us with the old promised hope that "when it gets a little older it will keep time."

23rd.—The whole atmosphere to-night vibrates with the sounds of preparation to advance. The new Secretary of War says "advance." We are getting daily dispatches from Gen. McClellan, asking, "Are you ready?" I have no faith We have received too many dumb-watches, which "will run when they get older."

27th.—Expectation is still on the strain. How long it has been kept up! But no order to move, and I doubt whether we get any soon. Indeed, I think now that we should not move. 'Tis too late. The roads are excessively bad, and for a long time we have been having an almost continuous storm of freezing rain and snow. An army could not lie out over night in this terrible weather, and be in condition next day to fight against those who had slept in good quarters and been well fed. The time has passed to move. But why are we not ordered to winter quarters? There seems to me to be great recklessness of the soldiers' health and comfort in this army. There is wrong somewhere.

A sad case has just passed under my notice. Three days ago, as I was busily engaged in attending to hospital duties, I entrusted, necessarily, the light sickness of quarters to others. As I passed out just after morning call, I heard one of my nurses say to a man, "You look sick; why do you not come to hospital, where we can take care of you?"— "That is what I came for, but the doctor says I am not sick, and has returned me *to duty.*" I passed on, but notwithstanding that there is scarcely a day that some "shirk" who is pretending to be sick to avoid duty, is not treated thus, that voice rang sadly in my ears. In ten minutes I returned, and inquired after the man. The drums had beaten to duty, and he was on parade.　I followed to parade ground, found him endeavoring to do his duty, on a "double-quick."　I took him from the ranks, examined him, and sent him to hospital.　Before they got him to bed he was delirious.　He has just died.　'Twas a case of typhoid fever, of which he had been sick for two days before I saw him.　I ask of army Surgeons,　Had you not better excuse ten "seeds" who are worthless, even when in rank, than sacrifice one good man like this, who believes he is not sick, *because you tell him he is not ?*

28*th.*—To-day I was admitted as a witness to the arcana of a field Court Martial, and of all the ridiculous farces in the name of justice, to excite mirth, indignation, pity, and disgust, commend me to a field Court Martial.　I will not spoil the ludicrous impression left on my mind, by any attempt to describe the scenes I witnessed to-day.　The grey goose has yet to be hatched which can furnish the pen capable of even approximating it.　Oh, talent of Barnum!　How does it happen that in all your searches after the wonderful and the curious, you have overlooked that nondescript of wonders, a field Court Martial?　Strike quickly on this hint, and there is a fortune ahead.

31*st.*—As a relief to the dullness induced by bad weather, and disappointed hopes that something will turn up to awaken the activity of the army, I am constantly amused by the merry chirpings of myriads of "crickets on the hearth."*　Now and then after night-fall a little mouse, nearly white, suddenly appears amongst them, and such a scampering, "such a gettin' up stairs I ever didn't see."　Mousey looks around for a little while as if surprised at their timidity, then

---

* My quarters are now, an old farm house with one room, with an immense rough stone chimney, and a flag-stone hearth.

sets up a beautiful little song of his own, much resembling the trilling efforts of the young canary. Yes, I have the reality of a singing mouse; and at all hours of the night, either he or the crickets may be heard, in their cheering and now familiar singings. A few nights ago I heard a sound as of some small animal struggling in the water. I arose quickly, and on striking a light, found my little musical companion struggling in the water-pail for dear life. He had "leaped before he looked." *I had him.* I warmed him, and dried him, and then I let him go. And why should I not have let him go? True, I sometimes see him gliding away with stolen portions of my dearly-bought cheese. Now and then the print of his little foot, just pulled out of Virginia mud, is found on my butter roll. Once, as I was preparing for breakfast, I found the little fellow taking his morning bath in my cream cup. But what are all these? The cheese I can afford to divide with him. I cut the print of his little foot from my butter roll, and enjoy what is left all the better. Though I lose the cream from my coffee, I become more attached to the cup, because it has afforded pleasure to my little friend. Have we any roses without thorns, good people without failings, or friends without faults? When I examine the catalogue of my friends, should I strike off every one who has a failing, I fear I should have *very* few left. Go on, then, little mousey, this world was intended alike for you and me. There is not a night but your little song more than pays me for all your depredations of the day, and for all my interest in and affections for you.

February 7th.—Still all is uncertainty here as to what is in store for us. Some are of opinion that we are to accompany the next squadron to the South; some that we go to Norfolk; others that we shall next week move on Manassas. My own opinion is that we shall remain where we are till about the first of April, then advance on Centreville, and if successful to Manassas, and thus to follow up our victories as long as we can win them.

To-day our Regiment is scouting. This morning a body of Cavalry went out from our Brigade, and returned about ten o'clock, bringing in six rebel cavalry men as prisoners. But some of our own men are missing. We immediately sent out two regiments to reconnoitre. They have returned with thirteen prisoners. Two of the Cameron Dragoons are wounded, but not badly.

9*th*.—The Court of Inquiry to examine into the conduct of my hospital affairs yesterday, decided that they would not investigate—that the accusations were the result of personal ill feelings. At least, so a member of the court informed me. I begged him to insist on an inquiry, and the court has reconsidered its action, and will investigate. I hope there will be a full *expose* of the whole conduct of the hospital. I have long desired it.

15*th*.—What a week of news, opening on us with intelligence of the capture of Fort Henry, with its list of high-bred prisoners. Scarcely had the sound of the cheers and the hurrahs died away, when Burnside startled us with an artillery discharge of news. To-day, whilst we were brushing out our "hollering organs" with alum swabs, when the startling intelligence from Fort Donelson, the most glorious of which is the capture of the arch-traitor, Floyd; and what a disappointment that not a throat in our whole Division can shout "Hang him!" loud enough for Floyd to hear it. Hold on for awhile; send us no more such news at present. As this poor old " grand-mother " of armies is to do no fighting, wait at least till the throats of our soldiers so far recover that

they can do the shouting over victories in which they are denied the privilege of participating. We have lain still here
till we have grown into old fogyism—gone to seed. So little
advance, so little progress have we made, within the memory
of any here, that should Methuselah offer us to-day a shake
of his hand, we should wonder whether it was yesterday or
a week ago that we parted from him, so little has been the
change *here* since his advent, and so much would he look
like all around him.

21*st.*—No grounds yet on which to base an opinion as to
when or where we shall go. One day brings us assurances
that our Division will in a few days go to Annapolis to join
the mortar fleet bound South. The next we hear that we are
to advance and take Manassas. To-day we hear that we are
shortly to go to Kentucky, and join the fighting army under
Buell. There is also a rumor here that the rebels are leaving
Manassas in great numbers. If that be true (the President
and Gen. McClellan both believe it), we shall probably advance
on that stronghold and occupy it ourselves until we are ready
for the " on to Richmond " move. But why, if we have been
staying here all winter to " bag the enemy " at Manassas, do
we now lie still and permit them to leave ? This " gives me
pause " in my opinions. I do not like such doings, nor can
I quite comprehend such Generalship. But it is not for me to
criticise the plans of educated military leaders. I presume
they know much better than I, what is best to be done, and
I shall still confide in their judgment and wisdom.

This morning Brigade Surgeon ——, of —— Brigade,
made the following statement on the investigation of my
hospital management and condition : " I was Surgeon of a
Regiment in the three months service ; since then I have
been Brigade Surgeon of four Brigades ;" (including 15

regiments) "I have seen no hospital fund anywhere as large as that of this hospital; I have seen none managed with more economy, nor any patients made so comfortable. I have seen no Surgeon anywhere who seemed to feel so lively an interest in the hospital and the welfare of his Regiment; I have seen no Surgeon who devoted so many hours in the service of the sick, as this Surgeon."

This statement, coming officially fiom a Surgeon whose duty it has been to supervise the care of the hospitals and the treatment of the sick; from an officer whose business has for the last ten months brought him in contact with half the hospitals of the army of the Potomac, and whose head-quarters have been for several months within sixty feet of my hospital, was gratifying to me, and entirely satisfactory to those whose duty it was made to investigate, and they so expressed themselves in dismissing the subject.

26th.—A pleasant little interlude to-day, to the troubles and hard work through which I have had to pass: At about twelve o'clock, a soldier stepped to the door of my quarters, and said that some friends wished to see me at the door. I stepped out and found my whole corps of hospital attendants, and the patients of the hospital who were able to be up, in a circle. The head nurse stepped forward, and in a very neat little speech, presented me, in the name of himself and the others, a very pretty regulation dress sword and belt. I replied to it as well and as appropriately as I could; the ceremony closed by a vociferous testimonial of kind feelings, and we parted. I confess that I have been highly gratified. The compliment was appreciated by the fact that it came directly from those who most intimately know me, both personally and officially.

27th.—Three days ago we received orders again to be

ready to move at a moment's warning. But here we are
yet. I was in Washington to-day. Went intending to
spend two days and witness the "doings of Congress." But
on my arrival got intelligence that Gen. Banks had crossed
the Potomac at Edward's Ferry; that the Government had
seized the Railroads here, and was sending off troops to his
aid, and not doubting that this would start us also, I immediately returned to my post.

28*th.*—All the stirring news of yesterday did not uproot
us. I begin to think that we are so deeply stuck in the mud
that nothing can get us out, short of the sight of a rebel.
That might galvanize us into a move.

This morning we received an order countermanding the
last one to be ready, so that we are again unready. This is
the last day of winter, and the coldest we have had. It
snows and blows, and this is probably the reason of the
countermand.

It seems to me a great shame that our soldiers have been
kept here doing nothing all winter, and yet not one in fifty
of them has been permitted to visit the National Capitol and
learn something of the *modus operandi* of the Government
for which he fights. Very few of them, I fear, will ever
enjoy another opportunity to do so.

March 3d.—In the way of petty tyranny, it seems another
Richmond has entered the field. Last week I was presented by
some of my friends with a very pretty sword, as a testimonial
of their respect and affection for me. To-day I am informed
by General ——— that this cannot be tolerated. All the
persecution which he and his satellites have heaped on me,
have not been sufficient to alienate the affections of those
for whom and with whom I have labored for the good of the
regiment; but all those who have had any part in the presen-

tation of that sword are to be punished, and this, too, at a time when all ranks, from Corporals to Major Generals, are receiving like testimonials! But (?) the head of this Brigade having failed to crush a Surgeon, aspires to a personal quarrel with privates and nurses. Magnanimous General! I have received a positive order, to-day, to ascertain the names of all who had any hand in the presentation of the sword, and to report them to headquarters, and I have just as positively refused to stoop to participate in any such dirty work. I leave all the honor to the Brigadier General, and after he has vented his malice on such of the privates as he can get other tools to hunt out for him, he is at liberty to try his hand on me again for this disobedience of his dirty order. The work is worthy of him, and of the tools he employs.

4th.—I returned from Washington to-day, and was met by Colonel ———, who told me that the Brigade Commander had ordered him to have every hospital nurse who had taken any part in the purchase or presentation of the sword to me, dismissed from hospital and returned to the ranks. Well, now, who is to do that? I shall not; and I am glad that our Commander of Brigade has had pride enough to rise to this trick to find out who they are, rather, than (pencil in hand) to go sneaking around, asking "Who did it?" But he will miss fire; I shall dismiss nobody. I would rather he would catch himself in the little act of nosing around for information. I doubt not he will do it, or even dirtier work, rather than let slip any opportunity to gratify his vindictiveness.

After I received this verbal order, I sat down and wrote a defiant letter to the General, giving him my estimate of such doings, but then, feeling that it might redound to the injury of my friends, who were sharing his displeasure with me, I suppressed it, and sent a request to the General to be permitted to see him on the subject. I received the manly reply: "When the order is carried out!" If we never meet till *I* carry out that order, these eyes will for a long time be relieved of performing a most disagreeable duty. He may perform the duty; I shall not. In the hope, however, of relieving my friends from his further vindictiveness, I determined on another attempt to mollify, and here record the attempt, with its result:

HEADQUARTERS MEDICAL DEPARTMENT,
—— Reg't —— Vols.

COLONEL :—

Permit me, through you, to lay before Brigadier General ————, the following statement of facts: During the autumn and early part of the winter, the sickness in our regiment was unusually severe. Often, one half of our nurses were sick, and the rest worn down by fatigue. Rather than draw more strength from the regiment to our aid, I, after my official duties of the day were over, did, for weeks together, spend the greater part of every night in the unofficial, and, perhaps, undignified capacity of nurse, sending the exhausted nurses to their beds, and ministering to the wants of the sick. I rarely retired before two o'clock in the morning. During this time I was so fortunate as to gain the affection and gratitude of those for whom I labored, whilst many of them were still feeble, scarcely able to leave their beds, they decided to express their gratitude for my personal efforts, by a new year's gift to me. They forgot that in becoming soldiers they ceased to be men, and gave vent to their feelings by presenting me a sword. If, in this presentation, there were "deliberations or discussions having the object of conveying praise or censure" for me, officially, as stated by the General, I have not been able to discover it. The circumstances attending—the spirit of the address—the inscription on the scabbard, all point to a different feeling and another object. With feelings of the deepest regret, I learn that this act of theirs meets the disapproval of the Brigade Commander, and that these men are to become the objects of censure and punishment.

For six months, these soldiers, by the direction of the Medical Director of the Army, have been thoroughly trained to the performance of those duties which are expected of hospital attendants on the field of battle, and I venture nothing in saying that the hospital under their care will show that they are second to no corps on the Potomac.

Under this state of facts, I respectfully appeal to the Brigade Commander, and beg that he will revoke the order dismissing these nurses and filling the hospital with inexperienced ones, at the moment when we are expecting to enter the battle field, and to need all the experience in our reach.

I waive all considerations of my own mortification, and will even cheerfully bear a public reprimand for myself. I put aside the consideration of the inconvenience which their dismissal will bring on me; I put aside even *their* mortification and disappointment; but, in behalf of the sick, the wounded, the dying of my regiment, I appeal for the revocation of this order.

I beg, Sir, to remain,

Respectfully, your ob't serv't,

———— ————,

Surgeon ———— Volunteers.

To COLONEL ————, COMMANDING ———— VOLS.

With this last appeal I close the labors of this day.

5th.—The deed is done. The blood-hounds tracked out at least a part of their game. The following will tell its own tale :

HEADQUARTERS ——— REG'T ——— VOLS,
Camp Griffin, Virginia, March 5th, 1862.

REGIMENTAL ORDER,
    No. 72.

Privates —— ——, —— ——, —— ——, —— ——, —— ——,* are detailed for extra duty in the Regimental Hospital. They will report to the Surgeon at the hospital forthwith, taking with them their knapsacks, arms, accoutraments, but no ammunition.

Privates —— ——, —— ——, —— ——, —— ——,† are relieved from extra duty at the Regimental Hospital, and will report for duty forthwith, to their company commanders.

The above changes in the attaches of the hospital is deemed necessary, on account of the late complimentary presentation, made by the attendants now relieved to the Surgeon in charge of the hospital. This was in violation of the spirit of the army regulations, and of the usage of the service.‡ Yet it is believed that in so doing the men were guilty of no intentional wrong, and were actuated by the better impulses of human nature; and there is, too, much reason to believe that they have been misled by the precedents which have been but too many in the volunteer service. While it is not intended to disgrace the soldiers above named, it is consid-

---

* Names of seven privates.

† Names of the ten of the hunted out.

‡ Everybody knows that statement to be false. 'Twas perfectly in accordance with the usage at that time and is yet.

ered that by making this present to their superior in the Medical Department, they have so embarrassed their relationship to that officer as to render the continuance of that relationship subversive of military discipline.

The relationship of officers and soldiers is that of instruction and command on the one part, and of respect and obedience on the other. All discipline is based upon this theory, and while the officer will receive in his own consciousness of duty discharged, and the disinterested approval of his superiors and peers, his sufficient reward, the soldier, by doing his duty in the defence of his country, will continually pay a greater compliment, and make a more acceptable presentation to his officer than handiwork can fashion or money buy.

By order of the Colonel Commanding,

—— —— ——, Adjutant."

Copy, Official, ⎫
—— —— ——, Adjutant. ⎬

Well, there is a good deal of rhetorical high-fa-lu-tin in all that; but after it shall have been laughed at, hooted and ridiculed by all who see it, I wonder how much comfort the poor soldier who has had his hip shattered or his spine dislocated by a shell, will derive from the recollection of this rhetorical sophistry, whilst he is being handled on the battle field as a bear would handle him, instead of by those hands which had for months been trained to a knowledge of the business, and now withheld for the gratification of a cowardly vindictiveness.

But take it all in all, the above is a remarkable document Nothing recognized but *order and obedience*. Affection for the commander is entirely ignored. It has been my boast and pride, that for months, not one of the ten men taken from me has been ordered. Their affection for me has anticipated my every wish as well as every necessity of the sick, and there has been a constant emulation amongst them as to who could best please me by contributing to the comforts of the sick. *This, it seems, is not consistent wi.h the good of the service, and they are all this day returned to the ranks!* Well, if military discipline ignores the impulses of affection, and of obedience from kindness, God deliver me from all such drill.

6th.—This morning as my newly appointed nurses came in, I was utterly disheartened. There is not a man amongst them who can make a toast or broil a chicken ; yet the sick must depend on them for all their cooking. Half of them are applicants for discharge on the ground of disability, yet they are sent to me to work over the sick, night and day, and to carry the wounded from the battle field. Not one has ever dispensed a dose of medicine, and yet I must depend on them for this duty. It is a dreadful thought to me that I must go to the battle field with the set which is now around me. Our sick, our wounded, our dying on the battle field will be from amongst my neighbors and my friends. To the parents of many I have made a solemn vow that their sons shall be properly cared for in times of trouble. Well, I will do the best I can, but when I have trained men to all the little offices of kindness and of care, even to the practice of lifting the wounded and carrying them smoothly on litters,* it is hard that they should now be taken from me, at the

---

*For months, it has been a daily practice to take the nurses to the field and train them to lifting the sick and wounded, and even to the proper step in carrying them off the field. None but those who have witnessed it can imagine the difference in pain or comfort, which a certain kind of step will communicate to those carried on litters.

very moment of expected battle, and replaced by such as *these.*

This morning the men dismissed from my service for the heinous offence of loving me, came in to bid me good bye. When a long time hence, I read this, I find it written that we all wept, I may then feel ashamed of the weakness. I certainly do not now.

7th.—Received orders to-day to draw rations for my hospital force for five days. This kind of an order is unusual. The roads are improving. Perhaps the dumb watch is nearly old enough to run.

9th.—All is bustle and confusion. Though there is no order to move, we are all packing, and ambulances are running with our sick to general hospital. This looks like clearing the decks for action. We are notified that when we do march, we shall do so without baggage or tents. So long have we been here that, notwithstanding we have been long impatient to move, it will be like breaking up our home. My home attachments are very strong. I shall feel sadly at breaking up, but I shall be glad to be again in active service.

Since the late ebullition of vindictiveness by Gen. ———, I have been schooling myself in the hardest lesson of my life —that is to sit and wait for orders, regardless of humanity, of everything, indeed, except the little eighty-seven dollars and fifty cents per month, and my own ease and comfort. This is a lofty ambition. A prize worthy a better patriot than I have ever claimed to be. Last night and this morning I labored in my hospital till three A. M. But that work is now over. We leave behind us those to whom my care and their suffering had attached me; and I will see to it that neither conscience nor humanity shall again so strongly attach me to the sick. It only lays me liable to indignities and insults.

March 10*th*.—Returned eaily last night ; but before midnight received orders to have two days' rations cooked, and be ready to move at 4 o'clock this A. M. Before I got dressed I found myself not only Regimental Surgeon, but in consequence of the absence of the Brigade Surgeon, I had charge of his duties also. My hands were full. I guess the watch is almost old enough.

We know nothing as to where we go, but a party of scouts who were out through the day yesterday, report that Manassas is evacuated, and that the rebel army of the Potomac has all gone South. About ten o'clock to-day we heard a terrible explosion, supposed to be the blowing up of some bridge to prevent pursuit. And has that army been so disrespectful to General McClellan as to go off without going into his bag ? Fie on them !

And now we are off. The sick whom I have nursed till my care grew into affection for them, are sent away. Those to come will be new ones. The last few weeks have taught me that in the army the Surgeon's duty is to take care of the Surgeon, and to leave conscience and humanity to take care of themselves. These, with the affections which are apt to accompany them, may be good enough in civil life; in the army they are obsolete, fit only for fogies. True, there are a few yet in the Regiment, for whom, should they be suffering, I might yield to the sheepish impulse of humanity, and even become interested in their comfort. But Surgeon —— first, is to be my motto now. Hurrah ! we are on the move !

CHAPTER VII.

March 10*th*, 1862.—Well, the Army of the Potomas is at last in motion. After having lain still with 150,000 men, comparatively idle, for nearly eight months, our National Capital besieged, its great thoroughfare blockaded by a foe of which we have habitually spoken with contempt, the Van Winkle-ish sleep is apparently broken, and we are at last in motion.

We left Camp Griffin at 4 o'clock this A. M, and now—4 P. M., are bivouacked in sight of Fairfax Court House. Freedom Hill, Vienna, Flint Hill, all passed, and we have met no enemy. We are within eight miles of Centreville, and are receiving reports that the place is already in our possession. There is nothing authentic, but we shall know to-night. We are within ten miles of the famous Bull Run battle field, within fifteen of Manassas. Ho! for Richmond!

We have had a most unpleasant march to-day. Rain, rain, mud, mud. The men have suffered much, and many have fallen out of the ranks. I have received another official reprimand to-day, and still another. I suppose I deserved them. Only last night I wrote a letter to ——, in which I expressed my *joy* that I had at last come to the determination that feelings of humanity should not again enter into any of my plans or conduct during the war—that I should now take the "Army Regulations" as my guide. They recognize no benevolence, no affection. Commands and obedience are all they know, and I left camp this morning firmly resolved that these alone should govern me in the future. Five miles from camp I overtook a poor, weakly little fellow who had fallen out of the ranks. He had unpacked his knapsack and thrown away his clothes, to enable him to keep up. My resolution of three hours' ago was all forgotten. I had his knapsack repacked, carried it for him till I overtook an ambulance and put it in. Captain ——, one of the General's staff, saw me put it into the ambulance, and I "caught it." This reminded me of my resolve, and I renewed it. I pushed forward, and overtaking the regiment I found F staggering under his load of knapsack, arms and accoutrements. Poor F., the pale boy, who had been my assistant since I joined the army, but now, through the arbitrary vindictiveness of a little military despot, reduced to the ranks; could I leave him stuck in the mud and in the enemy's country? I forgot again! Shouldered his gun and knapsack, took his place in the ranks, and mounted him on my horse to rest. I confess it was not very dignified to see a Surgeon—a staff officer—and at this time accidentally on the *General's staff*,* wading through the mud, with knapsack and musket, whilst *a soldier* was riding. "'Twas derogatory to the staff." So to the usual reprimand, the polite military addendum of "d–mn–d fool" was this time appended. Well, a man who will so often forget his good resolutions, deserves it, and I will *try* not to forget again, so far as to permit my kind feelings to derogate from the dignity of my commander's staff.

*I was acting as Brigade Surgeon.

Report of the evacuation of Manassas is confirmed. We got news of a terrible naval battle in the James River. Congress and Cumberland lost! Merrimac disabled! But to-day we have Fairfax, Centreville Manassas and Ocoquan; that pays for the work of the Merrimac.

11*th*.—Suffered more from cold last night, than on any other night in the army. The wind was terrific, and I slept out without any way to guard against it. Rode back to Camp Griffin to-day, to see to the sick and the hospital stores left there.

What next? No enemy here to fight or to watch. What shall we do? We can form no idea.

12*th*—On examining the fortifications at Manassas to-day, we find them mounting "*wooden guns.*" Subordinate officers have no right to ask questions, but if I were not a subordinate I should be strongly tempted to ask if, in eight to twelve months of anxiously watching the enemy, it were not possible to find out the nature of his defences? I really hope this oversight, or, rather, want of sight, does not indicate a *wilful* negligence on the part of some of our superiors.

13*th*.—A sad day is this. The effects of General ——'s vindictive meddling with the Medical Department are beginning to manifest themselves. When he took from me my well-trained hospital attendants and my experienced druggist, on the 5th inst., there were appointed in their places, men, worthless in the ranks, and without knowledge of the important duties which they were to perform in the hospital. The druggist knew not one medicine from another, and to-day three men are poisoned by a mistake in dispensing medicines. One of them is already dead; the other two suffering severely, though I have hopes that they may yet be saved.

Thank God, I was absent at the time, and had nothing to do with either the dispensing or administering ; and yet, should I write that the vindictiveness was not yet gratified, would the world credit it? It is even so. I have addressed to the General a respectful letter, setting forth the facts, and urging the restoration of my druggist, but he refuses ! Would he decimate his Brigade to gratify his vindictiveness?

Well, we have lain still nearly a year, "surrounding the rebel army," and, yesterday, when we went to "bag 'em," they were gone! One thing is gained, however, the Capital is no longer besieged, and the blockade of the Potomac is raised. "Great is Diana."

I visited some Virginia ladies at their homes to-day, took tea with them, and witnessed from their house the most beautful review of about 10,000 troops, that I ever beheld. The house is a fine old Virginia mansion, overlooking a large plain, where the troops were reviewed by Gen. McClellan. We all enjoyed it greatly. But I enjoyed more the pleasure of sitting down once more to a family table, and exchanging the boisterous society of the camp, for the quiet conversation of refined and civil life. Oh how I longed for a return of that peace which would enable the North, the South, the East, and the West, to feel again the fraternal bonds, and stop the desolations of war.

March 14th.—Received orders early last night to hold ourselves ready to move at a moment's notice. A few minutes after receiving the above notice, I was ordered to return immediately to Camp Griffin, to look after my sick there—to send such as could not be moved with the Brigade to General Hospital, and the rest to camp, and then to rejoin my Regiment. Our destination is still unknown to us, but we expect that we go either to Norfolk or to join Burnsid

E

in the Carolinas.   We have been outwitted here, and the rebel army which should have been captured has escaped us.

I fear that my mission here is a failure.   My friends expected me to be useful to the Regiment, and if I have had one predominant wish, it was that the expectation might not be disappointed.   "The setting of a great hope is like the setting of the sun."   I am in its deep, dark shadows, and fear it will be a long night before I can emerge from the darkness which envelopes the hope.   I shall go on and do the best I can in the face of the interference of the military department, but must not be held responsible for consequences, as I am but a subordinate.

Vienna, March 15th.—Did not lie down last night, but worked in separating and disposing of my sick.   Most of them I have brought to this place to embark such as cannot march to Alexandria, by rail.   The Brigade did not meet me here, as I expected, and I got to it at Flint Hill (where I left it) last night.   I cannot look upon our possession of this place and the railroad without deeply feeling how much we have been outwitted.   Here we have been held still with 150,000 to 200,000 men, since July last, by a little village mounting wooden guns.   Poor McClellan, I fear a wooden gun will be the death of him yet, though his failure here *may be* attributable to the interference of others.   I will not hastily condemn him.

Alexandria, 16th.—Received orders last night to march at 4 this A. M.   Simultaneously with the receipt of the order came a northeast wind and heavy clouds.   The clouding up kept pace with our preparations to march, and such a day of rain I have not witnessed in Virginia.   To-night, after a march of twelve miles through mud and rain, the men lie out without shelter, except the little tents debris, which in time of rain are good for nothing. I shudder when I think of them, exposed, after a hard day's march, to the driving storm. And whilst they are thus exposed, I feel almost guilty that I am in a fine hotel, by a fine coal fire, "comfortable and cozy." But sickness brought me here. For three nights I have not slept, and last night I had an attack of cholera morbus. This morning, being sick and worn out, I asked permission to return to Vienna, (two and a half miles), and come in by rail. Permission was denied me. Sick or well, I must march, and look after the management of ambulances, and transportation of hospital stores. Arose at three o'clock, working part of time, and the rest cholera-morbus-ing till four. Started with the Brigade, but at Fairfax, for the first time since I entered the army, had to fall out. Went to bed, slept two hours, arose, took a cup of coffee, mounted my horse, and pressing my way through dense masses of the army for five or six miles, overtook the Brigade. When within a few miles of this city I was so sick that I insisted on being permitted to seek lodgings out of the weather, and having received permission, came on here. Have got dry and warm, and am now feeling better. I am gratified to learn to-night that my two poisoned boys are doing well, though it will be a long time before they entirely recover.

When I left Fairfax this morning the scene was grand beyond description. The soldiery, densely filling the road, leading from the town, had been pouring steadily forward for more than two hours. I looked back, and as far as the eye could reach down the two roads coming in, the dense body blocked them in both directions. The three roads presenting a long blue line rendered more striking by the glare of the bayonets, which at a short distance looked like a solid body of glittering steel over the blue bulk below. How far back the lines extended, I could not see, but I pressed forward for six miles, through the dense crowd. Verily, the army is now in motion.

16th.—'Tis Sunday morning. Returned to my regiment this morning: found all quiet. No one yet knows our destination. But from the fact that some forty *river* steamers await us, we infer that we are not going to sea. A singular fact, worthy of note: On our arrival here to embark, *not a steamer had coaled, and there was no coal to take on ! !*— Why is this? 'Tis terrible to even suspect that treason may be at work in the very heads of our departments.

March 17th.—To-day our sick, instead of being put into General Hospital, are marched from depot to the camp. McDowell's Division is ordered back to Arlington Heights. We are sending to Washington for our tents. Our General Smith is building stables, and it looks as if we were again *settling down.* What does it mean? Is there another change of programme? and are we not to embark after all? Have we discovered the muzzle of another wooden gun, which we must besiege for nine months? Many of the troops begin to question McClellan's claim to infallibility. I have to regret that I have again failed to prevail on the Governor to interest himself in getting me transferred to another Regiment, where I could be much more useful. The opposition which I meet here from some of my superior officers, is rapidly destroying the interest which I have felt in the Regiment. (At night) a great hurrah and rejoicing in camp, in consequence of an order to prepare, *immediately,* five days' rations, and to be ready. This may mean, embark, but our Gen. McC. has so often cried "wolf" of late, that when the wolf does come, we may not be ready. Shall we embark to-morrow?

March 18*th.*—All quiet yet; no embarkation; no move.

March 19*th.*—The wolf has not yet come, and two of the five days' rations are consumed.

March 20*th.*—All quiet. No move.

March 21*st.*—Do., do.

March 22*nd.*—Ordered this morning to Washington to look up hospital stores and boxes, which are scattered "to the four winds." This is the first time since the organization of the Regiment that it has moved without my personally superintending the packing and forwarding of the hospital stores, and the first time they have got scattered. "What you would have well done, do yourself." I fear many of them will be lost.

In passing, I here note two circumstances, that I may not forget them. In addition to the poisoning of three men at Flint Hill by a mistake in medicine, yesterday I discovered that the dispenser, imposed on me by Gen. II——, was himself taking pills of Unguentum—blue mercurial ointment—instead of blue pill, which had been prescribed for him, and was giving another man saltpetre instead of the sulphate of cinchona—innocent mistakes, to be sure, but indicative of the fatherly care which our General is manifesting towards the soldiers under his command. He refuses to restore my druggist, though he is made aware of these repeated and dangerous mistakes. The other circumstance: During all winter, when no fighting was to be done, our Brigade held the advance of the whole army. All the hard and dirty work fell on us—picketing, chopping, ditching; but we held the advance, the post of honor, were to have the first chance in the fight, and we grumbled not at the hardship and exposure. The time came for attacking Centreville and Manassas. We were ordered forward, when, to our exceeding mortification, we found that 40,000 troops had been thrown in advance of us. Our Brigade has not been permitted even to see Centreville and Manassas. They were occupied by our army before we were started. What means this? Has our Brigade commander lost the confidence of his superior officers, and as a consequence been thus disgraced? We are now near Alexandria, but not in advance. There are from 40,000 to 60,000 troops in advance of us.

March 23rd.—At one o'clock this morning, met Major M. in Washington, who informed me that the absent officers of our Brigade had been telegraphed to rejoin their regiments immediately, to embark at 8 this A. M. Left on first boat for Alexandria, and found the most of my Brigade embarked. I had just time, before going on board, to write and copy the following note:

ALEXANDRIA, March 23, 1863.

MY DEAR ——: 'Tis Sunday, and here I am surrounded by all "the pomp and circumstance of war;" troops embarking, flags flying, martial music from a dozen bands all around me. My own Regiment is this moment marching on board the steamer Canonicus; and amidst the confusion and turmoil of troops marching, almost over me, transportation wagons wheeling within a few inches of my feet, and amidst every conceivable noise, I sit down in the street, with an old box in front of me, to write these few words, thinking that they may interest even you. * * * In a few hours the distance between us will begin rapidly to increase. How long will the increase continue? God only knows. I hope soon to be turned homeward.

This is such a time as Alexandria never saw—it is to be hoped may never see again. There seems to be but little interest or excitement in the city. Scarcely anybody out to witness this solemn—this imposing pageant. I know not what else to call it. Are the people here rebels at heart? I fear as much so as South Carolinians. We are not informed of our destination, but I still believe it to be Norfolk, and if successful there, then to Richmond. We are now ——— Called on board. Farewell ———.

CHAPTER VIII.

March 24th.—We have had a very fine run for about thirty hours, having left Alexandria at 6 P. M., on the 23d, laid too over night near Fort Washington, and at 10 P. M., after having passed Mount Vernon, Ocoquan, Aquia, and many other points noted in this war, have come to anchor off this point.

25th.—This A. M., at 6, weighed anchor, and dropped down to Hampton Roads, and disembarked at what was the little town of Hampton. If there be pleasure in the indulgence of sad reflections, how delightful it would be to have all my friends here, to enjoy them with me to-day. For a few hours, whilst the troops have been disembarking, and transferring the baggage and munitions of war from steamer to transportation wagons, I have been walking the streets of this once beautiful, but now desolate little city. Never before had I a conception of the full import of that word—desolate. Shortly after the battle of Bull Run, the rebels, fearing that we should occupy the town as our winter quarters, abandoned and burned it. This little city, amongst the oldest in America, and now giving evidences of a former beauty, possessed by no other I have seen in the South, *they burned !*

Oh, the demoralization, the misery resulting from this wicked rebellion. I would like to describe here the scenes I have witnessed this morning ; but the sad picture, so strongly impressed on the mind, would be blurred and rendered indistinct by any attempt to transfer it to language. I have already an affection for this little city, and a deep-rooted sympathy for its former citizens, now scattered and hunted, exiled and homeless. Its population, I should judge, was about 2,500. 'Twas compactly built, mostly of brick. The yards and gardens even yet, give evidence of great taste.

The walls of the old Episcopal Church, said to be the oldest orthodox church on the continent, stand almost uninjured, but not a particle of combustible matter is left about it. In its yard are the tombs and the tomb-stones of a century and a half ago. And what a place to study human nature, amongst the 50,000 soldiers strolling around. 'Tis low tide. All the tiny bays left uncovered by water, are crowded by soldiers "on all fours," sunk to knees and elbows in the slimy mud feeling for oysters. The gardens are full of soldiers, the church yards are full, each giving an index of his character by the object of his search and admiration. Whilst I have been looking disgusted and indignant at a squad prying the tomb-stones from the vaults to get a *look within*; at another squad breaking off pieces of the oldest tomb-stones as "*trophies*," my attention is suddenly drawn away from these revolting scenes by the extacies of a poor, ragged, dirty fellow, over a little yellow violet which he had found. He almost screams with delight. Just beyond him is a better and more intelligent *looking* soldier scratching among the ashes in hope of finding a shilling, or something else, which he can turn to some use :

a few seems impressed by the solemnity of the scene. Such are the varieties of human characters and of human natures. For myself, I cannot but think how worse, even, than Sodom and Gomorrah is the fate of this place. To think, whilst looking over the sad ruins, of the young persons who had grown up here, and whose every hour of happiness was in some way associated with their beautiful homes; of old men who had been born and raised here, and who had known no other home; of widowed mothers, with dependent families, whose homes here constituted their sole wealth on earth. To think of all these clustered together on some elevation in that dark and dreary night, turning to take the last sad look at their dear old homes; oh, what aching hearts there must have been there that night! What envyings of the fate of Lot's wife, as they were leaving the quiet, happy homes for—God knows where, and God knows what! My heart aches for them, and every feeling of enmity is smothered in one of pity. Before disembarking this morning, we got a look at the famous little Monitor. A raft—an iron raft, about two hundred feet long, lying from eighteen to thirty inches above the water, with its great cheese box on one end, with holes in it to shoot from. Were I to attempt a description I should say, it looked for all the world just like the sole of an immense stoga boot lying flat on the water with the heel sticking up. In the afternoon, left Hampton, marched about four miles in the direction of Newport News, and encamped.

26th.—Remained in camp all day, examined my hospital stores, and put in order what few I have left. At Alexandria, in consequence of my being ordered to Washington to look after the scattered ones, had to entrust the forwarding the few we had there to my assistants. On arrival here I find that they are nearly *all* left or lost, except the few I picked up in Washington and brought with me. Not a tent, not a cooking utensil, and scarcely any medicines. Hope that I may be permitted in future to look after my own affairs without too much help.

27th.—A day of excitement. We are near the enemy. Brigade left camp at 6 A. M.; marched ten miles along the beautiful James River. Almost every building on the route burned. Dreadful devastation. At 12 o'clock came upon the rebel pickets. They ran, leaving camp fires burning. In one tent found a boiler of hot coffee, in another a haversack of hot biscuit. Very acceptable, after a long and muddy march. Major L——, with two companies, was detailed on a reconnoisance. They have not returned to-night, and we fear they are in danger.

28th.—Slept on the ground last night, my saddle for a pillow. Greatly to the chagrin of all of us, after having driven in the enemy's pickets yesterday, we fell back a mile or two, and to-day fall back about seven miles.

> The King of France, with 40,000 men,
> Marched up the hill, and then marched down again.

Major L—— and party came into camp this morning, unharmed.

29th.—We are in camp again, about two miles from Newport News. Nothing doing, and this gives me an opportunity to realize the condition of my hospital. Up to the time of our leaving Camp Griffin in the early part of this month, we had not in all our moves, lost to the amount of a candle. Now, with only two moves since, we are here to-day, in the face of the enemy, expecting a battle, without a tent, an ambulance, a litter, a blanket, or a comfort for the wounded

—not even a reliable nurse at my command. Well, I suppose all this is a small matter, so long as the commanders who brought it about are comfortable. They can be taken care of, and why need they trouble themselves about the men?

30th.—Slept in the open air again last night; it rained, and I awoke in a pool of water. Strange that we do not take cold from such exposure. I never felt better, and I notice that very few of the soldiers take cold from any amount of exposure at this season of the year.

31st.—To-day, whilst all were expecting orders to move forward, I received orders to build a log hospital. What can this mean? The weather is beautiful, roads good, troops in fine condition, warm weather coming on, and here we are preparing as for a summer's stay. God help us and our little General, but put it into his heart not to remain here till the enemy, whom we have found, has time to fortify against our approach. We have been a long time accomplishing nothing. Although the weather is fine, and it is now first of April, not a forest tree has started its buds. I am disappointed, for I expected by this time, in this climate, to be as in mid-summer. But even the trees, and nature, seem to linger, and we should not blame our General.

I visited Fortress Monroe to-day. This is a great Fort, almost surrounded by *natural water*, besides being entirely enclosed within its own moat. The two walls which surround it are together from thirty to sixty feet thick, of solid granite masonry, and the two together are about three miles long, enclosing by a double wall about eighty acres. It mounts 480 guns, commanding the approaches in every direction. The transports are landing here from 15,000 to 20,000 troops daily. This is no doubt one of the causes of the delay of our army. We wait for the arrival of the remainder, that when we do move, we may march steadily forward without fear of repulse.   Start us, and twelve to fifteen days should place us in Richmond, only about seventy-five miles distant.   Whilst sitting on the parapet of the Fort, I had a good view of the Rip-Raps, an artificial island, built up in the sea, of huge stones shipped there, and on which is built Fort Wool.   These Forts are the key to the great, strong door between the Federal and the Confederate Governments.

April 1st.—An opportunity offers to-day to send letters to the dear ones at home.   This privilege is becoming less frequent, and we fear that when we move from here, it will be even more so than now.   Visited Newport News to-day. This, though a sad, was a pleasant visit.   There, within a stone's throw of our Fort and guns, stood, a hundred feet above the briny water, the graceful spars of the ill-fated frigate Cumberland, sunk by the iron-clad Merrimac.   It seems impossible that this monster ship, yet untried, should venture on her first voyage out, not only in presence of our armed fleet, but under the very port-holes of one of our most powerful land batteries.   I listened to many interesting anecdotes of this naval fight, or rather destruction, but I cannot record them now.   I could not withstand the temptation to visit what there was of the Cumberland above water.   Climbed into the rigging, and discovered at the very peak of the foremast, about one square yard of the American flag, still flying.   I determined, if possible, to have a piece of it, and started on the arduous task of climbing a hundred feet to get it.   By the aid of ropes, and spars, and rigging, reached the top-gallant.   The flag was still fifty feet above me, and there was no way of my reaching it but by climbing that slender, smooth top-mast.   I looked at the coveted relic

with longing eyes—thought what a treasure it would be—
looked into the ocean fifty feet beneath me—looked at a rebel
gunboat which was hovering near, as a shark follows and
hovers around a vessel with a cadaver ready to be thrown
overboard; *then* I looked at *myself*, and came to the sage
conclusion that there was *another relic* which wife and chil-
children might value even more than they would that flag,
though tattered in so noble a cause, and waving still an unim-
peachable witness to the bravery and patriotism of the noble
crew who went down with it, still floating aloft, they never
ceasing to cheer that loved emblem, till choked by the
gurgling of the water in their throats, when they sank, to
cheer no more forever.

About half a mile below the Cumberland, the wreck of the
Congress is just visible above the water. For want of time I
did not visit it.

We have no further revelations as to the programme of the
war. It looks to me, however, that the plan is, to conquer
the banks of the James River, making use of it as the base of
our operations till we reach Richmond.

Shall we have a fight at Richmond? I very much doubt
it. If we press rapidly forward, we must reach there before
the enemy can concentrate any large body of troops or make
any formidable defences. They will then, I think, fall back
on the Cotton States, luring us on to an enemy more formidable than their guns—rice swamps, hot weather, and yellow
fever. If we delay, however, giving them time to reinforce
and fortify, it may be otherwise. So much for a guess.

My Hospital Steward has been for a month under arrest,
and though I have constantly applied for the appointment of
one to temporarily fill his place, it has been refused me. This
has caused me much extra labor. In consequence of this I

have to-day disbanded my whole hospital force, sent my sick to quarters, and refused longer to perform the duties of Hospital Steward. Shall I be arrested for insubordination? We shall see.

2nd. Camp No. 4, in the field.—Our Brigade was reviewed to-day by Gen. Keyes, to ascertain if it was in order to fight. Verily, it seemeth to me that our Generals have reviewed us enough to know whether we are in fighting condition. All are anxious to be reviewed on the battle field, and to lay aside this silk glove war.

3rd.—To Newport News again to-day, to take some of my sick to General Hospital. For the first time during this war met Gen. Mansfield. Rode about three miles into the beautiful country with Brigade Surgeon Curtis. Picked up on the beach some relics from the wreck of the Congress, which I shall value highly. On return to camp found that my *insubordination* turned to good account. My old dispenser, who had been taken from me, is made Hospital Steward, and I shall again open my hospital and bring back my scattered family of sick. Found also an order to move to-morrow at six A. M. Our Brigade Surgeon O—— relieved to-day, and I, being next in rank, succeed him. I should have preferred to remain with my Regiment, but cannot.

4th.—Moved at 6 A. M.—After a march of twelve miles in direction of Yorktown, (at about 8 P. M.) came upon the enemy's entrenchments at Young's Mills. They fired a few shots, wounding one man of 5th Vermont in the shoulder. They then retired, giving us possession. Their barracks here were built of logs with good fire places and chimneys, and were very comfortable—far superior to any which our troops had had during the winter. We encamped for the night in sight of the deserted fortifications.

5th.—A day of cooling rain, and warming excitement. Marched three miles, and found the enemy strongly entrenched behind a line of fortifications, on a narrow neck of land between the York and the James Rivers. Artillery duel at long range began about 12 o'clock, in which we had quite a number killed and wounded.

6th.—Accompanied the Brigade to-day on a reconnoisance. Frequent skirmishes with small bodies of the enemy. One man in Company F received a slight flesh wound in the thigh—the first blood spilt by our Regiment in the cause. We encamped to-day near "Lee's Mill," on the narrow neck of land spoken of yesterday, and about four miles from Yorktown. The whole distance between the James and York Rivers here is only about seven miles. Warwick Creek, emptying into the James, rises about two miles from Yorktown, and a small creek emptying into the York River takes its rise amongst the sources of Warwick Creek, so that the two rivers are here nearly connected by these two creeks. These creeks have wide, marshy bottoms, now deeply overflowed by means of dams thrown across at short distances apart by the enemy. And the whole western border of these marshes, now lakes, are strongly protected by earthworks, mounting heavy guns. This lake, or marsh, we must now cross before we can advance on Richmond. The enemy's force here we do not know, but suppose it to be inconsiderable. This is a very strong point, and if well manned it is almost impregnable. My opinion is, that they have but a small force here. This, however, is a matter of conjecture. All are expecting a big battle at this point.

7th.—Some fighting to-day, by small bodies, with slight loss on either side. In the afternoon, finding our camps commanded by the enemy's guns, we started suddenly on a move of what we were told was to be a mile or two. The rain poured in torrents, and, instead of marching a mile or two, we kept on the move until late in the night. Many of the officers made the soldiers carry their (the officer's) tents on their shoulders, and this, in addition to gun and knap.sacks, and whilst the officers rode unincumbered. In the organization of an army under a republican government, was such a distance between officer and soldier ever contemplated? We halted about ten o'elock, drenched with the still pouring rain. The men are almost starved, having been for nearly two days entirely without rations, and lie to-night in pools of water.

8*th*,—There is almost a mutiny this morning. No rations, and unless there should be better things before night, I shall not be surprised at any violence. Before leaving Newport News I laid in a supply for myself and servant for two weeks, but for two days I have been dividing with my hospital attendants, and my supply is about exhausted. When I awoke this morning, my fire was surrounded by men and officers clamoring for something to eat. They had some how got it into their heads that the hospital should be able to remove all the ills that flesh is heir to. I cooked what I had, and distributed till all was gone. Although hungry, I think I feel better to-night, than if I had permitted my mess chest to have remained locked by the key of selfishness. At night—a few boxes of hard bread have partially calmed the angry storm which has been rising. But two or three hard crackers to a man who has not had a meal for three days, is but small satisfaction. We are promised, however, beef, pork, bread, sugar and coffee in the morning, and how many hungry men are hopefully looking for the morning, that the cravings of exhausted nature may be gratified. The rain still pours, and if it continues another day the roads will be impassable for teams, and we shall be compelled to fall back to some point where we can be provisioned by water. We are within four miles of two of the finest navigable rivers in the world. The mouths of both of them are held by us, and that of neither is twenty miles away; and here we are, almost starving for want of transportation. This all seems to me an indication of an unaccountable oversight somewhere—"shiftless!" If we had, before coming here, on our way, conquered twelve miles of one of these rivers, we should have had good water transportation for all our rations. But holding the mouths, we have advanced, satisfied to permit the enemy to hold the rest. What a climate for mud and rain; and what a country and people for poverty and indolence. Though we are almost in sight of the historical cities of Yorktown and Jamestown, the country is not half so far advanced in improvements and culture as the new State of Wisconsin, or even the still newer and wilder Minnesota. What a curse is slavery! I do not like the brigadeship. It places too great a distance between the sick and the Surgeon.

9*th.*—Rained hard all day. But little done to-day. 6th Maine regiment went out in afternoon, got one man mortally wounded in a little skirmish. Roads so bad that I fear we shall have to fall back to-morrow.

10*th.*—Fell back to-day about a mile and a half out of reach of enemy's shells. Patience and endurance of *everything*, without expression of thought, can scarcely be considered a virtue, even in a military subordinate. The Western Army is all activity and execution. No. 10 taken, Beauregard whipped on his own ground, all our armies accomplishing glorious deeds, except this poor old thing of the

Potomac, called an army. Nearly a year has been spent by us in squatting around in sight of the enemy, rushing forward to-day, till within fighting distance, to-morrow falling back, as if afraid that some one *might* get shot. Here we have been for five days in sight of the enemy we came to capture or destroy, and this morning, because they threw a few shells into our camp, we are falling back! We are within twenty miles of one of our principal military stores and depots, with our men and animals starving. My ambulance horses have not had a mouthful of *any thing* to eat for nearly three days, and to-day they are expected to draw the heavy ambulances over the worst roads I ever saw Yes, here we are, in a "cul de sac," the rivers on either side of us held by the enemy, the ground in front blockaded by them, and their pickets jeeringly calling across the little creek to know whether we are not most ready to fight. Who is to blame? Many of us begin to question the ability of General McClellan.

If we can get forage and rations here, I think we must make some kind of a fight before we get away. How much of a fight, I cannot tell. It is surprising how man is modified by habit. During the late skirmishes, we who are not engaged, sat in our tents, smoking, singing, jesting with as much indifference as we would sit by our fires at home and listen to the falling of the axeman's blows. True, we sometimes notice the sounds of a report heavier than usual, and "wonder how many that shell did for." Would such indifference have overtaken us, if we had been kept engaged in the ordinary duties of an army? I verily believe not. It is the offspring of a kind of desperation. We came to effect something. We have been disappointed, and are growing careless of consequences. Nor are the moral habits of the men less changed. Stealing is becoming a pastime with them, and is scarcely looked on as a crime.

General McClellan's command has dwindled down to three corps d'armee, and I regret to say that the opinion is beginning to be held by many, that he is not competent to the command of even this force.

No mail now for ten days. This is very hard; harder even than to sleep out and go hungry. Even now our families may be suffering, dying, and we have no means of knowing it. Well, in time of war this is necessary, and perhaps it is all for the best. God controls and directs.

11*th.—A mail to-day.* One, *only* one little letter from my home, and that thirteen days old! The bearing of General ———— towards me for a few days has been greatly changed? What is it to mean.* * *

Last night Prof. Lowe, the æronaut, staid with us. He went up in his balloon, and took drawings of the enemy's fortifications. Says they are the most formidable he has seen during the war. Nothing doing by the army to-day. Gen'l. McC. visits us. He has had a council of war. Result of it of course not known.

12*th.*—Am not well to-day. Have diarrhœa, and at mid-day had high fever. How much I miss the tender care of my family in sickness. Am much better to-night, but feel sad. Have been reading Ernest Linwood, and, by contrast, it has recalled pleasant family scenes, which I miss in my sickness. I wish I had not written my last letter to my family. I felt badly when I wrote it, and spoke harshly of officers. 'Twas wrong, but I cannot recall it. Oh, if every thought is a *material thing,* an entity, and goes forth to make a part of the great mental and moral atmosphere, how is it possible that, with the great preponderance of evil imaginations there can be moral or mental advancement ? We should be as careful of our thoughts as of our acts.

13th.—I have been made very glad by the receipt of a letter this morning from my dear M——. It is older than her letters used to be when they reached me; but whether old or new, *her* letters never lose their freshness. They are like the beautiful evergreens, standing in mid-winter amid the bare and ragged oaks. When I cannot get a new one I often go back to one of the old, and always read it with pleasure and instruction. But she does ask so many questions for me to answer.   *   *   *   *

At Fortress Monroe and at Norfolk lie the Merrimac and the Monitor, in sight of and watching each other, like two dogs with a bone between them, each wanting and neither daring to take it. By the side of the Monitor lies the Mystic, (now named the Galena,) and the little model of Stevens' battery —all iron-clad. By the side of the Merrimac lie four iron-clad gun boats. Either of these miniature fleets, unwatched by the other, could in a few days destroy the whole wooden fleet of the other party, and burn its principal cities. Either one, unwatched by the other, could change the whole aspect of the war, and work a revolution which would shake the world and indelibly stamp its future. For these reasons they do not fight. There is too much at stake for either to venture. Suppose a fight in which the Merrimac should prove successful; the mouth of the James and the York Rivers would be effectually closed to us, our supplies entirely cut off, this army starved out in a week, captured or destroyed, the iron fleet of the enemy free to go where it pleased, and, in twenty days, the destruction of Washington, Philadelphia, New York, Baltimore and Boston, would be as certain as that the enemy should wish to destroy them. The stakes are too large. We dare not risk the wager.

14th.—Have just received an order from Division Commander S———, to see that every regiment in my Brigade has a wagon set aside for the exclusive use of the hospital, to take steps at once to see that all of my regiments are amply supplied with every thing necessary for the comfort of the sick and wounded, and to report the sanitary condition of my Brigade early in the morning. This indicates a forward movement, and although a change of weather, or a variety of other circumstances may alter the plans, I doubt not the present intention is to go forward during the week. I am quite recovered from my sickness, and although I sleep in the hot and in the open air, generally, I never enjoyed better health. Visited Warwick Court House to-day, and spent much of the afternoon in musing over the musty records of two hundred years ago. Jamestown must have been a small affair then, and it has wonderfully "held its own." The date of these records runs back to within a very few years of the organization of the first government in Virginia, when the blue laws of Connecticut were recognized as patterns of wisdom, even here, and *tobacco was a legal tender.* Brought away a few sheets, over which I expect to while away many otherwise lonely hours. This country presents subjects of study and reflection, as well for the moral as for the physical historian. Compare its age with its progress, its appearance with that of other districts differently conditioned. The face of the country presents large tracts of low, wet land, intersected by extensive ridges of rich rolling timber—if in a proper state of cultivation, a beautiful farming country. It is surrounded on all sides by the finest navigable waters, with one of the finest climates in the world; nearer to markets, both foreign and domestic, than any country of the same extent on the continent, and though it has been settled for two hundred and fifty years, we may travel for miles through an almost unbroken forest ; or, if we chance to find an opening made by the work of man, it is some insignificant field worn out by the culture of tobacco till it would produce no more ; then, like an old horse, turned over to fate. This little field perhaps will have in its midst an old house, after the fashion of the peasantry of George the Second, which will exhibit to the eye the same broken panes which disfigured it a hundred years ago, and grate upon the ear the same harsh sound of rusty, broken hinges, which answered on the swinging of the door to admit the tax-gatherer of England's king, two centuries before. Oh, Slavery! if these be thy doings, and thou art doomed now, all the sufferings of widows and orphans, all the sins of this wicked world will be atoned in thy crucifiction. Aye, this war is but one of the links in the great chain of events wrought by Providence countless centuries ago, to draw forward the car of progress to its final goal.

15th.—Another fine day spent in camp waiting for better roads. I am getting out of patience with red tape. Since our arrival at Fort Monroe, we have been without many hospital stores absolutely necessary to the comfort of sick and wounded. Three weeks ago, drew for articles to make up our loss. Notwithstanding that we have been almost constantly since in face of the enemy, frequently fighting and constantly expecting a general engagement, the supplies are not furnished, but all this time spent in enquiring "how were they lost," as if that would comfort the suffering army. At night received orders to be ready to move at 7 A. M. to-morrow, and yet without hospital supplies. Poor men !

16th.—Left camp at 8 this A. M., Gen. Brooks' Brigade having the advance, with Gen. Hancock's at a respectful distance in the rear. Then came the third, under General Davidson, and so on. Marched one and a half miles, and halted in line of battle. At the same time, 10 A. M., our artillery (Mott's Battery) opened fire about a mile in advance of us. This is the first time we have had a near prospect of a general battle, and the effect on the bearing and conduct of our men surprised me. Were they burning with impatience to join their friends in the fight? In trepidation lest the danger approach nearer? Weeping to think how many of us before night must bite the dust? Rejoicing that this fight may terminate the war, and with it our privations, hardships, toils and dangers? Weeping over the fate of friends now falling in the fight? Not a bit of these. For myself, so soon as the firing commenced I rode up to Major ——, and we exchanged an expression of our wishes in case of serious accident to either of us. That arranged, he remarked, " Well, Surgeon, should you be killed it will be only for an hour or two. You will then wake up, (the Major is a Spiritualist) rub your eyes, look around you for the boys, but soon realize your new position." We parted. I rode along the line of Hancock's Brigade to see the effect on them. I first came on a group of men talking "horse talk," and playing with their horses. Whilst I was listening, General H—— rode up, gave some general direction about ambulances, and casually remarked that Mott was having a hard time. I asked, What? He replied *laughingly*, that his " big French artillerist " had been killed, and that he had several others badly wounded. This Frenchman is said to be the best artillery officer in the service, and thus is his death announced to those for whom he has fought and died. Who knows how many ties of home, of country, of family, he has severed in our cause ? I felt hurt, made no reply, but passed on to the 49th Penn. Regiment. Their band were lounging on their drums and horns as listless as personifications of ennui. Along the regimental line were quartettes interestedly engaged in the melancholy occupation of "old sledge." At the other end of the line the staff officers, including the Chaplain, were lounging around, and seemed to be digging into their brains for something to think about. The Sixth Maine exhibited about the same degree of interest ; whilst the 43d New York were amusing their Irish fancies by counting the reports, and now and then exclaiming, "By Jabers, but that shot tould some of your last stories," and other similar remarks, showing that they had not become quite as much hardened as those around them. Rode back to the head of the line to see if the Brigade Staff realized any more fully the importance of our situation. I, of course, expected to find in Gen. H—— about two hundred and fifty pounds of animated and dignified humanity, surrounded by his staff of well dressed, well mounted officers, dashing from point to point on the field, holding everybody and everything in readiness for the conflict. What an illusion ! I found the General stretched upon the dried grass, his elbow on the ground, his head in his hand—that laugh ! Why the General nodded so low that a stub of old grass has run into his nose, set it a bleeding, and he sprang up with such an oath as none but he could utter. The scene was so ridiculous that even the common soldiers could not restrain a "guffaw." Major L——, a few feet beyond, lies on his stomach so fast asleep as not to be disturbed by the loud guffaw of the soldiers. To such a state of hardened carelessness have we been brought by a few months of constantly disappointed expectations.

F

In the afternoon, moved down into the open field where the artillery fight was going on. Brooks' Vermont Brigade engaged the enemy, keeping up a sharp fire across the creek, (Warwick). The artillery firing became still more constant. Our sharpshooters picked off their gunners, our batteries dismounted several of their guns, and three Vermont companies dashed across the creek in the face of the enemy's infantry fire, drove a body of them from their rifle-pits, but were com. pelled to fall back (not being supported), leaving abont twenty of their number dead on the field. We have no better fighting men than this Vermont Brigade, composed of the 2nd, 3rd, 4th, 5th, and 6th Regiments. For the small number engaged this has been one of the most fiercely contested battles of the war. The engagements of artillery and musketry have been terrific.

10 o'clock, P. M.—The warring of the passions, the physical struggles and strifes of the day, are hushed in darkness. Oh, to how many, hushed forever! In the last half hour the firing has ceased. I have walked the round of my regiment, lying on their arms in the open field, to see if any were sick after the fatigues of the day; and having retired into the deep woods alone, and ate a little cold supper, now sit on a litter, bloody.dyed with the blood of the dead, whom it has been all day carrying, (my lantern between my knees) to make this note of the sad occurrences of the day. We attacked the enemy, and have been repulsed.

I have not had time to finish my article, commenced weeks ago, which was to write down the U. S. Sanitary Commission, and I am glad of it, for here again we have been made to feel that the Commission is a power for good. Whilst the officials have been wrangling over the question as to how the hospital stores of the army got lost in the move from the Potomac to the Peninsula, and whilst the soldiers have been suffering for want of them, this Commission has been actively devising means to supply the much needed articles, and, behold! right in the midst of the battle to-day, whilst Generals were inquiring of Surgeons: " Have you the necessary comforts for the wounded ?" and whilst Surgeons were anxiously enquiring what they were to do in the absence of them, this Commission drops down amongst us—from some where—their wagons are unloaded, and the wounded made comfortable. That " writing down" article will not spoil by a little more keeping.

CHAPTER IX.

17th.—When I dropped down last night on my bloody litter, new thoughts overwhelmned me, and I could not sleep. It was our first battle, and we had been repulsed. I never saw the stars shine so brightly through the leafless trees, and the scene was calculated to excite the active workings of the mind on the occurrences of the day. I wrapped my head in my blanket to shut out the view. When I uncovered it this morning, I looked around on new scenes. The beautiful level field between me and the enemy, which yesterday presented a surface even as a floor, was now thrown into great ridges, a quarter of a mile long, mounted with cannon, bristling with bayonets, and covered with men ready to renew the contest. Our army had thrown them up in the night, as a protection against the enemy's fire. Shortly after sunrise the troops were seen marshalling for the contest. The cannonading recommenced, but in a short time began to slacken. By eleven o'ciock A. M. all was quiet, save the tramp of men and horses, and an occasional oath from the commanding officers, and a little later we were all on our march *back* to the very ground we left yesterday. Why we have abandoned the contest I do not know.

I had a skirmish with my General —— to-day. He questioned my motives. I replied tartly. We quarrelled, and to-morrow I shall ask to be relieved from serving longer on his staff.

18*th.*—Severe picket firing occasionally through the night, by which the army was twice called out. No fighting to-day, but our troops are still throwing up earthworks on the battle field of the 16th. Wrote General H. to-day, asking to be relieved from serving longer on his staff.

19*th.*—A flag of truce on the enemy's parapet. A proposition to suspend hostilities and bury the dead. We crossed the creek and brought over the bodies of 35 (instead of 20, as previously stated) Vermonters, killed in the fight on the other side of the creek. Nothing of importance to-day. All quiet, remaining in camp.

21*st*—Occasional firing between the batteries on Warwick Creek to-day, without results worth noting. Sickness among the troops rapidly increasing. Remittent fever, diarrhœa, and dysentery prevail. We are encamped in low, wet ground, and the heavy rains keep much of it overflowed. I fear that if we remain here long we shall lose many men by sickness.

This neck of land, between Yorktown and Jamestown, it seems now is to be made the point d'appui of the armies in Virginia. If we can, and *will* break up this army, it will put an end to the war, and until this army is overcome or dispersed, be it a month or a year, there will be no progress in the direction of a satisfactory peace. We are getting forward our siege guns, concentrating forces, in a word, preparing for battle. My request to be relieved of the Brigade Surgeonship is to-day granted, and I return to the charge of my regiment.

22*nd.*—Nothing of general importance to day. There was

an alarm, and in anticipation of an attack we were held in line of battle for about half an hour in a driving rain, then dismissed to quarters.

23rd.—A week ago to-day was the battle at Lee's Mill, and though there has been daily fighting ever since, and calls to arms almost every night, sometimes two or three times a night, there has been no battle worthy of the name. The artillery have been firing at long range, with occasional infantry firing. Two Federal officers, Col. Cassiday and Major Crocker, deserted to the enemy to-day. Charles F., of Company K, had his leg shattered by a musket ball—the first man of our Regiment seriously hurt by the enemy, although we have now been in the field nearly eight months. Whilst I was dressing his wound a little circumstance occurred illustrative of the tender sympathies which some military officers feel for their men. Gen. H—— was passing and looked in. "How are you, my man?" asked the General. "Oh, General, I am suffering terribly; but just set me up before the damned rebels, and I'll fight whilst I breathe." "I am sorry to see you wounded my man. *We need your services* in these times." That's it; not a word of sympathy for his "suffering terribly;" not a word of approbation for his bravery; no thanks for his having done his duty like a man. All sorrow for loss of service. He has fought his fight, and henceforth is a useless appendage to the army. "Poor old horse, let him die!"

The newspapers, containing accounts of last Wednesday's fight are now being received by us. They state our loss at thirty-two killed, and speak of our artillery as "mowing down the enemy by acres." Now, this is all stuff. We might as well tell the truth. Our cause does not need the bolstering aid of falsehood. I have myself seen over fifty of the killed. And, then, I was by the side of our batteries during the hottest of the fight, within five hundred yards of the enemy's fort, not a twig intervening, and at no time could there be seen an average of fifteen men to "the acre." What ever others there might have been there were so concealed in rifle pits and behind parapets as to be entirely secured against the "mowing down" process of our artillery. This system of falsifying and exaggerating is a positive injury to our cause. The soldiers are losing confidence in reports, and even in official statements. Even the newsboys are being infected, though I heard one this morning, wittily burlesquing the reporters by crying "Morning Republica-a-n. Great battle in Missouri. Federals victorious. Their troops *retreating in good order!* Wonder if it will not awaken the reporters to a sense of their ridiculous statements.

If we have another battle here, it will be a desperate one. No stronger position could have been selected by the enemy, and they are well fortified. Jeff. Davis is here, and in the field. Magruder is here, and they are being rapidly reinforced. I do not like this way of marching up to an enemy, and then sitting down quietly and waiting for him to get ready before we attack him. 'Tis not the Napoleonic style. But there may be good reasons for it which I do not comprehend. I am not a military man, and shall be careful how I condemn the plans of my superiors; but I do not like that style of fighting. Would it not be singular if Yorktown should decide the fate of this revolution, as it did that of "our revolution?"

24*th*.—Comparatively quiet to-day, with only occasional skirmishing along the lines. Sickness rapidly increasing;

yet government furnishes no medicines, no appliances for comfort of sick and wounded!

25th.—Still men are occasionally shooting each other along the picket lines, but nothing of general importance.

26th.—News reaches us to-night of a pretty severe skirmish two or three miles off, in which *it is said* about fifty of the enemy were killed. I have very little confidence in these "it is saids." We lost four men killed. I went to Ship Point to-day, and made the acquaintance of Doctor Mc-Clellan, (brother to General,) and Surgeon General Smith, of Pennsylvania—both agreeable men. Our army have done a wonderful work here, in the last few days. They have built a "corduroy road" all the way to Ship Point, eight miles, through a most dismal swamp. Over this road we are now transporting all our supplies and munitions (having got possession of York River, up to the neighborhood of Yorktown.)

27th.—We hear very heavy firing to-day, in the direction of Yorktown, but at night, have not learned the purport of it; though there is a rumor that several of our gun boats arrived there this morning, and that the enemy's batteries opened on them. Our whole Division is ordered out at 6 A. M. to-morrow. What means it?

28th.—Marched out this morning, to support our pioneers, who are cutting out a brushy ravine, which has afforded cover to the enemy's pickets, from which to inflict much damage to ours. We met with resistance, and have had quite a brush of a fight over it, but succeeded in driving the enemy out. Here, again, I am astonished at our men's indifference to danger, and their apparent insensibility to the suffering of their comrades. During the fight, our whole regiment were lying on the ground, laughing, talking, whittling and cracking jokes, as unconcernedly as if they were preparing for a frolic ; and, yet we were constantly receiving intelligence of comrades falling within a few rods of us. So near were we to the fight that we could occasionally hear the rebels calling to the " damn-d Yankees to come on." Sometimes when a wounded or dead soldier was brought by on a litter, the soldiers would discuss the question whether they would rather be litter-bearers or litter-borne, and would even get one of their number on a litter, with litter-bearers, and "play wounded." Such is the demoralization of war, and it is one of the least of its evils. War may be necessary, but—

> " Och ! it hardens a' within,
> An' petrifies the feeling."

29*th.*—A quiet day. Men seem cheerful and happy, but sickness increases. No medicines nor hospital stores, except those furnished by Sanitary Commission. I must take the liberty of thinking our Medical Director deficient in—something. What should we do now without the Sanitary Commission ?

30*th.*—Still quiet to-day, with exception of an occasional report of artillery along the line, and some picket firing. A. B. Millard, Co. G, 5th Wisconsin, brought in to-day, badly wounded in the shoulder. He lived about four hours after being shot. He is the first man killed from that regiment, though it has been eight months in the field. Am not well to-day. Have diarrhœa, and threat of fever.

General Washington's rifle pits extend for miles in front of our camps. The state of perfection in which they now are, after the lapse of eighty years, is surprising. A road runs by the side of the ditches, and were it not for the immense pine trees growing on the embankments, they would be taken for modern works to drain the road. These rifle pits surrounded Cornwallis at Yorktown, and from them was fought the closing battle of the revolution. May they serve the same good purpose for us now!

May 1st.—Awoke this morning, feeling very badly—*sick.* How I wish I could now be nursed a little by my family. Heard yesterday of the capture of New Orleans. This ought to have made me well, but it has not. Attended to a little business in the afternoon, but was very feeble. Hope to be able to work to-morrow. My wounded men are taken from my immediate control, and placed in what *is called* a brigade hospital. This is an outrage, and if we were not in expectation of a fight, I should resign at once. If it were found necessary to send the wounded away from the field to a general hospital, we would not complain. But they are simply transferred from one tent, under charge of their own Surgeon, sent here by the State to look after them, to another tent alongside, under charge of some other Surgeon, whom they know nothing about. It is an outrage on the men, simply to raise the importance of "red tape."

2nd.—Firing to-day in the direction of Yorktown. A report says that a general battle has commenced there. I think not, as we are moving our camp. If there were a fight we should have been ordered to hold ourselves in readiness, (which we have not.) Great rejoicing in camp at the report that Stevens' battery and the Vanderbilt have captured the Merrimac. But these camp reports are very unreliable, and have to be repeated many times before they are believed. We have increasing indications of a fight soon. I this moment hear a man inquiring after my health. He is sorry

"*the old gentleman*" is not well. "Fine OLD gentleman."
Am I really growing old? I am not well, but better.

3rd.—Considerable firing, all day, towards Yorktown.
Increases towards night. I learn that the heavy firing is
mostly by the enemy. Can it be possible that they contemplate an evacuation, and that this firing is to cover their intention? The camp ground *we left* yesterday is being shell-
ed to-day.

CHAPTER X

May 4th.—Sun-rise brought us the intelligence that during the night the enemy had evacuated Yorktown, and their Warwick Creek fortifications. Now for a chase. Immediately started—whole army in pursuit—and on overtaking the rear guard had considerable fighting through the day, in which, though we get reports of our victories, I am inclined to the opinion that we came off "second best." We have had a very hard march, many of the men being compelled to fall out. But we have Yorktown, without a fight. As the telegraph speeds this over the country, what relief it will bring to thousands of anxious, aching hearts! If the relieved feelings of anxious fathers, mothers, brothers, sisters, friends, lovers, could be told on paper and started to the loved ones so long exposed to danger here, what a burden of mail matter our good uncle Samuel would have on his shoulders!

A few incidents of the chase are worth remembering. Our cavalry started at a dash past the nearest abandoned fort, but suddenly under their feet burst a shell in the road, killing two horses and one rider. The *savages* had planted the shell in the road, and when struck by the horse's foot it exploded. There was an immediate halt, the road was examined, quite a number of shells exhumed, and the chase resumed. The infantry, after bridging the creek near Lee's Mill, pushed forward. A march of three miles brought us to the handsome *new* brick mansion of Captain Dick Lee, nephew to the General, and a large property holder here. I did not withstand the temptation to leave the ranks and take a look at the house. *Our Vandals* had been there, and all was chaos; furniture broken to pieces, books and papers scattered to the winds. At a short distance from this new building, into which the family had but lately moved, stood an old, weather-beaten, moss-covered wooden building, till recently their residence. I there found one relic which even Vandalism had respected—the leaf of a diary dated "May 3rd, 1862." "Oh, my dear, dear home, the home of my childhood—my life! Oh the old time-beaten, moss-covered house where my eyes first saw the light, and my 'tongue was taught to lisp its first prayer; how I have watched your decay, and my proud heart has been ashamed of your age. My own wicked spirit is now humbled, and I come to you to-day where my first prayer was uttered, to offer up the last in the home of my former *happiness*. Farewell, dear home, forever." This was written in a lady's hand. So the people here *were happy* once; but I suppose they did not know it, else why this wanton, wicked war, carrying misery into so many homes? Captain Dick Lee and all his family had left. Capt. Lee was only an hour ahead of us, and is, I hear, a prisoner to-night. His family were in Williamsburg yesterday. To-day they are doubtless flying in a pitiless storm before a pursuing army, homeless and houseless. Oh, Capt. Lee, think of that happy family one year ago, and now! We had two running fights, in one we were repulsed; in the other we drove the enemy, killing and wounding many of them. Our loss is stated at 40 to 50 in killed and wounded. But I am learning to put but little reliance on the reported results of a battle. We always exaggerate the loss of the enemy, whilst we lessen our own.

At sun-down we arrived at Mill Quarters, the residence of a Mr. Whittaker, about three miles from Williamsburg, formed Hancock's Brigade into line of battle, and skirmished till night. Then we laid on our arms in front of the first line of the defences of Williamsburg.

5th.—At 10 o'clock last night, I left the front line of battle, withdrew about half a mile, laid down on the ground by the side of a negro house, and about 2 this A. M., was made amusingly conscious of the fact, that underneath the eve of a roof is not a pleasant place to pillow one's head during a heavy rain. I was not in the least *thirsty*. I crawled into a cellar near by, laid upon the damp brick floor, with my wet blanket over me, fell asleep and dreamed I was a "toad and fed upon the vapors of a dungeon." But I was not a toad, though I own up to the vapors a little in the morning.

Detached from my regiment this morning to establish and organize a large army hospital at Whittaker's. * * * *

It has been a bloody day. A battle has been fought and our enemy driven; but we have suffered terribly. About 7 A. M., Generals Hooker and Heintzleman came upon Fort Magruder, with our left wing. The enemy came out and met us. He seemed eager for the fray, which we had supposed he was running to avoid. He seemed determined and confident in his strength and position. Falling on Sickles' Brigade, he decimated it at once. By noon, the battle on our left wing became general. General Hooker lost twelve guns, and by three o'clock our left wing was whipped and retreating in confusion.

At this time General McClellan, who, for some reason unknown to me, had been in the rear, was coming up, and met our flying battalions. By the active aid of his staff and a large escort, he succeeded in rallying our defeated army. He ordered up reinforcements, and sent them back to the field, where, though they could not drive the enemy, they maintained their ground. They retook Hooker's lost guns, and captured one from the enemy. General Peck's Brigade suffered severely, but he held them to the fight. The headquarters of the army and the large hospital of which I had control, were about two miles from Fort Magruder, around which the hottest of the fight raged. Shells were frequently falling and exploding in uncomfortable proximity to us, and by 3 o'clock could be heard ominous whispers about the necessity of abandoning our quarters, preparatory to a general retreat. The greatest anxiety now prevailed as to the fate of our army. The left could not hold out much longer without further reinforcements. The center had not been engaged. I hear that a dispute arose between Generals Sumner and Heintzleman, as to their rank, and that in the confusion resulting therefrom, the centre was not brought forward, nor were any of them sent to reinforce other parts of the line. (Strange that the Commander in Chief should not be with his army in a time like this !) The enemy were sending off forces to flank our right, and should they succeed in this movement and get into our rear, our whole army must inevitably be destroyed. The right wing was weak, consisting of only two brigades of General Smith's Division—the first composed of 5th Wisconsin, 49th Pennsylvania, 6th Maine and 43rd New York, and the third composed of the 7th Maine, 33rd, 49th and 77th New York, all volunteers, with two batteries. General Davidson, who usually commanded this third brigade, being absent, the whole was under command of General W S. Hancock. For some reason, the third brigade had not come up, and when the enemy's detachments of six regiments, supported by a well mounted fort, the guns of which were in easy range of our lines, attacked our right, we had only the first brigade and the two batteries to contend against them. This was the position of affairs when, at half-past three o'clock, I left the large hospital crowded full of the wounded, to go to the right wing. Up to this time I had supposed our army invincible, at least by an enemy fleeing from us, and now I was utterly astounded to find our officers clearing the roads of teams, men and everything which could impede the retreat of our army, and bodies of our artillery collecting in front of all the gorges, to check the speed of a pursuing enemy. I dashed past all these, crossed Queen's Creek, when a short ride brought me out into a large plain, in full view of our right wing, in line of battle, just as four regiments of the enemy emerged from the woods to the extreme right of our line of skirmishers. *We were outflanked !*

This was the most exciting moment of my life. Our left had been whipped, our centre had been passed, the Commander in Chief not on the field, the officers in command, instead of concentrating all their energies, were quarreling about their respective ranks, and had failed to reinforce the right, which had again and again sent for support, the enemy on the point of outflanking us here, and getting in our rear, in which, if successful, our army must be cut to pieces. At this moment, five companies of the 5th Wisconsin were skirmishing in the advance. Two of these companies on the right had just opened fire on the four regiments advancing. General Hancock had just given an order to fall back;

the batteries, which were in advance of all, instead of falling
back, leisurely and in order, were whipping their horses,
whooping, hollering, running from the field as if chased by a
thousand devils; three of the four regiments of Hancock's
brigade were falling back in obedience to the order; whilst
the Fifth Wisconsin, not hearing the order, or determined
not to abandon their skirmishing on the field, was continu-
ing the fight against the immense odds of four to one.
Nobly did it fight, every shot seeming to tell on the advancing foe.   But just then, as if to add to the certainty of our
destruction, two other regiments of the enemy emerged from
the abattis on the left of this wing, and were bearing directly
down on the little band so nobly fighting under such disad-
vantage.   Between these two regiments and the fighting columns was one company of the Fifth Wisconsin,
skirmishing under command of Lieutenant Walker.
His quick eye told him that the only hope of salvation for
our army was to prevent the uniting of these forces with those
now fighting, and with his little band of sixty brave men, he
boldly confronted the advancing fifteen hundred, supported
by their fort, not six hundred yards off.   At this critical
juncture, there is a moment's relief.   Our third brigade is
seen in the distance—but it is too far away to afford effective
aid.   Again the eye reverts, as the only hope, to the fighting
battalions.   Lieut. Walker is manœuvring his handful of
men into fighting position under cover of a fence, from which
they delivered their shot into the approaching mass with
wonderful effect; but still the mass advanced, and he was
seen passing along his line amid the rain and the lightning of
the battle, whilst his voice was heard above its roar.   Suddenly a flash along the whole fort's front, a roar of cannon,
and the shrieks of shot and shell, made my blood run cold as

I saw the Lieutenant whirled into the air and disappear among the rails and rubbish. The little band fell back; the cheering voice was hushed—but for a moment. Instantly he was seen emerging from the rubbish—the voice was again heard—back rushed the little band to the fight—the two bodies of the rebel army failed to connect—the battle of Queen's Creek was won—and the army of the Potomac was saved. But in recording the part taken by Lientenant Walker and his brave band, I must not omit to fix ₊permanently the heroism displayed by the main body of this regiment, who carried on the fight with the four flanking regiments of the enemy. Every man seemed most of the time to be fighting after his own plan, and on his own responsibility. The five companies skirmishing were under the general command of Lieutenant Colonel Emery, to whose firmness and coolness much of our success is to be attributed. The remaining five companies were in line under Colonel Amasa Cobb. The fight was commenced on our skirmishers,* who slowly fell back, contesting every inch of ground till they reached their supports, who now joined in the fight, slowly falling back to the main line. The relative positions of the 5th Wisconsin, the enemy's advancing line, and our regiments which had fallen back on the order of Gen. Hancock, were such as to prevent the rear regiments from aiding the 5th Wisconsin. It was precisely between them and the enemy, and a fire from them would have been destructive to our own men. Why Gen. Hancock did not change their position, I cannot imagine, unless under the excitement, *he forgot it.* To me his sole object seemed

---

* In this skirmishing, the companies of Captains Wheeler, Evans, Bugh, and Catlin, were engaged. Every officer, as well as every soldier, proved himself a hero.

to be to get the Wisconsin regiment *out of danger.* The enemy were pressing it. It was sending its vollies with the deliberation and precision of marksmen at a shooting match, and at every one, the ranks of the enemy were literally mowed down. It still fell back towards the main line, firing and fighting. By the time that it reached this line the enemy's ranks were so thinned that our success was now certain. It reached the main body, and one volley from our entire brigade ended the fight. At this moment, an order to " charge " was given, but simultaneously with the order, the enemy displayed a white flag, and the order was countermanded. No charge was made, the firing instantly ceased, the battle was won. In twenty-one minutes from the time that the firing commenced, these four regiments were so utterly destroyed that the two regiments which Lieutenant Walker had held in check, saw the futility of a further endeavor to reach them in time, and they, too, fell back. They left in dead and wounded about seven hundred on the field. The main body of the enemy, which had been so severely punishing our left, seeing our right driving their friends, fell back on Williamsburg, leaving their dead and wounded, their fortifications, and the field in our possession. Thus ended the great battle of Williamsburg, including the battle of Queen's Creek. The loss has been heavy on both sides, but the extent of it has not yet been ascertained.

After the battle closed, I spent the evening and night in caring for the wounded of my regiment, for whom I organized a separate hospital, keeping charge of them myself. I had seen so much indiscriminate amputating of limbs, that I determined it should not be so in my regiment, so long as it could be avoided by any efforts of mine.

6th.—It is ascertained to-day that although we were

entirely successful yesterday in driving the enemy from the field, and from his entrenchments, we did it at great cost. The aggregate loss to both armies cannot be less than 15,000 in killed and wounded. As far as we can now judge, this loss is about equally divided. Reports are rife to-day that Gen. Mugruder has surrendered with 12,000 men. At this report their is great rejoicing in camp, but it is not authenticated.*

I have spent this day at hard work amongst the wounded, not only of my own regiment, but of the army generally. Am very much now out to-night. †   Was visited to-day by Medical Director Tripler, with whom, after inspecting my own hospital, I went to General Hospital, at Whittaker's.

7th.—Magruder has not surrendered. This day has been spent by the Surgeons in care of the wounded, and by the troops in rest and rejoicing, at the favorable result of the battle of the 5th, which for a good part of the day threatened us with disaster. The enemy has evacuated Williamsburg, and we are in possession. Gen. Franklin, with his corps d'armee, yesterday left Yorktown on transports, for West Point, to get in advance of the enemy and cut off his retreat to Richmond. If he will be prompt, and accomplish this, it will end the war by mid-summer. We are now receiving Gen. McClellan's telegraphic reports of the late battle. He exaggerates. Amongst other things he says that "Hancock's success was gained with a loss of less than twenty in

---

* Since writing the above, I have heard it stated that Major Larrabee was not at his post during the fight. It is due to Major Larrabee to state emphatically that he was not only in the fight, but actively engaged wherever there were symptoms of wavering, and where duty called him.

† Early in the fight the gallant Captain Bugh, of Co. K, 5th Wisconsin, fell, badly wounded by a musket ball through the upper end of the thigh, shattering the bone badly. A braver or a better man never went to battle.

killed and wounded!" Why will Gen. McClellan undertake thus to deceive the country? Is it to elevate some favorite General? He cannot do that without, by comparison, depreciating others. Gen. Hancock had eight regiments under his command on that day. In one of those regiments alone I counted seventy-nine killed and wounded. True, the whole eight regiments were not actively engaged in the fight. True, too, that the regiment referred to suffered more than all the rest, but there were others killed and wounded; and even if there were not, the loss to this regiment alone quadruples the number reported by Gen. McClellan. I wish he would not do so.

8th.—I spent this day chiefly with other Surgeons and Assistants in getting the wounded to the river and on transports. My former estimate of the casualties was certainly not an exaggeration, and I now think the loss to the two armies is not much short of 18,000. We hear that General Franklin had a fight with the enemy near West Point this afternoon, and was repulsed, The hope that he would intercept and destroy the army is blasted.

9th.—We started at 5 this A. M., in pursuit of the retreating army. Found the road lined with fragments of wagons, gun carriages, and baggage of the retreating army, showing great haste. At night we are fifteen miles farther on the way to Richmond. I to-day had my knee-pan dislocated by the bite of a horse, and am suffering great pain to-night.

10th.—Another march of fifteen miles to-day. Have seen nothing of the enemy. We hear that General Franklin remained twenty-four hours at West Point before disembarking his troops, permitting the enemy to pass, and then attacking them in the rear! Has delay and procrastination become a chronic disease with our Generals? I hope he will be able to give a satisfactory reason for his course.   It begins to look as if, when this Army of the Potomac can find no apology for digging, it will hunt up other excuses for delay.

I have had to ride in an ambulance to-day, in consequence of lameness from the bite of the horse yesterday.

11th.—No move to-day.   Nothing of importance transpiring.   Atmosphere filled with all kinds of rumors of battles, but nothing authentic.   We are in a beautiful country, and about thirty miles from Richmond.   I am not surprised at the enemy having made a point at Warwick Creek.   It separates the most God-forsaken, from the most Godly favored country.   From Newport News to Warwick is truly forbidding; but on crossing that stream we strike into a country the natural advantages of which are extremely inviting; but still the same antiquated appearance of the improvements prevails, and there are no evidences of thrift or economy. We are having warm days, but the nights are cool and invigorating.

12th.—No move to-day.   Still encamped near West Point. Selected out our men disabled by sickness, and sent them off to general hospital.   This is usually the precurser of active work.   The crisis approaches.   Let it come.

CHAPTER XI

13th.—Again pulled up stakes and moved five or six miles, and brought up at Cumberland Landing, on the Pamunkey River. Here, on a large plain, surrounded by an amphitheatre of bluffs, were collected about 70.000 of our troops, presenting from the high ground a most magnificent sight. Spent the afternoon and night here.

14th.—At White House. Marched here to-day. It is known as the "Custis Estate," and is now owned by the rebel General Lee, nephew of the wife of General Washton, and has on it a large family of negroes, about 300. 'Twas here that General Washington overstaid his leave, the only time during his eventful life that he was known to be guilty of a breach of military discipline. Here he courted and married his wife. It is a most beautiful place on the banks of the Pamunkey river. It consists of about 5,000 acres and we now pasture our horses in a field of 1,000 acres of the prettiest wheat I ever saw. 'Tis waist high, thick on the ground, just heading out, and stretches away down the river as far as the sight can reach. By the side of it is an immense plain of rich and luxuriant clover, on which is encamped our army of about 80,000, with all the concomitants of horses, mules, ambulances, transportation wagons, &c.

Close by our encampment runs the Pamunkey River, up and down which a crowd of transports, gun boats, steamers, schooners, and all manner of water craft, are constantly passing. And here again we get another view of the blasting influence of the institution of Slavery—the most beautiful country on earth, with a fine navigable stream opening to it the markets of the world, and yet in its whole course of 100 miles, it has not, in two hundred and fifty years, built up a town of one thousand inhabitants.

We found and captured on this farm five thousand bushels of corn and seven thousand bushels of wheat. On this place, too, crosses the railroad from Richmond to West Point, making it a strong strategic point.

One circumstance occurred on our arrival here this morning, showing the distance between officers and men, and so characteristic is it of the man, that I cannot refrain from recording it in my journal, as "food for thoughts" hereafter. We found some negroes drawing a seine in the river here. Some soldiers made a bargain to make a draw for them, fixing price and paying for it. The men had been on short rations of hard bread and salt meat for several days. Being compelled to carry their provisions in their haversacks, they can carry nothing but this simple food, whilst the officers, having transportation at command, take with them all the comforts of the country. Well, the net was cast, and whilst the drawing was going on, General H—— rode down to the beach and watched the operation with much apparent interest. The draught was nearly at shore; the hungry mouths, and watching eyes of the soldiers were being gratified by the anticipations of a joyous feast, for it was now beyond doubt that the net was cast at a propitious moment, and was coming in loaded with herring, shad and eels. But what right had common soldiers to indulgences like these? The General's mouth watered too. The instant the draught was brought to land, the bayonets of the General's guard bristled all around, and the *General's capacious bags received every fish.* Off they were carried for himself and friends, without even a nod in acknowledgement. How ungrateful common soldiers must be not to love their commanders! How abject common soldiers are when compelled to submit to indignities like this, and dare not murmur! Now there was scarcely a soldier on that beach who would not have deemed it a pleasure to relinquish his right to what he so much coveted, *at the request of his General,* but to be driven from his rights by the bayonets of his legitimate protector!

Rains hard this P. M.

15th.—A raw unpleasant day. Hard rain, with east wind. We do not march, and in consequence of the heavy rain we may be compelled to remain here several days. The enemy is in force on the Chickahominy, and the two armies are gathering their hosts within ten or fifteen miles of each other, probably for a final struggle. The crisis approaches, and how the army pants for the time when they are to try conclusions! It was much worn out by the long delay at Camp Griffin. The detention at Warwick Creek was by no means refreshing, and now they naturally feel that every day's delay is irksome.

16th.—Quiet at White House. Nothing worthy of note.

17th.—But little worthy of note to-day, except the increasing impatience of the army. They begin to complain of the Commander in Chief, and, I fear, with some ground of justice. This morning the whole plain of 80,000 men, with its five hundred wagons, ambulances and carts, its five thousand horses, and all the paraphenalia of the army, was ordered to be ready to move at 12 m., precisely. At 11 we ate our dinners; then came the details of men for loading the heavy boxes and chests, striking, rolling and loading tents, which, by hard work, was accomplished by the hour fixed, and noon found us all in column; the word "march" was given, and off we started; moved about fifteen rods, wheeled (teams and all) out of the road into a beautiful field of wheat; wheeled again, and in a few minutes found ourselves right where we started from, with orders to unload and pitch tents. A few regimental groans went up as complimentary of the movement, and in two hours we were again settled. *The object* of this movement is now known to me, and so small and contemptible was it, so mixed up with the gratification of a petty vindictiveness, that, for the honor of the army, and some of its sub-commanders, I leave it unrecorded, hoping to forget it.

18*th*.—Last night, after we had retired, the aids-de-camp of the several brigades, rode through the camp, and calling up the company commanders, read aloud: " Orders from Headquarters. Roll will beat at 5 in the morning. Army will move at half-past six, precisely." All was bustle. The chests and boxes which had yesterday been packed for a move, in the morning, unpacked in the afternoon, were again packed at night, which showed how eager our soldiers are to get to work. The roll, at 5 this morning, instead of calling them from their beds, summoned them to breakfast. They were ready, but had not finished their hurriedly prepared meal, when it was announced through the camp, "Order of last night, to move this morning, is countermanded." If the oaths then perpetrated were recorded in heaven, the recording angel would certainly have been justified had he have "dropped a tear upon the page and blotted them out forever." Our army swore terribly, but their ruffled feelings are now being calmed by the beautiful notes of Old Hundred, exquisitely performed by our band, and recalling, oh! how many sweet recollections of homes where many of us have, for the last time, had the warring elements of our souls soothed into quiet submission by the "peace, be still," of this master piece of sacred music.

We are now in an intensely malarious region, with the sun's scorching rays pouring on us, and our men coming down by scores daily. We have been nearly twelve months in the field, have fought but one battle, and I fear that General McClellan's plan, to win by delay, without a fight, is poor economy of human life, to say nothing of the minor subject of wear and tear of patience; of the immense debt accumulating for somebody to pay, or of the major one of the effects of a protracted war on the morals of a nation.

19*th.*—Marched to-day about eight miles, but by a road so indirect, that we are only five miles nearer to Richmond. I am to-night again detailed from my regiment, with orders to report for duty at the general hospital at White House.

20*th.*—Army moves at 7 this A. M. In the P. M., in obedience to the order of yesterday, I returned to White House, where I was received with the gratifying remark of the Medical Director, that when he needed the interference of my General in his hospital, he would let him know it. To-morrow I shall return to my regiment, and hope to be permitted to remain with it.

21st.—From White House, returned to camp to-day. I really believe I am becoming attached to this kind of life, though I did not feel it till to-day. When I reached the spot where I left the army encamped yesterday, and found it deserted, with the camp poles still standing, (although I had staid there but one night,) the desolateness of feeling was strongly akin to that experienced on returning to an old and loved home, and finding it emptied of all that had made it dear. The army had left, I followed, and am now with it, encamped within ten miles of Richmond, near the Chickahominy. We have had some firing in the distance, towards Richmond, this P. M.

22nd.—A quiet day in military matters. No movement of the army. Ballooning all day ; discovered large force in front of us. Unless the fear of McDowell or Banks, in the rear, should induce an evacuation, we must expect hard fighting here. Heavy thunder storm this P. M.

23rd.—No movement. Should this journal, after I am gone, fall into the hands of persons, who shall undertake to read it, and shall complain that these everlasting records of " no movement," " all quiet," and " thunder storms," are dry food for the mind, I answer them now : That the hardships which we suffer in this world, instead of awakening a sympathy for others in the same condition, are more apt to call up unworthy comparisons, with a remark, that " they need not complain; they are no worse off than we are." And just so at this moment, I find the physical man of the army answering the complaints of mental man in civil life, finding fault with the dullness of these records. Try, says he, long camping and disappointed expectations, amid the swamps of the Chickahominy, living on half rations of hard

crackers and salt beef, and you will then be able to appreciate the hardships of dry food, and the difficulty of assimulat-
ing from it moist ideas.

But, at 5 P. M.,—*an event.* Our Balloon is up, with Pro-
fesser Lowe and General McClellan, taking observations of
the enemy and his movements. Boom—speaks a big gun
from away beyond the Chickahominy. Bang—a little cloud
of smoke just over the balloon, and the fragments of a shell
hiss and screech in all directions around it! Ah, General,
are you thinking. Eight hundred feet above the earth, how
quickly that shell, or the one this moment coming in search
of you, by a passing touch with the gossamar web which
holds you suspended above your fellow men, would ex-
tinguish all the hopes and bright visions of political or military glory, which *sometimes* form the brightest jewel in the
crown of patriotism? Or are you reflecting on the solicitude with which you are now watched by the tens of thousands of humble but anxious men, praying, without one selfish feeling, to the God of the patriot, to protect and preserve you, on whom they feel now rests the solution of the
greatest problem, in the moral as well as the political history
of the world? I wish I *knew* your thoughts just now. I
wish I could *know* that they are as far above the grovelling,
selfish ambition of some of those now watching you, as you
this moment swing higher than they.

And now, oh General! look down, I beseech you, from
your airy height, on your little army below, and devise
means to preserve it from the temptations of the world, the
flesh and the devil. Particularly guard from those evils,
your officers; and most particularly your journeyman
Generals. Teach them that it requires more than
accidental promotion, or even accidental success without

merit, to make great men of little ones. Teach them, I beseech you, the folly of vanity; whilst you inculcate the fact that many of your officers are doubly blessed with permission to carry *all* their brains in their shoulder straps, leaving their heads unincumbered, and to be used for substantial purposes.

Teach your men to be not only obedient and respectful, but submissive to the whims of their superiors; that they have no right to any of the comforts to be gathered by the wayside; that should they find the fishes,* the fruits, the poultry and other delicacies of the country guarded against their approach, for the comfort of their Generals, to remember that these Generals were never confined to hard bread and dried beef, on long marches, and can therefore never appreciate the wants and the sufferings of the common soldiers, who are; and that their might gives right to appropriate all these to themselves. Teach them that when, at the close of a hard day's march, through mud and rain, should a " double quick " be required of them, their commander, being well mounted, can know nothing of the impossibility of obedience, and that terribly profane oaths are at such times the only *gentlemanly* invigorators known to Generals. Teach them that obedience from *submission*, and not from principle or affection, is the only rule to be recognized in your army; that in becoming soldiers they ceased to be men; and all for thy glory and thine honor.

24*th*.—Another day of inaction near Gaine's Mill, on the Chickahominy. An instance of petty despotism occurred to-day. I was sick, confined to my bed. We were approaching Richmond, with prospect of a fight. The

---

* See record of May.

Division Surgeon procured an order from General Smith, detailing me to organize and take charge of a hospital at Liberty Hall. I reported sick. The order was repeated; the report was repeated. The order came the third time, with the same result. General ——— took the matter in hand, and ordered me from my quarters, as a non-effective, to this hospital, or house, unorganized, without any provivisions for the sick, now packed full of soldiers, suffering with infectious diseases of the worst kind. From this order I had to appeal to the Division Commander, who at once had it rescinded, and the "amiable General H——" was cheated of his victim.

25th.—I had a dream last night. There is nothing being done to-day, and as Dr. Franklin, when he gave as one of his rules of conduct, "Never tell your dreams," did not add, never write them, I here record mine. "Like master, like man." Master McClellan had his dream published for the the world; I see no good reason why I may not record mine for my humble self. It was part vision, part dream— part retrospective, part prospective: I saw Buell, and Halleck, and Grant, and Pope, and Foote, battling successfully. I saw some slight errors in their conduct. I saw Grant resting securely at Shiloh, made careless by his former successes, and I saw the terrible consequences of his self-reliant carelessness, and yet with all the draw-backs, and the terrible responsibility, the aggregate of all the efforts in the West and Southwest, had resulted in a great progress of our cause. I saw some of the gigantic projects of Fremont, at first sneered at and ridiculed; afterwards adopted, and become the most powerful agents of our success.

"A change came o'er the spirit of my dream," and I saw the Army of the Potomac at Bull Run scattered in flight

—routed, massacred—when it should have been successful. I saw the terrible slaughter at Big Bethel—so great that the Government never dared to tell it—greater than any of us had ever imagined. I saw thousands of our best men driven to the slaughter at Ball's Bluff without the possibility of either success or escape. I saw in my vision what I had witnessed in reality, our fight at Lee's Mill, when about two hundred of our brave men were sacrificed by being led against an enemy of the strength and position of whom our leaders were ignorant, I saw the army fall back, and die by hundreds in the swamps and ditches, waiting for the enemy to leave. I saw the pursuit from Warwick to Williamsburg, in which we rushed upon a body of the retreating army, and were repulsed with the loss of fifty men. I saw again Hancock's little Brigade drawn up in line of battle, about sun-set of the same day, under command of Col. Cobb, in sight of Fort Magruder, and distinctly heard the voice of General ———— ask the Colonel if he would take that fort with his little Brigade "now, or wait till your men have had their suppers?" I saw the men, tired and hungry (for they had not ate a mouthful all day) throw off their knapsacks right in the field where they stood, and go forward to "take that fort before they had their suppers." And then I saw what had not been visible to my eyes awake, 15,000 of the best troops of the Confederate army lying in and around that fort, the strongest I had ever seen, and our little, jaded, worn-out brigade of three thousand on their way to take it. And how clearly then did the dream show me the incompetency of the leaders on whom these devoted men were pouring out their whole confidence. I saw *a Providence* lead the brigade astray into the enemy's abattis, entangle and detain it there till after dark, then lead it across an open field into another abattis, impassable even by daylight, and there compel it to remain till morning, complaining of the very fate which was preserving it from entire destruction. I saw the impossibility of escape for a single man, had they passed the abattis and attacked the fort. I saw Gen. Hooker next morning, groping about, ignorant of the position of the rest of our army, and of the strength and position of the enemy, until he stumbled on them, and found himself unexpectedly engaged with a force which he was unable to withstand. I saw him with his corps fight as rarely ever man fought before —his brave men and officers falling around him, unflinching and unaided, calling in vain for succor on whole divisions of the army, who were looking on as idle spectators, *but I looked in vain for the commander-in-chief*, or some one with authority to order up these idle but anxious brigades. I saw Hancock's Brigade engaged without plan, and without order, the General, secure behind the walls of the fort, ordering his regiments to fall back from before the advancing foe, and that same Providence inspiring *one* regiment to stand fast, despite that order, to fight the battle to the death, to save the army, and to win for their General a reputation which he had not courage to risk in the unequal combat. So much in retrospect. My dream reached ahead, and I saw Gen. McClellan at the head of a large army marching into Richmond. Suddenly we came upon a fort thrown up by the enemy. I got upon an elevation, and saw a few thousand troops there. A balloon was in the air; my dream transported me to this balloon; I looked into Richmond; there was a small army there preparing to evacuate; the citizens were hurrying to and fro, packing up and leaving the city; some were already crossing the river. The few troops who were there, marched out, presenting a bold front, as if to delay our advance till the citizens could have time to escape. The æronaut dropped a note to the commander to hurry forward, and he would not only take the city but capture an immense spoil. My eye followed the fall of the note, and what was my surprise to see breastworks had sprung up for miles in length, in front of our army; men, dead and dying, were lying in the ditches, and thousands of spades and shovels were burying them there without winding sheets or coffins, whilst the Commander-in-Chief, with folded arms, stood looking on. A shout arose, "Hurrah for McClellan!" and a response, so deep and sudden that it shook the very ground! "What has he accomplished." I awoke, startled more by the idea conveyed in question, than by its noise. I immediately arose, and having thought for a few minutes over the retrospection of my vision, caught up my diary and wrote it down with this addendum: "Now here we are in the sight of Richmond, preparing for the great battle which is perhaps to decide the fate of free institutions for ages, without any more idea of what we have to contend against than we had at Lee's Mill or Fort Magruder. Have we no way to discover the enemy's strength and position as he does ours? If after all I have witnessed I have misgivings as to the result, it should not be wondered at, nor should I be blamed for my want of confidence. Whilst I hope for the best, I keep prepared for the worst; only whatever is in reserve for us, let it come and relieve this suspense."

26*th.*—To-day, was so far recovered that I reported myself for duty at the Liberty Hall Hospital.* I found there about four hundred sick, about one hundred of whom were crowded into the house. The rest were lying about in stables,

* Liberty Hall is a large dwelling, the birth place and home, during his life, of Patrick Henry. It is about eight miles from Richmond.

alive with vermin—chicken houses, the stench of which would sicken a well man, on the ground, exposed alternately to beating rain and the rays of the scorching sun. There were no beds, no blankets, no straw, no cooking utensils and nothing to cook. The sick were lying on the bare floor, or on the bare ground, without covering, and this was the third day they had been in this situation without food, or without any one to look after them, except as they could mutually aid each other. All kinds of diseases prevail, from simple intermittent to the lowest camp typhus, complicated with scurvey ; from simple diarrhœa to the severest of dysentery. My first effort has been to separate the simple from the infectious diseases. To pitch what few tents I have, and to get as many as I can under shelter, I have before me, in the organization of this hospital, a Herculean task for a man not quite recovered from a spell of sickness. But what I can, I will do.

27th.—Resumed my labors in the hospital this morning, making requisitions for provisions and cooking utensils. Some of the men have now been without food, and are in a state of starvation. I have not had to-day half the help I need, and in consequence of my over-work, am sick again to-night, and have been compelled, so to report. Surgeon Jayne, of one of the Vermont regiments, is detailed to take my place.

29th, 30th and 31st.—I am still too unwell to resume charge of this hospital, and as I hear of no action in the army, I have nothing to record.

June 1st.—Am so much better, to-day, that I have to report for duty. Am instructed to remain at my quarters near the hospital till further orders. I think I can foresee a plan in this to keep me at this hospital during the fights before

Richmond.   It is a dangerous thing in this army for a subordinate officer to think.

2d, 3d, 4th.—Taking my ease and riding about the camps, not having received any further orders as to duty. The army remains in "statu quo," the large hospital, or rather its patients, in suffering state, though Surgeon Jayne seems to be using every effort to improve the condition of things.

CHAPTER XII

JUNE, 1862—(ACROSS THE CHICKAHOMINY)—INCIDENT IN HOSPITAL—ACKNOWLEDGMENTS.

5th.—This day Franklin's Corps crossed from the left to the right bank of the Chickahominy, and encamped near Goldon's farm. I was again ordered to the charge of Liberty Hall, Surgeon Jayne and most of my assistants withdrawn.

This is as I expected. Our wing of the army has crossed, no doubt in anticipation of a battle soon, and I am again detached from my regiment in the hour of its trial. I called on the Medical Director this morning, and stated in the strongest language I could command, my wishes to be with my regiment when it went to battle. The reply was that it would not be consistent with the good of the service to have me withdrawn from the large hospital at this time. I then asked to be permitted, in case of a battle, to ride to my regiment, after I had seen and cared for all the patients in hospital, to remain with it what time I could, and return to hospital in time to again see all the patients, during the afternoon and evening. The Director hesitated. I urged, stating that, in consequence of my having been so much separated from my regiment by orders, the friends of the regiment at home were complaining of me for it ; that it was being noticed even in the public papers, to my prejudice. Besides, I had many intimate personal friends in the regiment, the sons, too, of my neighbors and friends, who looked to me for aid and comfort in the time of trial, and I would like to be present, even if only long enough to receive their dying messages. *I did not get the permission.* I have returned to my hospital sad and discouraged, but with the determination that, if I am denied the privilege of caring for those under my especial supervision, I will do the best I can for the poor fellows here who are accidentally or rather arbitrarily under my charge.

6th.—Yesterday I resumed my duties in hospital actively. On examining the Steward's Department, I found *almost* nothing to feed the starving five hundred men on my hands —*absolutely* nothing *suitable* to feed them on; that for days there had not been a cooking utensil belonging to the hospital, for these five hundred sick, larger than a soldiers tin cup. To-day, I have set myself actively at work. I have called on Quartermasters, Commissary, Medical Directors, and Generals, for the proper authority to procure the necessary supplies; the promises are profuse, but the interminable "red tape" must be followed out, even though the men starve. Plenty of supplies in sight belonging to the government, and soldiers dying of starvation! I have not half nurses enough to care for the sick and dying. To-day I asked for a detail of half a dozen men, as cooks and nurses. "They could not be spared from the lines." I immediately went to the top of the hospital, from which I counted over fifty muskets in the hands of our able bodied soldiers, guarding the vegetables, the fruits, the flour, the pork, the beef of rebels, (now in line of battle, in sight of where I stood) whilst our poor men were dying for the want of these very things. I came down and asked for a detail from these guards who were not "in the lines" to assist in nursing the sick and burying the dead. *I could not have them !* Verily, the unfortunate sick of an army must be interlopers; they can have no business there. I close this writing, and retire with loathing and disgust of what I must see here; but not till after I have written a letter to the Medical Director, setting forth the occurrences of this day in language as strong as I am master of, and asking to be either sustained in my efforts here, or returned to my regiment.

8th.—I am threatened this morning with dismissal from the service, and my letter of yesterday is held up as a piece of intolerable insolence, and as one good ground for my being dishonorably relieved. Well, I am a Surgeon of a large hospital, in which are about five hundred brave but unfortunate men, who, under their almost superhuman efforts to sustain and defend a government have broken down and sickened. They are from home, from family, from friends; they are suffering for want of the commonest attention ; the dead and the dying are lying together for want of proper and sufficient aid to dispose of them otherwise. The living are dying for the want of the necessaries of life, which, in great abundance, are in sight, part owned by the government, part by the rebels ; that owned by the latter carefully guarded by men withrawn from our lines, lest some of these suffering sick should, in desperation, crawl from their beds, get in reach of, and take enough to snatch their languishing bodies from suffering, and, perhaps, from death. But worst of all, I have taken the liberty of stating these things plainly, and, as a penalty for my insolence in holding up a mirror to the eyes of a superior officer, I am to be relieved! By me, " this is a consummation devoutly to be wished." Will they dare to try it ? We shall see. (I have a mirror which will reflect other sights not less hideous than this. Perhaps they would like to look at it ?)

(This month was the one in which commenced the retreat, or "change of base,") from before Richmond. The constant call on my time, from the last date to the 25th, prevented my keeping a full journal of events, and I therefore state, generally, that after having been compelled, for three weeks, to witness an amount of unnecessary suffering, which I cannot now contemplate without a shudder, I at last succeeded, by the efficient and cordial aid of my Assistant Surgeons, Dickinson, Tuttle, Freeman and Brett, (the last two named coming in at a late date) and by my " insufferably insolent demands" on my superior officers, in getting the hospital wel[1] supplied with provisions, stores, bedding, &c. The Assistant Surgeons named above, have my acknowledgements and my grateful thanks for their ever willing and well-timed support of me in my efforts to relieve the sufferings of brave men under our care. I wish, too, to make my acknowledgement to Medical Director Brown, for his courteous and cordial support of my efforts. Nor can I pass here without bearing testimony to the ever-ready and humane efforts of the Sanitary Commission to aid, by every means in its power, in the proper distribution of comforts for the sick and wounded. On arriving at Washington, shortly after entering the service of the United States, I became much prejudiced by statements made to me against this organization, but it required but a short time to satisfy me that my prejudices were groundless. I have uniformly found the members both courteous and humane, and am satisfied that the privations of the soldiers would have been incomparably greater but for the aid received through them. From this Commission we received, about the 15th June, amongst other things, a generous supply of bed sacks.   These, by the aid of the convalescents in hospital, were filled with the fine boughs of the cedar, pine and other evergreens, which made very comfortable beds, and in a few days after this every man was comfortably bedded, and between clean, white sheets.*   About the time of this change in the condition of the hospital, patients unable to be moved to the rear began to be sent in here from other hospitals.   The removing of convalescents to the rear, and the breaking up numbers of hospitals and massing their very sick in one general field hospital, always indicates some active army operations.   'Twas so in this case.   But the condition of the patients sent in was shocking in the extreme, and a disgrace to the officers by whom such things are permitted. Poor fellows, wounded in battle, had been neglected till their wounded limbs or bodies had become a living mass of maggots.   Legs were dropping off from rottenness, and yet these poor men were alive.   Yet if the Surgeons had have protested against these things, *perhaps* they would have been threat-

*A little incident here.   Amongst the loads of hospital supplies furnished by the U. S. Sanitary Commission, were many articles of clothing and bedding marked with the names of the persons by whom they were donated.   After the new beds were all made and severally assigned to those who were to occupy them, I was supporting a poor, feeble Pennsylvanian to his bed.   As he was in the act of getting in. he started back with a shriek and a shudder, accompanied by convulsive sobs so heart-rending that there was scarcely a dry eye in the ward.   He stood fixed, staring and pointing at the bed, as if some monster was there concealed.   As soon as he became sufficiently calm to speak, I asked what was the matter?   With a half-maniacal screech he exclaimed—his finger still pointing—"My mother!"   Her name was marked upon the sheet.   Three days after the poor fellow died with that name firmly grasped in his hand. The sheet was rolled around him, the name still grasped, and this loved testimonial of the mother's affection was committed with him to his last resting place.   This circumstance was published at the time, in a letter from myself, and I have seen it also stated in several papers, extracted from letters written to friends by soldiers in the hospital.

ened, as I was, with dismissal, and have been told that it was
"bad enough that this should be, without having it told to
discourage the army." There is no necessity for it, and the
Surgeon who will submit to being made the instrument of such
imposition on the soldiers, without a protest, deserves dismissal
and dishonor. I must be permitted to insert here my most solemn protest against the action of *any* Governor, in promoting,
at the request of (7x9) party politicians, (and in defiance of the
remonstrance of those acquainted with the facts,) officers, and
particularly surgeons, whose only notoriety consists in their
ability to stand up under the greatest amount of whisky; and
also against their re-appointing surgeons under the same influence who, after examination, have been mustered out of
the service for incompetency. Under such appointments humanity is shocked, and a true and zealous army of patriots
dwindle rapidly into a mass of mal-contents.

24th.—To-day General Hooker advanced his picket lines
about one mile nearer to Richmond, and the incessant roar
of artillery, with the constant volleys of musketry and the
cheers of fighting men, wafted to us from beyond the Chickahominy, tell that it is being done, not without cost of the
blood and suffering of brave and good men. At night we
hear that Hooker's movement has been a success, crowned
with a victory. General Hooker rarely undertakes a thing
which he does not accomplish ; but I fear our loss has been
heavier than is now admitted. These frequent reports from
our Commander-in-Chief, of great victories with little loss,
subsequently contradicted by the real facts, begin to shake
the confidence of a large portion of the army in his infallibility.

25th.—All in the hospital having been made comfortable,
we set to work yesterday to take care of ourselves. Arrang-

ed our tents, and to-day find ourselves a band of contented Surgeons, assistants and nurses, willing *now* to remain where we are. The above lines were written at noon, and before the ink dried, an orderly rode up with a note, the first line of which read: "Surgeon, you will report for duty with your regiment, without *delay.*" So the fat of my content is all in the fire. I suppose there is another hospital to be organized. This constant change from newly established order and organization, to unorganized, chaotic confusion, is very trying. To establish a large field hospital, provision it and put it in good condition for the comfort of sick and wounded, in the short time allowed and with the disentangling of the red tape, is a big work, which I have been so frequently called on to perform, that I am heartily sick of it. No sooner do I get all comfortable, and become interested in the men under my care, than we must separate, perhaps, never to meet again.

On receipt of order to join my regiment, immediately mounted my horse in obedience, leaving behind me my tent, trunk, books, mess chest—everything but a case of surgical instruments, and reported at headquarters on the Richmond side of the Chickahominy. Found all quiet on the surface, but there was underneath a strange working of the war elements, which I could not comprehend. Officers spoke to each other in whispers—there was a *trepidation* in everything. There was "something in the wind." But it blew no definite intelligence to me. I received no order for duty; only to hold myself in readiness for whatever might be assigned me.

CHAPTER XIII.

26th.—The forenoon of to-day passed something as did the afternoon of yesterday. Asked for transportation to bring my tents and baggage from Liberty Hall. Cannot have it till to-morrow; so, having nothing to eat, nor any place to shelter, have lived on the kindness of my friends.

About 2 o'clock P. M., "Stonewall Jackson" and General Ewell, from the North, and Generals Lee, Longstreet and Hill, from Richmond, having united their forces to the number (reported) of about one hundred thousand, made an attack on General McCall's division, which was strongly posted and fortified about a mile and a half east of Mechanicsville, on the left bank of the Chickahominy. This is about four miles from where we are encamped on the right of the river. The fight was severe, every musket and artillery shot being distinctly heard at our quarters. Our excitement, during the whole of the afternoon, has been intense. The firing ceased at about 9 o'clock in the evening. A few minutes later, orderlies and aids-de-camp were dashing from regiment to regiment, reading a dispatch from General McClellan, that "Stonewall Jackson is thoroughly whipped." Great rejoicing and cheering in camps. But, strange—one regiment to whom it was read, never, during the whole excitement, raised a cheer or manifested one symptom of elation. That regiment is the Fifth Wisconsin Volunteers. It has been under General McClellan's personal friend and relative, Brigadier General Winfield Scott Hancock, for whom it has won whatever of reputation that Brigadier General claims to have. Can it be possible that this favorite regiment has so far lost its confidence in the Brigadier as to distrust the statement of his friend, the Commander-in-Chief? However this may be, I have heard several of them remark that "it will be time for us to cheer when we *know* it is true." Significant.

27*th.*—There has been great rejoicing in camp all night—no sleep for the troops. But one regiment, seeming to be callous to the good news reported last evening, by General McClellan. At 8 this A. M., I started with wagon to Liberty Hall, for my tents and other baggage. The fight on the other side had commenced two hours before. I learn that in the reports to me of yesterday, the rebel forces had been greatly overrated; that they had only about twenty-five thousand men in the fight, on McCall's single division, of perhaps eight thousand. But both parties were strongly reinforced last night, Lee having swelled his army to about seventy-five thousand, whilst General Porter had come to the aid of McCall, with about thirty thousand. After fighting for about an hour and a half on the ground of yesterday's battle, Porter and McCall commenced falling back, and when I crossed the Chickahominy, between 8 and 9, this morning, I passed squads, batallions, regiments, brigades of our soldiers, apparently in disorder; but as I had heard nothing of Porter's falling back, I paid but little attention to them. I passed on without discovering what was the matter till I came so near to the advancing enemy as to barely escape capture. Riding back to the groups and brigades which I had passed, I learned that they were our scattered army, retreating before the advancing enemy. They had already fallen back about three miles, were rallying near Emerson's Bridge, and were preparing to give battle and to prevent the farther advance of the enemy. Should we be defeated here, the railroad from Richmond to West Point, now held by us, must fall into the hands of the enemy. White House, (our base of operations), with its immense supplies and munitions, must also be lost. General Porter was preparing for a desperate struggle, which, at farthest, could not be many hours off. General McClellan, *I hear*, telegraphed to General Porter, now in command on that side of the river, to know whether he needed reinforcements, to which he replied that he did not; that he could hold the enemy where he was. For this, whether true or not General Porter is to-night being highly censured. He felt that it was his fight, and was unwilling that a ranking officer should be sent to him to take or share the credit. Six times the hosts of the enemy came down upon him like an avalanche, and six times were repulsed. The seventh assault has been successful, and the army has passed our lines and has proceeded in the direction of White House. As Liberty Hall was in the line of our retreat and the enemy's pursuit, it was captured, and I of course lost everything, except the clothes I wore.

About 1 o'clock P. M. the fight commenced on our side of the Chickahominy (the right bank) at Golden's farm, between the batteries, at long range. I had just returned from my attempted trip to Liberty Hall. Our infantry was in line of battle between the opposing batteries, all the shot and shell from both sides having to pass over it. In passing from our artillery to our infantry, it was necessary to face the enemy's shells, which were exploding with almost continuous roar. These flashes, as they burst around me, reminded me of the wonderful " shower of falling stars" which occurred in 1850. Many of our own shells exploded as they passed over our infantry, killing a number of our men. Through this shower I had to ride, and it now seems that nothing but an interposition of Providence has saved me uninjured. About 7 P. M. the artillery ceased firing, and in a few minutes commenced an infantry fight, by the enemy's opening fire on about one mile of our line of battle. This has been a trying day—the fight on the left bank of the river under Gen. Porter, on the result of which depended our holding or losing our base of supplies, with immense stores. That on the right bank, directed by Gen. McClellan, in which it was thonght, if we succeeded, we should march unimpeded into Richmond, only six miles off. We are repulsed on the left bank ; we have driven the enemy on the right bank. Shall we lose White House and the Railroad as a consequence of our defeat on the left? Shall we march into Richmond as the result of our success on the right ? To-morrow will tell.

May God preserve me from another *battle in the dark*. The sight is grand, but terrible, beyond my wish to witness again.

28*th*.—This morning opened brightly and beautifully ; the elements calm and peaceful—not so the passions of the parties, for we on the right bank, where the enemy attacked us and were repulsed last night, were again attacked in our little fort by Toombs' Brigade—Toombs in person leading it on. He was repulsed with considerable loss, whilst we suffered but little.

Our army had now abandoned the field on the left bank,

leaving the enemy free access to our base, and we were massing our forces on the Richmond side of the river. But whilst our defeat on the left admitted our enemy to our supplies, their repulse on the right did not, as we had hoped, admit us to Richmond. The necessity of a general retreat is now becoming evident to the men, though nothing is heard on the subject from our officers. At 10 A. M. our right (Hancock's Brigade) moved its quarters about a mile and a half professedly to get out of the reach of the enemy's shells, which were falling and exploding in the midst of our camp. My opinion is that the real object of the move is the massing of our men preparatory to a general retreat. Our troops to-night are very much worn out. The rejoicing all night of the 26th, at the report of the "thorough whipping" of Stonewall Jackson, repulse on the north side, and the night fight of the south side on the 27th, the morning fight of this day, with the subsequent marching and moving of camps, being all the time on short allowance, is telling sorely on the energies of the men. The losses of yesterday to the two parties cannot have been less than 25,000 to 30,000 men.

29th.—'Tis the Sabbath—the appointed day of rest. To us how little of rest, of quiet, either to mind or body, it has brought! After the fatigues of the last three days and nights, our army lay last night on its arms, and this morning, at 3 o'clock, without breakfast, we were on the march, and as the first light of day revealed to us the immense heaps of commissary stores abandoned by the road, the truth that we were stealing away could no longer be concealed. The burning of these stores would disclose the fact to the enemy, and they were therefore left to fall into their hands. Are we then to give up all the anticipated pride of a triumphal march into Richmond ? Must we hang our harps upon the willows, and forego the pæans which we were to sing here on the down-fall of the Rebellion ? Must we abandon the remains of the thousands on thousands of our comrades, who have perished here in the ditches, unhonored and unknown, without having been permitted to strike a soldier's blow for government against anarchy? There is a retribution for some one. Till now this want of efficiency has been attributed to the powers at Washington. At present much of the blame is being laid at the door of our Commander-in-Chief, and I fear he deserves it. He has certainly committed many errors. His vast army, the best of modern times, has accomplished nothing. Early in the day it became evident to us that the watchful enemy was aware of our movements and was on our track, and everything of value was now destroyed. Runners were sent ahead to dam up the little streams near ammunition depots, to wet the powder and to drown the thousands of boxes of cartridges there deposited. Thousand on thousands of new muskets, of Springfield and of Sharp's rifles, were bent and broken over logs and stones. Barrels containing whisky, molasses, sugar, were broken in, bridges destroyed, and locomotives blown up. Delayed by work like this, by marching and by countermarching to protect our long transportation trains, 4 o'clock P. M. found us only about four miles from where we had started. For thirteen hours we had marched, after a night of watching, and the men had not yet had their breakfasts. On our arrival at Savage's Station we found the large building crowded with the wounded of the battles of the two days previous. Hundreds of tents were pitched around, from all of which came the groans of the sufferers, and the yard was filled with our poor mutilated men, with an army of surgeons and nurses moving amongst them. As we left this Station the booming of cannon in our rear told us

H

that this day, too, must have its fight. In the terrible heat of the day we moved on. We had not, however, proceeded more than a mile when we were overtaken by couriers calling us back to reinforce the rear, which was now preparing to engage the pursuing enemy. Back we marched. On again reaching Savage Station we found two immense lines of battle nearing for the conflict. We had a long line of batteries in position just in the edge of a wood fronting an extended plain over which the enemy was advancing. In rear of artillery our infantry lay in ambush. Our artillery was the coveted prize, and over the level plain came rushing on the long lines of the enemy at a full charge of bayonets. Our batteries had anticipated this, and were charged with grape and cannister, which they withheld till the mass came within easy range, then belching forth their iron hail, the whole front was absolutely shot away. For a moment the enemy recoiled, but it was momentary as the recoil of the ocean's wave as it breaks on the impending rock, then down they came again, but again belched forth the angry cannon, and again a line was swept away. But to this immense host of enthusiastic pursuers numbers were nothing, and a third time it came rushing on. They were now too near for our artillery to be effective, but at the moment up rose in its rear our long line of ambushed infantry, and the setting sun was saluted by the roar of a hundred thousand muskets. Again reeled the staggering foe, and "*forward, charge !*" and the battle of the 29th—the battle of Savage Station—was ended. The enemy were repulsed with immense loss, and we resumed the march, leaving the dead and wounded and our large hospital filled to overflowing in the hands of the enemy. All night we marched, stopping at 2 in the morning, and after a march of twenty-three hours, almost without food, rested for about three hours.

30*th.*—The night's march had placed a considerable distance between us and our pursuers. The morning opened bright and balmy. Again our division had to be brought to the rear, and we continued to march and to countermarch for position till about noon, when we halted in line of battle, and waited till our troops and transportation had all passed up. We had thrown out our videttes and pickets, and had lain down to keep out of sight. We began to stretch out our limbs for a little rest, when instantly, and almost simultaneously, fifty-three of the enemy's shells burst upon us. I doubt whether the Malakoff, in the "infernal fire" which reduced it, witnessed such an opening of a cannonade. Mott's battery was almost instantly demolished; most of his horses and some of his men killed by their first fire. Just here a little incident occurred, and which was rather amusing, if anything can amuse in such circumstances. I had taken my hospital corps and litter bearers some distance in the rear, in a deep gorge, where they could be out of danger, and where we could have plenty of water for the convenience of our wounded. I had left them and gone to the line. The burst of artillery came. I ran back to see that litter bearers were ready, but arrived just in time to see their backs as with the litters they passed over the hill on a full run. I ran to the top of the hill, ordered them to halt, but on they went. I ran on calling to them, and sent three pistol balls whistling after them. On they went. At a moment's reflection, I raised my voice, and uttered a great mouthful of oaths—not natural, but got up for the occasion. They stopped as if an iron wall had dropped before fore them. They returned, and were surprised to find me alone. 'Twas difficult to convince them that it was I who swore. They did not believe "that any man in the army, save our Brigadier, could utter any such oaths as that." I felt flattered, and thought that I had earned promotion. Immediately on the opening, our whole line was on its feet. We were ordered to change our position. We started on the double quick, directly *away* from the enemy. The order as to the position we should take was misunderstood, and we moved rapidly for about a mile. The day was intensely hot, but the men marched well and vigorously. Suddenly an order brought us to a halt, made us aware of our mistake, wheeled us to march back towards the enemy, and it is surprising what a difference was made in the vigor of the men, by marching west instead of east. Directly on their being faced to march towards the enemy, the sun's rays pierced so violently that they commenced falling from sunstroke. The effects, however, were not serious, for as soon as the column had marched by, the fallen men arose and starting again away from the enemy found themselves so well that most of them ran from ten to eighteen miles before night.

We got back into line, facing the enemy ; but from some cause unknown to me, they commenced withdrawing their forces from our wing, and swung them over to our left, on White Oak Swamp, about two miles to the southwest of us, where McCall, Porter, Sedgwick, Hooker, and a host of others were battling for life. McCall's Division is badly cut to pieces. We learn to-night that he is himself a prisoner, and that of all his staff, but one is left to tell the story. Our troops held their position, and after night had drawn a curtain betwixt us and our pursuers, with whisperings and hints of the necessity of capitulation, we resumed our march, nor halted till the sun was lighting up for the resumption of our perilous task of defence.

CHAPTER XIV

July 1st.—The march of last night was full of terrible
anxiety and danger. We marched through an enemy's country, pressed by them on all sides, and momentarily expected
when passing through some dense pine forest, to be attacked
from ambush and cut to pieces, without the chance of a
chivalrous fight. This would be murder of the worst kind,
and we feared it.

We reached the James River this morning, at Carters'
Neck, just below Malvern Hills, where the army expected
to cross at once, and be again on ground of rest and safety.
We were allowed three hours to cook, eat and sleep, and
again we moved. But instead of crossing, we found ourselves marching directly away from the river, and the roar of
artillery ahead told us of more work yet to be done. Our
men, who had now for five days been limited to an average
of two hours' rest a day, pressed forward with an alacrity
truly astonishing. After a march of about two miles, we
halted on the slope of a hill which concealed us from an immense open plain stretching out in our front to Malvern Hills.
Here was progressing a battle which will be famed in history,
so long as battles are fought on earth. I doubt whether one
so bloody, in proportion to numbers, or so obstinately con-

tested, has been fought since the invention of gunpowder. Here Hooker, and Kearney, and Heintzleman, and, I hope, Porter, (though I have heard hints of his misbehaving) and Stevens, with others, have gained imperishable renown. Our Division was drawn up in line on the slope of the hill referred to, just so as to be concealed by its brow from the plain in front, yet so near as to perceive the advance of an enemy approaching over it, and here we lay all day in reserve, expecting our main body to be driven back on us, as their supports, and the eagerness with which our jaded and worn out troops now watched with a welcome for the foe from which we had been so long flying, is to me as astonishing as it is unaccountable. Here we felt secure, and here we have remained all day, chafing for a part in the deadly conflict going on so near us.

6 P. M.—The battle of Malvern Hill still rages, and what carnage. Hand to hand the fight goes on. The dead and the dying lie heaped together. Charge after charge is made on our artillery, with a demoniac will to take it, if it costs them half their army. Down it mows their charging ranks, till they lie in heaps and rows, from behind which our men fight as securely as if in rifle pits. Nearer and nearer approach their batteries, till the two lines of artillery are mingled into one, but pointing in different directions. In places the wheels of gun carriages of the opposing armies become nearly locked together, and the cannoniers leave their guns and sabre each other in a hand to hand fight. The slaughter is terrible, and to add to the carnage, our gun boats are throwing their murderous missiles with furious effect into the ranks of our enemy. By their shots huge trees are uprooted or torn into shreds, which whip the combatants to death. The combatants seem infatuated with excitement,

and the very terror of the scene lashes them into a love of the conflict.

As twilight approaches, the noisy eloquence of battle becomes subdued ; at 8 o'clock 'tis hushed, and the enemy is driven and routed. We are too much exhausted to pursue ; and, relying on the assurance of our leaders that we are here secure, we at 9 o'clock stretch ourselves at length to take the full enjoyment of a long night's rest, which our condition so pressingly demands.

2d.—What relief it was, last night, at half-past 9, after the six day's of excitement, fatigue, fighting and famine, to lie down once more, secure of a good long night's rest! What a surprise, the whispered call, in just three hours, to rise *quietly* and resume the march! And what was our astonishment, when daylight revealed to us the fact that we were now retracing the very road by which we had been trying to escape. On discovering this the men began to waver in their confidence. But soon we left this road and bore off " down the river," and of the scene which now followed, neither Hogarth's pencil nor Hall's pen could render the faintest idea. The rain was pouring in such torrents as I never saw the clouds give down. The men at every step, sank nearly to their knees in mud. The officers, either sulky or excited, were driving them to a double-quick, which it was impossible for them to maintain for more than a few rods. They began to fall out, and, in half an hour, every field, and all the open country, as far as the eye could reach, presented the appearance of a moving, hurrying *mob*. I was here strongly reminded of my school boy imaginations of the Gulf Stream. This swaying, surging mass presenting the idea of the ocean lashed into irregular fury by driving storms, whilst a part of General Smith's division, moving in unbroken column through the mass, could not but recall the picture of that little stream as from the beginning of time it has preserved its quiet course, in despite of all the convulsions and conflicts of the warring elements. So great was the demoralization at this time, that I have not a doubt that an unexpected volley of either musketry or artillery would have produced a stampede which would have shamed Manassas. I saw no officer so calm, so collected, so perfectly himself as our Division Commander, General Smith. By the teachings which I had received at Camp Griffin, I had been made to believe that he could never be a man for an emergency. At the most trying moment of the day, I bore him a hurried message from two miles away. He saw me coming on the full run, through the heavy rain and mud, and as I rode up he received me with a quiet, pleasant bow of inquiry. I delivered my message, which was important, and involved the fate of his Division, without the least hurry or the slightest hesitation, and in the very fewest words which could make it forcible, as if he had known the object of my coming, and had his answer prepared, he gave me his orders, and calmly resumed his other duties. The prejudices planted and cultured at Camp Griffin were all dissipated.

I did see him, however, once during the day, a little excited. We were hard pressed by the enemy on all sides of us. We had repulsed him in every fight, protecting our immense train of wagons, *now seventy miles long*. But so critical had become our situation that it was decided that to save the army it was necessary to abandon the transportation; Gen. Smith rode along the line of his own transportation, clearing the road of the wagons that the rear guard of infantry and artillery might pass. He once or twice ordered a teamster out of the road. The man did not obey. 'Twas no time to

arrest him ; he grappled him by the neck, and for half a minute kept him in that peculiar state of gyration which a hungry soldier often communicates to the body of a rebel rooster
about midnight. He had no more trouble with that teamster.
But the confusion of those teams! I thought Mons. Violet
in his stampede of buffaloes had got up a description of confusion which no reality could ever approach. I had formed
vague ideas of Bedlam, of Pandemonium; but a million of
buffaloes on a stampede, Bedlam turned loose, and Pandemonium "on a bust," all mixed and mingled, could form no
approximation to a train of teams, seventy miles long, on a
" skedaddle."

But all day the rain poured in torrents: men dropped by
the wayside and were left. Some died from exposure; some
dragged themselves into camp, and many were captured by
the enemy. The night of the seventh day has come. The
question of capitulation has been heard in whispers all day.
But now that we are once more in camp, and in a position to
offer or accept battle, most of the men scoff at the idea of
capitulation, and say "fight it out." Nearly all the men, in
the retreat, have thrown away their knapsacks and blankets,
and have thrown themselves down in their wet clothes, and
in mud and water which nearly covers them, hoping to get a
little rest after the incessant fatigues of the week. The wind
blows damp and chilly, and I fear the poor fellows are to have
a hard night of it.

3rd.—This morning the men looked haggard and worn.
Some slept; more shivered with cold the night through, and
in my morning round to look after the health of the regiment, I found men standing upright, without any support,
and *fast asleep.* There was no wood within half a mile of
us to make fires. Not a step could be taken without sinking

to the ankles in mud and water ; and thus opened the day of the 3d of July.   All felt depressed, but there was little or no murmuring.   What a wonderful army !   And yet it has been a whole year in the field and has accomplished nothing.   Who is to blame ?   We are in a bow of the James River, with the enemy in our front.   We can retreat no further, and when, early in the morning, a few vollies of musketry were heard, all felt that the trying time had come, and that the death struggle must be had to-day.   We were mistaken.   After the few vollies, the firing ceased, and all has been comparatively quiet.   The thirst had been quenched, and the flow of blood, at least for the day, is checked.   *To-morrow will be the Fourth of July*, and the calm of the 3d portends that this Fourth is to be a day of travail, and, *perhaps*, the birth-day of another nation.

4th.—The fourth has come and gone, but brought no fight, and our great Republic has passed another anniversary, if not in safety, in integrity, for its flag yet floats over the loyal men of every State, and the sunset salute of *thirty-four* guns, proclaims that we are yet an integral.   But for the bombast of General McClellan's proclamation of to-day, we should feel sad.   That makes us laugh.   Shut up in a little bend of the James River, not daring to venture a single mile from his encampment, he commences digging and peeping from his ditch to see that Lee is not in sight, he cries thus :   " On this, our Nation's birthday, we declare to our foes, who are rebels against the best interests of Mankind, that this army shall enter the Capital of their so-called Confederacy."   Stuff !   Has he forgotten that last winter he promised that under him we should have no more defeats ?

4th.—The President, I see, has made another call for three hundred thousand men.   Before this war is over, we shall have to resort to drafting. I regret that it was not done in the first place. Then the vast majority of the able bodied men willing to go, would have shamed down the unwilling ones from complaining. As it is, now that most of the willing ones are in the field, I fear that a draft will cause trouble. I should much have preferred, as it is put off to this time, a conscript act, requiring all able-bodied men to organize and hold themselves ready to act when called on. This would have given us an irresistable army, and all would have been treated alike.

Our regiment, which has heretofore borne, more than any other, suffered terribly in the late retreat. I am vain enough to attribute this to the change of sanitary measures adopted during my month's absence. General ——'s pride could never brook the small show of my regiment on his "dress parades." My plan was, that when a man began to sicken I took him at once from all duty, and had him nursed and cared for till well. Hence, in time of quiet, I always had a large number excused, but when we came to action, or to a hard march, there were few regiments in the army which could compare with us, either in numbers or endurance. During my absence of a month, this thing was reversed. Men were kept *on show* as long as their legs would bear them up, the General's vanity was gratified, but when we came to a forced march, we were found to be in most miserable plight.

CHAPTER XV

12th.—This night closes the period of one year's service in the United States. One year ago to-morrow, our regiment changed its situation from State to United States, and when I review that period, and recall the sufferings I have witnessed, the treason and incompetency which have thwarted the well laid plans of the government, the repeated failures of our leaders to embrace most favorable opportunities to crush the rebel armies and to arrest the war, I despair of accomplishing decisive results till we have a change of leaders. But I have a gratifying consciousness of having, up to the ability which God has given me, performed every duty to my country with as little selfishness as man's frailty will permit. I cannot recall an instance where fatigue, the fear of danger, or even sickness, has been permitted to interpose between my comfort and my efforts to relieve the sufferings of the soldier in whatever form presented. I have had much reason to regret that my efforts were not more effective, but never that I have neglected their performance ; nor has it been a source of less thankfulness to me that I have been so small a portion of time unable to labor.

13*th*.—One year ago this day, the —— Regiment of —— Volunteers entered the service of the United States. It then numbered between ten and eleven hundred of the finest troops that ever went to battle. Its history in that brief period, though sad, is briefly summed up. On the 19th of June, 1861, the regiment was organized. On the 24th of July following, it took up its hurried march, to aid in arresting the tide of retreat which was rushing from Bull Run on Washington, and was, I am told, the first Western regiment which passed through Pennsylvania to support our beaten friends. Early in August it reached Washington, was shortly after brigaded under command of General R—— K————, a Commander in all respects worthy of the position he held. The measles, in its very worst form, had broken out in camp, before the regiment left the State of ————, and from severe exposure on a most hurried journey, much sickness prevailed for a time after its arrival at Washington. General K——, being endowed with feelings which could never witness suffering without sympathy, fully realized the fact that sick and feeble men were an encumbrance to the army. He was constantly on the watch, and every means in his power was employed to preserve the health and energy of his men ; nor did he permit either vanity or vindictiveness to interpose between his Surgeons and their proper duties. The restored health and vigor of his men responded beautifully to his care and his efforts.

Some time in September the regiment was transferred to the brigade of Gen. —— S——, and although after this transfer their position subjected them to more labor and exposure, their health and comfort whilst under his command were looked after with such care and solicitude that their efficiency continued to improve, and on the 1st of October, not a man had died in camp, or had been killed or wounded in battle. About that time they were transferred to the brigade of Gen. ————. This General showed himself possessed of one very Napoleonic trait of character, that when an object is to be attained the lives of men are not to be estimated. The men were exposed and hard worked. The efforts of the surgeons were not seconded. Their advice was disregarded. Sickness increased. The men became jaded and dejected, and the frequent passing of a squad to the solemn tread of the dead march, and with arms reversed, told sadly that another foe was at work. The cool days of November brought hopes of restored health and vigor, but continued severity of discipline and disregard of sanitary demands, blasted the hopes and brought even more frequent processions to the grave.

The New Year came without a death on the battle-field, but with greatly thinned ranks. The winter passed with constant work and constant exposure, without an enemy in our field. The men sickened of the work of the menial, and panted for that of the soldier. The battle of Drainesville was fought in our hearing, but we were not permitted to participate. Their spirits were buoyed up by promises that soon we should have the enemy at Manassas "in a bag," and then we should have only to go forward and capture them. But notwithstanding these promises we were compelled to chop, to dig, to do picket duty, and to see them going away before our very faces without being permitted to prevent it. So great had been our losses that recruiting officers had been sent off, and men were added to the regiment sufficient to swell its original number to between eleven and twelve hundred.

On the 23d March, 1863, the regiment (in the same brigade) embarked at Alexandria, for the Peninsula between the

James and York Rivers. On its arrival, hard work, hard marches and exposure seemed the order of every day. Numbers were discharged from service daily, on account of constitutions broken by excessive demands on the nervous energy of the men. They were anxious, whilst able, to be led to battle, but for them only drudgery was reserved; and although for weeks our regiment has been within sight of the enemy, or within hearing of his guns, never to this day has it been permitted to attack.

At Williamsburg it fought on the defensive, and scarcely had it engaged till it was ordered to fall back. By declining to obey that order it at last found an opportunity of its long wished for ambition, to distinguish itself in fight. In that fight, despite the order of its General, it saved the battle of Williamsburg—the Army of the Potomac. The regiment lost in the fight nine killed, and seventy-one wounded. It fought that day under Gen. Hancock, and this is the battle in which Gen. McClellan telegraphed that "Hancock's success was won with a loss of less than twenty in killed and wounded!" Was the Commander-in-Chief ignorant of the facts about which he telegraphed? Or did Gen. Hancock need some "setting up?" However this may be, the Commander-in-Chief publicly declared to this regiment that to it he owed the victory, and promised that it should have "Williamsburg inscribed on its banner." Notwithstanding this promise, "Williamsburg" got on to other banners, but never found its place on that to which it was promised. Why?

Experience seemed to have taught no good lessons. Large demands continued to be made on the energies of the men. They sank under the efforts, and on the retreat before Richmond, when at the battle of White Oak Swamp, and Malvern Hills, all the force of active and robust men were needed. This regiment which had brought to the field eleven hundred of as good men as ever went to war,* which had not lost thirty men in battle, now tottered feebly into line with only two hundred and twenty-seven muskets, borne by men feeble, emaciated, and as nearly spiritless as it is possible for ambitious and energetic men to be.

I omitted to record, in the proper place, that though the regiment was in the fight on the night of the 27th of June, doing great execution, not a man was killed, and only twelve wounded.

This is an epitomized history of one regiment for a year.

The signs of the times portend that we have done " playing war." Our Generals have now been taught a lesson of realities, which it is to be hoped will be heeded. Our muskets will hardly be seen guarding the property of rebels, whilst these are shooting down our men in the battle. Contrabands are being taken into the employment of the government, and are relieving the soldiers of much hard and depressing labor. As matter of economy, the regimental brass bands are being discharged. This is pretty hard, but as economy is necessary to a proper and successful prosecution of the war, we submit cheerfully. Our good band then will no more carry us forward in pleasing imagination to the land of " Dixie," nor backward to the melancholy " days of Auld Lang Syne," the "Star Spangled Banner," will not again wake our drowsy energies " At the Twilight's Last Gleaming;" nor shall we be awoke in the " Stilly Night," by the romping, rolicking music of " The Girl I Left Behind

---

* The physical superiority of the Western over the Eastern regiments was illustrated in the athletic exercises on first of January, at Camp Griffin. [See journal of that date.]

Me." We shall part with regret, not only the band, but with particular members, whose conduct has on all occasions been courteous and gentlemanly. Their leader has also made himself useful by his peculiar talent for scouting, often learning almost instinctively the position and strength of the enemy.

18*th*.—I regret exceedingly to feel that there may be too much truth in the following extract of a letter received to-day: I would not libel my fellow officers, but I have no hesitation in declaring that, notwithstanding I have spent fifty years of a life of excitement in this little world, I have witnessed more drunkenness amongst officers of the army within one year, than I have seen in the *same class of men* in all my fifty years of civil life. The letter says: "After you left me I was lonely, rarely having any of the officers call at my tent. I spent my time, when not engaged in official duties, in reading and in writing. This was rather agreeable, notwithstanding I could hear in all the tents around me the social hiliarity of officers visiting each other. It seemed pleasant to me, and I sometimes almost envied them. One morning there could be seen in my tent three boxes. On the end of one, in large print: "Prime Bourbon;" on another, "1 Doz. each Old Q and Cogniac;" the third, "Fine Sherry." On top of the boxes sat three bottles, each marked correspondingly with the box from which it was taken; and by side of the bottles, glasses, and a bucket of ice water. It soon began to be found out that I had the shadiest, *airyest* tent, and that I was one of the most jovial fellows on the ground. Privates, who had previously frequented my tent for instruction and advice, disappeared, cocked hats and shoulder straps crowded about me; I had a good cook, and occasionally my friends dined with me. *   *

* * * Can you imagine how, after my long seclusion, I enjoyed this change of socialty? Let me tell you: I have become most supremely disgusted with myself, my liquors, my comrades, and almost feel that the world, or at least the military portion of it, is a failure. Thank God my liquors are gone; my friends and I now *know* each other, and those who loved me for my good liquors will love me no more forever. A few with whom I was thus brought into contact, are fine fellows, and our intimacy will continue."

The enemy are attempting to blockade the river below us, and thus cut off our supplies. Should they succeed, we must capitulate, or fight our way to Fortress Monroe, a distance of seventy or eighty miles, without provisions.

In the year that we have been in the field our fine army has been frittered away, without having accomplished anything. I fear General McClellan is a failure. I would not be an alarmist, but I fear that without a change of leaders our cause must be abandoned. The ring of General Pope's proclamation is right, just right; I cannot take one exception. But the expediency of its coming from General Pope is questionable. I have not too much confidence in the disinterestedness of our Potomac officers, and this proclamation may be applied by some of them personally, and make trouble. Nevertheless, the tone of it is right. I hope he will be able to come up to "the sounding tenor of the munifesto."

22nd.—I have received letters from my family to-day. One of them says, "We are not feeling well this morning." "Who is not, and what is the matter? It is a dreadful thought that we must be thus separated from family without the slightest prospect of being able to see them when we know they are suffering.

24th.—No active work to-day, save of my mind. The

condition of the country and of the army, past, present, and prospective, is the material on which it has worked. Notwithstanding that one year ago our little army had been repulsed at Bull Run, and the heart of the nation was sorrowful, yet the " whole broad continent was ours." And with our little army in spirits, though momentarily baffled, we were almost unembarrassed to go where we pleased. The country, confident in its leaders, had risen as one man to sustain the best Government the world ever saw. Three hundred thousand troops were called for, and the question was not who shall be obliged to go, but who shall have the privilege of going. A few weeks later, this "Grand Army of the Potomac," two hundred and twenty thousand strong, had, like the spirited steed, to be restrained by the strong arm of power from rushing forward to the contest. Summer passed, amidst impatient appeals of the men to be led against the enemy. Winter came, with joyful assurance that we were not to go into quarters, because they were soon to advance upon the enemy and to end the war. But spring found them still in canvas tents, impatient for the word to move. At length, with 130,000, shortly afterwards swelled to nearly 160,000 men, such as no General ever led to battle, we sailed and marched till me met the enemy, about three thousand strong, entrenched at Young's Mill, when we turned around and marched back. After waiting till they had left, we again took up our march, and overhauled them at Yorktown, now increased to seven or eight thousand strong. Instead of crushing them at once, we settled down and digged, lest they should crush us. After they had tired of waiting for us, they quietly packed up and left our General, with his one hundred and forty thousand men, to enjoy his diggings in the swamps of Warwick. They went to Williamsburg, and having had plenty of time, they had swelled their force to about thirty thousand men. They gave us no time to dig here, but came out to meet us. They punished us severely, but were driven, and instead of following actively in pursuit, we settled down and cried for help! The patience of the soldiers was exhausted; their patriotism was worn out. The malaria of the marshes, and the fatigues of digging, produced low grades of fever which began to carry off the men. And on the 25th of June, although the muskets and the bayonets and the artillery of the enemy had scarcely marked our army, we brought out to meet the opposing foe, which had now swelled to a monster army, less than eighty thousand of the one hundred and sixty thousand men. One half of this eighty thousand dragged themselves to battle, but yet fought like heroes. And now that noble army, instead of moving where it pleased, as it could a year ago, is shut up in a little circuit, with a radius of less than a mile and a half, and cannot leave it. I am induced to hope that in all this there is nothing worse than incompetency. But I doubt the ability of any other set of honest men to use up such an army with so little fighting. There is another call for three hundred thousand men, but before it is filled I fear the hydra-head of party will rear itself and give us trouble. But in whatever manner raised, here this remnant of a great army must remain besieged until a new one is drafted, drilled, and brought to relieve us. Somebody has failed. The men have not.

29th.—It is a source of unspeakable gratification to me that after my long fights, the comforts of the suffering soldiers are being heeded; whether on account of my much importunity, or from the fact that the necessity of this course has become apparent to the Military Department, or that the new Surgeon General has directed his attention more particularly to it, it matters not. When I call for aid for the hospitals under my care I get it. All the surgeons in this department now have only to call for help to procure enough to clean, drain, and sweep camp grounds every day, to ask for the necessary food, medicine and furniture, and if *they will then give their personal attention to it,* they can have it. The scurvy has been rapidly increasing with us, but we have now the means of arresting it. Thanks to U. S. Sanitary Commission for the larger share of them.

Some mysterious movements are going on in this army. At night we look over a large flat covered with tents, lighted by camp fires, resonant with the sounds of living soldiers. In the morning that same flat is deserted and still, as if the angel of death had enjoyed a passover. What has become of the busy actors of the night, none who dare speak of it can conjecture. In fact, in the present perilous condition of the army all purposes are necessarily secret. Some think the troops thus disappearing are crossing the river and marching on Fort Darling. Some think they are moving down the river to possess ourselves of a fort which is being built to blockade the river and cut off our supplies. Others think Washington is again in danger, and that a part of this army is being shipped thither, whilst many others are of opinion that we are slowly and secretly withdrawing our forces, and that Gen. Smith's division is to be left here as a blind and sacraficed to save the balance of the army. This would seem hard; yet when it becomes necessary, Gen. Smith will be found to be the very man, and his the very army to submit to the necessity without a murmur.

I am, however, of the opinion that the bulk of the rebel army has withdrawn from about us, and is after General

Pope, and that we are taking advantage of their absence to escape from our present perilous position. General Pope's antecedents warrant the belief that whatever is in his power to do for our relief will be accomplished to the utmost of his ability.

30th.—Rumors of battle have to-day, waked up our drowsy energies, and put all on the qui vive. Orders at noon to " be ready for action at any moment." The enemy's gun boats are coming down the river, and a land attack is anticipated. Humiliated as we feel at being shut up here on the defence, there is a kind of " let 'em come" defiance in every heart and on every face. My own opinion is that it is a feint, and that we shall not be attacked. My experience in the late retreat, has fully gratified all my curiosity to see a great fight. For five days and nights I was not out of sight of our lines; in fact, never left the field of battle. It will require more than idle curiosity to induce me to undergo the same again.

August 1st.—The month was ushered in by the opening of a cannonade, precisely as the clock struck twelve, on our shipping, from the south side of the river. For a short time the firing was very brisk. It was from some batteries of flying artillery which had taken position during the night. They were soon silenced, but not till after they had killed and wounded a number of our sailors, and done some damage to our shipping.

2nd.—What numbers of letters, and from home, are lost en route! Can it be possible that the private letters of soldiers and officers to their families and friends are " vised?" Many suspect it; and should it prove true, woe betide the authorities which should attempt to justify it. West Point wields a mighty influence in this army. But this would be a dangerous assumption, even though the attempt might be made to justify it under the plea of the "necessity of war." There are whispers in camp that we are to commence another retrograde movement. Should we attempt it, and an attack made on us in retreat, I should fear a total route without even resistance. Since our Generals showed such want of confidence in the soldiery as was hidden under terms "change of base," "change of front by a flank movement," the soldiers are correspondingly distrusting their commanders, and I verily believe would not again fight under them on a retreat. Should they be brought by an advance to the battle, it would be a different thing. I think they would fight as they ever have fought, like heroes. I have heard hundreds say that if we are to retreat again, they would prefer to be captured as prisoners, than disgraced as fugitives.

6*th*,—I am just in receipt of the following letter, and lest I may some day be disposed to charge the friends of those for whom I labor with want of appreciation of my efforts, I record it in my journal, with the hope that my eyes may often fall on it. I am almost daily receiving similar letters, and how they brace me in my efforts to do my duty, despite of the embarrassments which are unnecessarily thrown around me!

[Letter omitted in the publication of this journal.]

Do surgeons in the army ever realize that often friends of the soldier, at home, are as great sufferers from this war as the soldier himself? Do they ever think of the comfort, of the happiness they may with a little effort, impart to those whom they never saw, but are perhaps as active participants in the war as those actually in the lines! and do they begrudge the little time and labor required to impart this comfort or consolation?

13*th*. We are now all packed ready for a move, awaiting only the final order to march. Where or how we go, we do not yet know. We learn, however, beyond a doubt, that the regiments which disappeared so mysteriously a few nights since, embarked on transports under cover of the darkness, and have gone down the river. Their destination is not certainly known to us. From present appearances the plan seems to be, that the army, with the exception of Smith's Division, or perhaps Franklin's Corps, are to embark on transports, leaving us to escort and protect our immense transportation train overland to Fortress Monroe. Should this conjecture be true, we shall have a hazardous time, unless General Pope shall succeed in keeping the enemy so busily engaged as to relieve us. I have full confidence that he will exert himself to the utmost to relieve us in this manner.

Our leaders here are rapidly losing the confidence of the army and becoming objects of ridicule to the enemy. At White Oak Bridge, when we retreated. we left our pickets at their posts, without notifying them of our movements. They were of course taken prisoners. They have been paroled and are returning to camp. They say that immediately on being captured, they were being examined by a rebel Colonel, when Stonewall Jackson came up and upbraided the Colonel for spending time with the prisoners. "Let the prisoners go," said he, and "press on after the enemy. So accustomed have they become to digging that if you give them twelve hours' rest, they will dig themselves clear under ground." Flattering, truly! I hope General McClellan will note it. But these things must not be talked about. Oh, no! We must see army after army sacrificed, the bones of hundreds of thousands of our bravest men bleaching on the plains, the nation draped in mourning, and not speak of it lest we shake confidence in our Generals, who through selfishness or incompetency, I will not *yet* say treason, are so frequently subjecting us to such contumely and sacrifices. History will make sad revelations of this war. I verily believe that, could its abuses be fully told, it would arouse the people to an enthusiasm which no acts of the enemy can excite. Under our present leaders, God knows what is to become of us. I have lost all confidence in them. In only four months from the time we landed on the Peninsula we had lost nearly two-thirds of the vast army brought with us, without one decisive battle! Since the 20th March we have landed here about 160,000 men. I doubt whether we could to-day bring 45,000 into action! At any time between October and June last, it has been in the power of this army to crush out this rebellion in a month; and yet the rebellion is more formidable to-day than at any previous time. Even now we are receiving reports of the discomfiture of Pope's army, and, notwithstanding that its struggles are for our relief, it is unmistakeably evident that the report gives pleasure to the staffs of McClellan and Hancock. It may be so with other staffs; these are the only ones I have seen. Jealousy, jealousy—what will be the end of this? God preserve us.

Whilst I am noting down these abuses, a strange feeling possesses me; I lose all sense of my determination to abandon this rotten thing, and I resolve here to fight to the bitter end. Oh, if we had a Wellington, a Napoleon, a Scott, or even a Jackson, to do—something—anything, but dig and watch and — ! falsely report!

Just as I close this journal of the day, a man rides up and tells me that General Pope has had a fight, and " holds his own." I hope this is true, but I cannot forget that on

I

the 26th of June, General McClellan made the army boisterously joyful by his assertion that McCall had thoroughly whipped Stonewall Jackson. On the next morning at daylight, it was claimed that McCall had only "held his own." Two hours later we find that instead of even holding his own, he had retreated four miles, but it was only a "strategic movement," and next day it became necessary for the whole army to—not retreat—but—"change its base." All this it required to tell the simple truth that we were overpowered, whipped, and on the retreat. I hope it may not now be the beginning of a like history of General Pope's movements.

14th.—At 9 P. M. received orders to be ready to move at daylight to-morrow morning, with two days' rations in haversacks. The crisis approaches, and whilst the men are cooking their rations, I note this, and then go to packing.

15th.—Called up at 2 A. M., to be ready to move at daylight. Eight o'clock comes, but no order for us to march; 10, 12, 2, 4, 8, 10 o'clock at night, and still here. One day's rations consumed, men wearied with watching and impatient expectation; no tents, no comforts, men dropped on the ground to rest, whilst other regiments, brigades, divisions, are marching by. Many fires kept brightly burning through the night, and many soldiers would not lie down, but kept watch, momentarily expecting a call to march. This excitement and waiting, I find, is more wearing to the soldier than active duty.

16th.—Morning came, and found us still waiting orders, whilst immense trains of teams and masses of soldiery, sick and well, are pushing past us. Our division are again to bring up the rear, and receive the attack, if one is made.

This is said to be the post of honor: but we are beginning to feel that we may be "honored over-much."

At 5 P. M. came the expected and anxiously looked-for order, and we are on the road down James River. Not being a military man, I may be hypercritical, but it does seem to me that it should not require the forty-eight hours which we have taken for that purpose, to get out of camp with an army no larger than ours ; or, that if so much time is required, the leaders should adopt some system in leaving, so as to call the divisions successively to get ready ; not to call all at once, and wear out the rear guard with watching and with expectation, whilst the advance is passing. Two days ago our division was ordered to be ready to march at an hour fixed, and to have two days' rations to march on. The two days expired without further order to prepare rations, and the hour of starting found our rear guard, which is to stand the brunt of battle, worn out, and without rations to march on ' "Shiftless."

At 11 P. M. we reached Charles City, an *extensive* capital of one of the oldest and richest counties in Virginia. This Charles City contains one dwelling house, with three or four buildings for "negro quarters," and a court house of about 20x35 feet, and one story high. In Virginia, they must have very little legal justice or very little need of it. From the direction of our march so far, I judge we go to Fort Monroe, and that we shall cross the Chickahominy at its main junction with the James.

17th.—Left Charles City at 5 1-2 o'clock this A. M. Beautiful day ; clear, windy and cool, but terribly dusty. At 3 P. M., crossed the Chickahominy near the mouth, on a pontoon bridge.* Pontoon bridges are a success. To-night

* A pontoon bridge is thus built : Narrow, flat-bottomed boats, about

we lie at the mouth of the Chickahominy, under protection of our gun boats. What a commercial world this State of Virginia should be. Its navigable waters are nearly equal to that of all the Free States combined; yet there are single cities in the North which have a larger commerce than the whole of the Slave States. Why is this? Has the peculiar institution any thing to do with it? If so, God, nature—everything speaks aloud against it as a curse. The ground which we now occupy is one of the most beautiful, as well as one of the most desirable sites for a city in America, high and dry, with an easy ascent from the water, presenting three fronts to the navigable rivers, with fine water views in all directions, as extensive as the range of vision, with business amounting to one house and a few cords of dry pine wood, which seems to be the article of export from this part of the State.

There is no longer a doubt that we are leaving the Peninsula. What now becomes of the statement that our retreat was only "a change of base?"

18*th.*—Left camp this morning at 6 o'clock, on the Williamsburg road, and at 12 to 1, passed in retreat over the scenes of our first hard fight, where my regiment, by its firm and unyielding bravery, won the promise that it " should have Williamsburg inscribed on its banner ;" a promise richly merited but never fulfilled.

When passing through Williamsburg I, in company with Surgeon Frank H. Hamilton, stepped aside to take a stroll

twenty-five feet long, are anchored in the stream. They lie side by side, from ten to fifteen feet apart, so as to make a row of boats from one bank to the other. From one to the other, clear across the stream are tied stringers, on which are laid down heavy planks, about sixteen feet long, which makes the bridge, and which is sufficient to bear up any number of teams which can be crowded on it.

through the halls and rooms of old William and Mary, the oldest college, I believe, except Yale, on this continent. There still stood the students' desks and seats, at which Virgil and Ovid and Horace had kindled whatever spark they possessed of poetic fire, and Livy had evoked many a curse at his dry detail. There were the black-boards on which the mysteries of Euclid were solved into the unwavering language of distance and of measure, and there was the old chapel, with the benches still in situ, from which for more than a century, hopeful youths had sat and listened to prayers for their usefulness and prosperity, whilst they laid plans of mischief against the supplicators for their good. But the places of the Professors were now filled with the inevitable Commissary and his aids, with their barrels and their boxes, whilst the benches of the students were crowded with clamors for their bacon, beef and beans. I mused for a while over thoughts of the learned men who had passed forever from these ancient halls, and of the influences they have left behind them.

> " Their heads may sodden in the sun,
>   Their limbs be strung to city gates and walls ;
>   Bnt still their spirits walk ABROAD."

They certainly do not walk *here*. The sight would be too painful for sensitive and sensible spirits to bear. But these thoughts were dissipated as I looked again on the places where for the first time any number of our regiment had met death on the battle field, and on which it won laurels which shall be green forever!

At 2 o'clock we encamped on the east bank of King's Creek, a small stream about three miles from Williamsburg, on the banks of which repose the bodies of thousands of the

Federal army—of those brave men, who, flushed with hope and patriotic enthusiasm, rushed boldly to the contest, and were permitted to be swept away by hundreds, unsupported by commanders, who, with their hosts unengaged, stood calmly watching the slaughter.

19th.—Moved at 7 this morning. Marched to-day over much of the same ground which we travelled over on our way to Richmond. But strange! There was scarcely a spot which I could recognize. Heretofore my memory of places has been almost wonderful. Why could I not now recognize? Has age impaired my memory, or was my mind at the time of passing so occupied with weightier matters that ordinary scenes and circumstances made no impression?

At 12 M. to-day we reached Yorktown. How wonderfully our minds deceive us in estimates of places and things associated with great events! Whoever heard of Yorktown, that city on the banks of the noble York River, on the sacred soil of the great State of Virginia? The famous city where Lord Cornwallis took his stand to crush out the American rebellion—the city in which was fought the last great battle for American independence—the mother of a nation, and which lives to have witnessed the growth of that nation through youth to maturity, from the feeble efforts of infancy to the power of a giant, and still lives to look on her offspring sent by the convulsive struggles of its own strength, perhaps to final dissolution. I ask what mind can contemplate a city associated with all these events and recollections, without being possessed of ideas of its vastness and its splendor? But what the reality? Yorktown is a little dilapidated old village, which never contained a population of over 200 or 300, and at the commencement of this war not over 150. When I look on its insignificance, or rather on its significant littleness, I find it difficult not to detract from the ideas of greatness, associated with the great men who figured there. How wonderfully have the great advantages which nature has lavished on this State been prostituted to the one great idea of maintaining her peculiar institution, which she has nursed and defended against the approaches of the world, as she would protect and encourage the whims and weakness of a sickly girl.*

A circumstance occurred to-day so painful that I should like to forget it, yet so suggestive of the trials of this army and of the discouragements which has occasioned much of their indifference to events, that I feel it a duty to record it, that it may not be forgotten. On the late retreat from Richmond, most of the men found it necessary to throw away everything which impeded their progress, even their canteens. During our stay at Harrison's Point they had not been fully replaced. This morning we started early. The day has been intensely hot, the dust almost insufferable. Gen. H——— was in command of his brigade. We had made a rapid march of about ten miles. The men were fatigued, foot-sore and thirsty. In many instances, two or three having to depend on one canteen, it was soon emptied, and when we stopped to rest after the ten mile march, we were in sight of a large spring of beautiful cold water. But the General ordered that not a man should leave the ranks to fill his canteen. It was hard to bear, but the men submitted in patience till they saw the soldiers from other brigades passing from the

*I think that all the towns on this noble river, from its source to its mouth, will not amount in the aggregate to a population of 2,000 souls! And the same may be said of the James River, from Richmond to its outlet; and yet these rivers pass through one of the finest agricultural regions in the world. There is not a spot of earth, the wheat from which can compete in market with that of the James River.

spring with their canteens filled. This was too much, and they commenced crying out "Water, water." Immediately the General dashed amongst them, proclaiming "mutiny," and demanding the offenders. Of course no one could tell *who they were*. He then turned upon the Regimental and Company officers, "damned them to hell," and spent some time in consigning the soldiers to the same comfortable quarters. After he had got them all labeled for that kingdom, he told them that their officers were "not worth a G—d d——n," and having exhausted his vocabulary of gentlemanly expletives, calculated to encourage subordination, he called the men into line and put them through the evolutions of a brigade drill for about half an hour, and thus were they rested to resume the march. These men—this remnant of a fine army, who had been dragged through the putrid swamps of the Chickahominy till they were more like ghosts than men, were thus rested, thus drilled, thus marched, thus abused. Surely the end is not yet.

20*th*.—These men, who were yesterday worn out and abused, who needed all the rest they could get, were ordered up this morning at half-past 2, to march at 4, and then, after being formed into line, were kept waiting till 6. The Surgeons dare not say, "General, permit me to suggest that this is rapidly exhausting the nervous energies of the men, and that last night, we had to leave over sixty, overcome by the fatigue of the day." It would have been deemed insolent and insubordinate in a Surgeon to have suggested that the two hours which the soldiers spent on their feet, waiting for their officers to get ready, might have been spent with great benefit to their health and energies, in bed, and the Surgeons must be dumb and the men sick.

We are to-day passing over some of the places of our former

defeats—Big and Little Bethel, and the localities of some of our unsuccessful skirmishes.

21*st.*—Camped last night in sight of Big Bethel, and left this morning at 5 o'clock. After a brisk march of four hours, we reached Hampton, (12 miles.) As we reached the summit of a ridge and the Roads, and the shipping two miles off suddenly burst upon the view, how intensely did I realize the feeling of a scarred leader in a ten year's war, when, on his return he caught the first glimpse of his native land—

" Italiam, primus conclamat Achates."

CHAPTER XVI

On Board Ocean Steamer Arago,
In Chesapeake Bay.

August 23rd.—We have now, at least for the present, bid farewell to "the Peninsula," the land of blasted hopes, the place of our disappointments, the hot-bed of disgrace to the finest army of modern times. General Pope having drawn off the rebel army to give us an opportunity to escape from our perilous position, we passed from Harrison's Point to Hampton without a fight or without a hostile gun being fired. Never since the retreat of Napoleon from Moscow, has there been so disgraceful a failure as this Peninsula campaign; indeed, not then. For, although Napoleon failed in the object of his enterprise, before he retreated he saw the Russian Capital in flames and his enemy abandon his stronghold, whilst we witnessed the daily strengthening of the enemy's capital, and were driven out of the country we went to chastise, without having accomplished a single object of our visit.

Our destination is not yet revealed to us. We suppose it to be Aquia Creek, thence to reinforce General Pope, but I fear it will be such a reinforcement as will not benefit the country or raise the reputation of our already disgraced army.

The jealousy of our commanders towards General Pope is so intense, that if I mistake not, it will, on the first occasion, "crop out" in such form as shall damage our cause more than all the cowardice, incompetency and drunkenness which have so far disgraced our campaigns. General Pope's advance proclamation was construed into a strike at McClellan's manner of warfare, and, notwithstanding that the former has publicly disclaimed any such intention, there has existed an intense bitterness between the friends of the two ever since, nor is it lessened by the subsequent failures of McClellan and the reported successes of Pope. It is interesting, but saddening, to witness the brightening of countenances among some of the staffs of the army of the Potomac, whilst listening to or reading the reports of the repulses of General Pope. Stonewall Jackson's official report of his "splendid victory" over our army of Virginia, has caused more joy amongst them than would the winning of a splendid success by McClellan himself. Our Generals seem to have forgotten that this is *the people's* war, not their's; that it is waged at the cost of the treasure and of the best blood of the nation, not to promote the ambitious views of individuals or parties but to protect the people's right to Government. I begin to fear that patriotism as an element of this army is the exception, not a rule. Many years ago Pelham said to an officer during a European war, "If you would succeed, conduct yourself as if your own personal ambition was the end and aim of the nation. Let others take care of themselves." Bulwer was a judge of human nature.

The more I witness of the workings of this government, and of its influences on men and on their aspirations, the more do I become satisfied that time and increase of population must ultimately bring a separation of the States. There is more territory than can be satisfactorily governed in republican form.   This State of Virginia alone possesses all the requisites of a great nation.   Its navigable fronts communicating with the ocean, exclusive of its sea coast, equals that of almost any nation on the globe.   No one, who has not actually traversed its great Chesapeake, its Rappahannock, York, James, Elizabeth, Potomac, Ohio, and other rivers, can form the least idea of the vast commercial resources and advantages of this great State.   Add what might be, must be, will be, its agricultural and mineral wealth, and it becomes a mighty nation of itself.   Look again at the vast Northwest, at the immense region south of Mason and Dixon's Line, at the great Pacific slope, and we see a territory capable of sustaining its hundreds of millions.   With all this vast population, under a republican government, each individual eligible to and struggling for power, not limited in numbers by a circle of nobility, and no power on earth can hold together, in brotherly love, so vast a crowd of strugglers for place.   Separation of the States or formation of a stronger government, is, to my mind, but a question of time and of denseness of population, and I cannot but look on the present struggle more as a war for the maintenance of government against anarchy than as a determination to hold in one Union, and under one Government, sister States, which can never live together in amity.   Let this war be prosecuted and fought to the bitter end, let us establish beyond all controversy, the now questioned fact, that man is capable of self-government, under a republican form, and then, if a part of the States are dissatisfied with a government which they cannot control, call a convention of the States or of the people, and let the "wayward sisters depart in peace."   During the contest for the annexation of Texas, I opposed it on the ground that we had already more territory than republicanism could govern. For the same reason, the present secessionists advocated the measure. The Mexican war was brought about for the same purpose, and as a link in the great chain, the annexation of Cuba was eagerly sought after.

We are feeling sadly anxious for our little army on the Mississippi. We seldom hear from them directly, and scarcely know what credit to give the newspaper accounts. Even official reports can no longer be relied on. Pope and Jackson have just fought a battle at Cedar Mountain. Each, in his official statement of it, has caused great rejoicing amongst his friends. Do they both tell the truth when both claim a " decisive victory ?"

24th.—The great size and draft of our ocean steamer made it necessary for us to lie by last night, and we are this morning running into Aquia Creek.

When we arrived we found no orders awaiting us. Immediately dispatched the steamer Montreal to Washington for instructions. Whilst waiting for dispatches from Washington, we have listened to a good sermon on deck, from our Chaplain. At half-past 12 o'clock the dispatch boat returned from Washington with orders to proceed immediately to Alexandria, and disembark.

Five months ago yesterday, we embarked at the very dock at which we now lie, to take Richmond. Now, at the end of the five months, we have arrived at the same spot, with nearly a hundred thousand less men than we took away, having expended $70,000,000, and accomplished nothing else which we undertook. It is vain to deny that our campaign has been a monstrous failure, that the men have lost confidence in their leaders, and that they are feeling, in a great measure, indifferent to the result. At 5 p. m., we are again ashore at Alexandria, and the scream of the locomotive, the rattling of the cars, the voices of women and children, with other signs of civil life, break so strangely on our ears. I feel deeply anxious as to the result of General Pope's fight yesterday. The enemy have got between him and Washington. We can hear nothing from him, and all is uncertainty in regard to his little army. God help him!

25th.—At 1 o'clock this morning we stopped two miles from Alexandria, on the Fairfax Pike, and bivouaced. I threw myself on the ground and slept an hour or two; woke up shivering with cold. I arose, walked a mile to start the circulation, then found a large gutta percha bed cover, wrapped myself in it, and contrived to sleep warmly till the bright rays of the sun in my face called me to consciousness again. Our regiment is very much dispirited, and almost reckless.

26th.—I have been to Washington and Georgetown to-day, and really enjoyed the scenes of civil life. There is a rumor to-day that our worn-out regiment is to go to Baltimore to guard the Fort there. To the regiment generally this would be a god-send, but I confess that for myself I prefer the active duties of the field.

27th.—One year ago to-day I received notice to be ready to march with three days' rations, at a moment's notice; and three days less than a year ago we settled down near this place to bag the army of rebels at Manassas and to close the war. We then stayed settled till they left us. We followed to take them wherever found; overtook them at Young's Mills, on the Peninsula. After a while we followed them to Yorktown. Again sat down and dug holes to bag 'em. They went away, and we followed to take them at Richmond.

but they getting out of patience at our tardiness, stopped, and we blundered on them at Williamsburg, where they saved us the trouble and mortification of digging, dying and waiting, by coming out and attacking us. Having blundered into this fight, we followed on to Richmond. For weeks and weeks we digged and died again, giving the enemy time to collect his forces from all parts of the country, when he came out, and instead of being quietly bagged, drove such of us as were living from our pits, and now here we are back again with our National Capitol in sight on one side, and the guns of the pursuing rebels in hearing on the other. Last night he burned one of our bridges between here and Manassas, and this morning it is said and believed he captured, within our hearing, a brigade sent out to aid Gen. Pope, whilst here sit we idle all the day. Have the people yet begun to question the infallibility of Gen. McClellan? If ever there was an abused army on the face of the earth, this is one, and it will yet pass into a by-word that McClellan holds the army, whilst his Generals abuse it or use it for their own ambitious or mercenary purposes.

It now looks as if we need not leave this ground to fight, but that the enemy will advance and give fight on this very spot. Even now, whilst I write this sentence, five of the 12th Pennsylvania Cavalry, of a company left at Manassas, ride into camp. They say they were surprised this morning, (the old story,) and that these five are all that escaped. Pope they say is surrounded by Jackson. I admire this man Jackson. He has snap in him, and deserves to succeed. Admiration of him, and of his energy, are unmistakable all through our lines. Our men are discouraged, disheartened, and constantly express the wish that they had such a General to lead them to honorable battle.

Late at Night.—Oh! could I have been proved a croaker, an alarmist, an anything rather than witness what I have seen to-day. Another Bull Run. My writing has been arrested by the noise of teams on the road. What a sight! The road for miles crowded with straggling cavalrymen, infantry, and hundreds of contrabands with their packs and babies, all fleeing from the fight begun last night at Manassas. Miles of teams, batteries of artillery, retreating here in sight of our Capitol, before an enemy whose Capitol we were to have danced in a year ago! Have I misjudged our leaders in my frequent bewailings? Have I croaked without reason? Would to God I had, instead of having to witness the scenes of this day. I am impatient for the advance of the enemy, and hope he will be at us by the next rising of the sun. After the late disgraceful scenes, my mortification prompts me to wish that we may settle this matter now and here. What has this Army of the Potomac done? What attempted? But hold! A rumor is just here that Gen. McClellan has stopped the running of the ferry boats between Washington and Alexandria, and that he has ordered all the water conveyances now in the river to lay alongside of the docks at Alexandria. What does it mean? Is it only a camp rumor? I hope so, for if true it can mean nothing short of a preparation to embark the retreating masses. I will not believe this, for it would imply that we mean to yield our defences here—our strong forts—without any attempt at defence. I will not credit it, for give the enemy possession of Arlington Heights, and Washington cannot hold out a day. Eight months ago we boasted an army 700,-000 strong. Where are they, and what doing? We are driven back here. Buell is in danger at the South. Forts Henry and Donelson surrounded for want of troops to defend them. Morgan unsupported in Kentucky. At this rate what will be worth that political advancement for which our Generals plan and sacrifice each other? What place will the nation have worthy a man's ambition? If it be through tribulation that a nation is perfected, what a perfect nation we soon shall be. I have for a long time wished to resign, but I cannot now; my regiment is in danger, and I must see it through. Then for home.

28*th.*—The news of the morning confirm the rumors of yesterday in reference to our disgrace at Manassas. The enemy caught the garrison there asleep, took eight guns, and captured or routed our force there almost without a fight. The Jersey Brigade, which left here yesterday morning, having no knowledge of the taking of the place, went up and were captured. Pope's communication with Washington is entirely cut off. If I am not mistaken in the character of Gen. Pope and his army, Jackson and Longstreet will have a lively dance before they succeed in capturing him. McClellan, they say, is in high glee. Significant!

29*th.*—Struck tents near Alexandria, at 10 A. M., and have marched in direction of Fairfax Court House, I suppose to go to Bull Run, to reinforce General Pope, who with fifty thousand men is now engaged with Jackson and Longstreet's army, over one hndred thousand strong. I hope to God that may by our destination, and that we may be in time. We have marched to-day only about six miles. The day is beautiful and cool, the roads fine. Why do we not go further. Is it because we have other destination than what I hoped?

30*th.*—We can distinctly hear the fighting beyond Centreville; yet we move slowly, and in that direction. This fight has been going on for two days, with great advantage of numbers and position on the side of the enemy, and yet we stop to rest every half hour, when no one is tired. The troops have had no marching for a week. What *can* our delay mean? God send it may not be the jealousy foreshadowed in a letter written to my wife a week ago. Go on! go on! for God's sake, go on. The whole army says go on, and yet we linger here. We stop an hour in the suburb of Fairfax, whilst the sound of the fight is terrible to our impatience, and we tarry here.

5 p. m.—We have just reached Centreville. The battle rages in sight, yet we stop again to rest when no one is tired, but all anxious to rush on. After having "rested" for two hours, we moved slowly forward for two miles, when we met a courier, who exclaimed: "Oh, why not *one hour* earlier!" Close on his heels followed the flying crowd, again overpowered, beaten and whipped at Bull Run, the disastrous battle field of last year, and we too late to save it.

Alas, my poor country! and must you at last be sacrificed to the jealousies, the selfishness, the ambition, the treachery or the incompetency of those to whom you have entrusted your treasure, life, honor, every thing? Grouchy failed to come. So did Hancock, Franklin and McClellan. There may be good reasons for our delay, and we not be permitted to know what they are. The subordinate is forbidden to discuss the merits or the motives of his superior, but we must not be blamed for *thinking*. Pope was whipped. Thousands of our neighbors and our friends died on that bloody field, whilst struggling to hold it till we could reach and save them, and the joyous faces of many officers of our Army of the Potomac *made* us think that the whipping of Pope and the slaughter of his men, had something to do with their joy. We could not help thinking, and the army regulations will be lenient with us, if we will only not tell our thoughts. But there is one subject connected with this, on which I am inclined to think that, if spirits ever talk, those of the slaughtered there will cry aloud, in spite of the army regulations. Whilst we rested for hours in sight of the battle field, couriers came to us from the Medical Director of General Pope's army, asking that our Surgeons might be sent forward to the aid of the wounded, as they were suffering dreadfully and falling faster than their Surgeons could take care of them. On receipt of this message, I saw a Surgeon ride up to General Hancock (who was lying on the ground) and asked permission to go to their aid; the General abruptly ordered him back to his regiment! *I could not learn that a single Surgeon was permitted to go forward !*

Having met the retreating crowd, and night having come on, we fell back about two miles, now tired and dispirited, and threw ourselves on the ground in and around the fortifications at Centreville, and by 12 o'clock we were all resting, preparatory to another fight to-morrow.

31st.—We were awoke this morning at daylight, by the pattering of rain on our faces, and at once went to work preparing to meet the foe, and perhaps to fight the battle decisive of the war and the fate of our poor "friend-ridden" country. Oh, my country; both you and your friends are making a history, and when it is written, may I be there to help. * * * But we are preparing for fight. Must all of our great battles be fought on Sundays ?

10 1-2 A. M.—"Fall in, fall in." The rain pours whilst we march and counter march for an hour, forming into line

of battle. Why spend so much time at what could have been done in twenty minutes. No need of delay, *now that Pope is whipped*.

We have remained all day at Centreville. No advance by either party. I have a bad cold to night, and lie down with wet feet, and between wet blankets, and yet with this discomfort, how enviable my condition compared with that of thousands whom, and whose families our tardiness has doomed to a life long intensity of pain or misery.

Monday, Sept. 1st.—The defeat which we met with on Saturday, seems to have been a very decisive as well as a very destructive one. Our loss is heavy, though I am not without hopes that the official report will restore many of our lost men, and even place us in possession of the battle field. These official statements are powerful weapons, when well wielded.

We are under a flag of truce all day, removing the dead and wounded from the battle field. I have listened to more than a hundred funeral sermons to-day, each preached in a single second. A dozen muskets at a single volley, tell most impressively and laconically the last sad story, and the spirit of the departed soldier looks down with sad interest on the country which his body can no longer defend.

The enemy can be seen on the move, some eight miles away, and no doubt we shall soon be called to arms.

At 4 P. M. I went down to aid in the hospitals, worked for a short time, and was just prepared, with sleeves rolled up and knife in hand, to excise the shoulder of a poor fellow whose joint had been shattered, when a call to arms arrested further proceedings, and I returned to my regiment. Now, as I write, all is packed and ready, and we are ready to fight or run. The Lord knows which we shall be ordered to do, but presume we shall make another "strategic movement," and "change our base of operations," by falling back in the night on Washington. I was so severely reprimanded for saying that we were whipped at the battle of Mechanicsville and Gaines' Mill, that I shall not venture to write that we are whipped now, but only *think* we are.

A tremendously heavy shower and hard wind set in about 5 o'clock, and continued till nearly dark, the men sitting in line and taking it as they best could. * * * At about 8 o'clock we took up our line of march *towards Washington*. The roads were terrible, the night very dark, yet it was a subject of frequent remark that, notwithstanding these embarrassments, we are led much faster from the enemy than towards him. After travelling about five miles, we found ourselves on the ground where a battle had been fought in the afternoon (Chantilly) between Gen. Stevens and the rebels who had got in our rear and were trying to cut off our retreat. The enemy was repulsed, but Gen. Stevens was killed, and his son wounded.

We marched through the rain during the night, and at 2 o'clock A. M. (when I dropped down and slept between my wet blankets for about three hours,) we had reached to within one and a half miles of Fairfax Court House. I now get no letters from home. This being deprived of regular mail matter from their homes, is one of the most cruel of all the impositions inflicted by government officials on the soldiers. If these office-holders could but know the deep interest with which the most illiterate soldier watches for the mails to hear something, anything from the dear home which he despairs of seeing again, it would move his heart, if he has one, not to throw out the soldiers mail to make room for the civilians.

12 o'clock.—More bad news. The dead body of General

Philip Kearney has just been sent in by the enemy. He was killed yesterday, in the fight at Chantilly. This is a great loss. "He was the noblest Roman of them all." If McClellan only possessed his dash, this war would not now be on our hands. Not an hour before his death, I saw him dashing along his lines, then quiet at Centreville, whilst his soldiers rent the air with shouts of gladness at the sight of him! How proud and happy he seemed at the huzzas of his "fighting division." He little realized how short-lived the pleasure. He started for this place, (Fairfax,) fell in with the enemy, who had got in our rear, engaged and repulsed him, and lost his own life, and never fell a braver man or better fighter.

Our brigade is here, as on the Chickahominy, the rear guard of the army, to protect the rest from a pursuing foe. It seems strange that we should so long be exposed in this perilous position. After this defeat, I fear General Pope's army will be demoralized. 'Tis very sad to listen to the tales of bravery and destruction of his devoted troops at Bull Run, on Saturday. Again and again, whilst being borne down and pressed back by superior numbers, on being told that McClellan's army was in sight and hurrying to their support, would they rally, cheer, and dash themselves against overpowering numbers, and struggle with almost superhuman effort, to hold the field till we could come up ; and all this while we, the "Great Army of the Potomac," were looking on, dallying with time, many, no doubt, praying for the very disaster which happened. Am I prejudiced that I think thus? Had I not written it in this journal, a week before it occurred, I might have hoped so.

10 P. M.—Again in the camp which we left to go to the rescue of General Pope. 'Tis hard to write of what seems to me

the infamous closing up of this short campaign; but it must be done. At 4 o'clock P. M., we left our camp, a mile below Fairfax, and before 10 o'clock, had accomplished a march which had occupied over a day and a half in our hurried march to save Pope's army from destruction, our country from disgrace, our fellow-soldiers from slaughter! A day and a half towards the enemy, five hours to get back! There, it is written; it must tell its own story. I have no reflections to journalize. We are in camp, and the leading officers of our army are preparing *for a good night's rest.* I do not think many of them will be disturbed by thinking of the groans of the wounded and dying whom they saw butchered, and reached forth no hand to save. God grant them sweet repose and clear consciences.

3rd.—Moved our camp this morning, to Fort Worth, about two miles from Alexandria, a beautiful locality, overlooking city and river; and here, report says, we go into garrison for the winter. I would much rather be in the field, and now that my regiment is not likely to be exposed to active danger, I think longingly of home.

4th.—"All quiet on the Potomac."

5th.—10 o'clock P. M. Have just received an order to cook three days' rations, and be prepared to move at a moment's notice. I do not know where we go, but presume into Maryland, to resist the advance of Lee and Jackson, who we hear are crossing at Harper's Ferry and pushing towards Frederick, and perhaps towards Harrisburg, Pennsylvania. If they have crossed with their hundred thousand men, and we cannot now, with our large force, hem them in and capture them, we deserve to be beaten. Will General McClellan *let* us take them, if we can?

CHAPTER XVII

6th.—We cooked our rations yesterday, as ordered, but are being still to-day.   I this afternoon rode down to Alexandria, (2 1-2 miles,) remained a short time, and when I returned at 4 o'clock P. M., found the army in line, ready to march. About dark, we started, no one seeming to know whither we were going, but at 10 o'clock at night, found ourselves on the south end of Long Bridge, opposite Washington.   Having crossed the river, we marched with the pomp and boldness of a victorious army up to the house of the Commander-in-Chief, (General McClellan) and inflicted many long, loud cheers; and what an infliction it must have been!   Just one year before, he had in a speech to the soldiers, promised them that if " you will stand by me, I'll stand by you, and there shall be no more Bull Run defeats."   And here we are, on a skedaddle of a most shameful " Bull Run defeat," celebrating the anniversary of the bomastic, yet puerile speech. We are eight miles farther from Richmond than when the promise was made, and worse still, Generals Lee and Jackson have pushed us aside at the Bull Run defeat, gone past us into Maryland, and threaten Baltimore and Harrisburg. Yet, amidst all my mortification, I have been unable to restrain a laugh at the ridiculousness of our position, as we pass through Washington. For weeks, we have, by night, been stealing away from the enemy in such trepidation that the breaking of a trampled stick would startle us, lest the noise might discover our position to the pursuers. Whilst crossing Long Bridge to-night, General Hancock ordered all the music to the front, and as we marched through the streets to the tune of " Hail to the Chief who in *Triumph* Advances," I could not for the life of me, restrain a laugh at the thought of some poor old dung-hill cock, whipped till feathers were all plucked and ruffled, running away from his victorious antagonist, then perched on his own ground, and peeping from behind a bush to see that no *little chanticleer* was in hearing, would raise himself up and perpetrate his biggest " cock-a-doodle-doo."

" Hail to the Chief who in triumph advances."

Having crowed this big crow on the threshhold of General McClellan's house, we passed on through Washington and Georgetown, and as no army was endangered by our delay, we have marched all night, stopping at daylight near Tennally Town, Maryland.

7th.—Having marched all night, I slept until awakened by the city bells, the first I had heard for nearly eight months. How forcibly I felt the application to the wilderness in which we had been, of Selkirk's soliloquy :

" The sound of the church-going bells
These valleys and rocks never heard,—
Never sighed at the sound of a knell,
Nor smiled when a Sabbath appeared."

K

It has been a beautiful Sunday, and we have been all day "lying around loose," (no tents pitched) awaiting orders.

Had it not been for this move, I should now have been packing up for home. We supposed that we were to remain idle in garrison this winter, and my Colonel promised that he would approve and aid me in getting the acceptance of my resignation. On appearing at his tent four days ago, with my resignation, I received orders for this march. I did not present it, and do not know now when I shall; but not on the eve of battle.

Yesterday, (I learn,) General McClellan was made Commander-in-Chief of the combined armies of Virginia and the Potomac. This looks very much as if there was some truth in the statements of his friends, that he had been held back and controlled in his movements by the President and General Halleck; very much, in fact, as if it were an acknowledgment that General McClellan had had but little voice in the management of the war, and that his superior officers were in the wrong. Should this prove true, I shall have much to atone for in the wrong I have done him in this journal. How gladly will I make all the amends in my power, should he only now prove to be the man for the occasion, and close up this war, as he has promised to do. This prompt and sudden move, too; this all night march in pursuit of the enemy, on the very first day of his accession to the command, gives additional ground for a belief in the hypothesis. God grant that it may be true, and that our General may by saving the country, retrieve his own waning popularity.

8th.—Marched again last night. Started at dark, and moved till about midnight. Were called before daylight this morning, started early, passed through Rockville. Stopped to rest for two or three hours, left knapsacks and baggage, and pushed forward. Verily, there may be mettle in General McClellan, after all. This is so different from our wont, that we appear to be under another dynasty. The army is elated. Let us hurrah for McClellan! But we must do it cautiously ; we are not quite out of the woods.

Having lightened ourselves of our baggage, we moved on, our transportation wagons keeping up with us.

9th.—At midnight last night, we had but just got to rest, when we were called up to unload our wagons, taking out only such baggage as would be absolutely necessary on a forced march. The rest was sent back by teams. This lessening of transportation of leaving of packs, looks as if our leaders expected work to-day or to-morrow. I think we shall not have it so soon; but our leaders are at least on the alert. May this energetic stir be continued to a decisive result! Many think that we shall have no fight here at all, that the rebels have crossed in considerable numbers, with the view of drawing us away, but that their chief army is at Alexandria, ready to attack it so soon as we are enticed far enough away.

Six weeks ago we held almost the whole of Eastern Virginia ; now, not a spot of it securely, unless it be a little piece around Alexandria. But with a continuance of the energy manifested for the last few days, we can soon retake it.

At present, the darkest shade cast upon the country is by our currency. These five cent shin-plasters I do not like, and I like less the false pretence under which they are issued. Why call them "postal currency?" What have they to do with "postal" affairs? 'Tis time the government had quit cheating the people by disguising facts. If five cent issues are necessary, say so frankly, and make them, but let us have no more of this miserable deceit, with the more miserable looking rags.

We marched this morning through Darnestown, and there turning from the main road to the left, proceeded towards a ford in the Potomac, expecting to meet the enemy there and dispute his passage. Finding no enemy, we bivouaced for the night on Seneca Creek, a beautiful stream, at this point about two miles from the river, Crouch's division lay in front of us. Much diarrhæa amongst the troops. In consequence of a scorbutic tendency in the whole army, the free indulgence in the green fruits found by the way side seems rather to alleviate than to increase the diarrhæa.

10*th*.—Returned to the main road this morning, followed it for a short distance, then turned to the right, towards Frederick, by the way of Sugar Loaf Mountain. For two days we have been marching in full view of the Alleghany spurs, and to-night sleep within three miles of the foot of the Sugar Loaf. These mountains present a spectacle both grand and sublime, when viewed at a distance. 'Tis worth a half a life of travel to see them. The men, to-day, have been forced beyond their power to endure, and very many of them have fallen out. Indeed, some regiments are reduced, to-night, to less than half the numbers with which they started in the morning. Rumors vague as vast, in reference to the strength of the enemy in Maryland, meet us to-day. They are variously estimated by those who have seen them, at from thirty thousand to two hundred and fifty thousand—a great margin, truly. We meet to-day, occasionally, our wounded cavalry men, coming in from successful skirmishing with the enemy's outposts about Poolesville and Sugar Loaf; but they have fallen in with no large body of troops.

11th.—Generals Hancock's and Brook's brigades started this morning, on a reconnoisance towards Sugar Loaf Mountain. There is no longer a doubt that the enemy is in possession of Frederick, and has been for some days. Reconnoitering party discovered no enemy in force. It has rained to-day, and I now prepare to lie down, sick and tired at the foot of the mountain.

12th.—Dreamed last night of social scenes and comforts, and woke up a little home sick. I was not made better by the appearance of a cup of wishy-washy coffee which was set before me; but, observing my old man carefully washing himself, after he had served my breakfast, I enquired of him, why so particular to wash after cooking. He replied that he had not water enough at first to wash and get breakfast, too, so he concluded to use what he had for cooking, and to get some to wash him afterwards. This, of course, settled all daintiness in regard to the poor coffee, and I took my breakfast with a relish, thinking no more of home and its comforts. My home sickness was cured.

At 12 o'clock to-day, we moved again, starting in the direction of Frederick, but after a short march we bore away to the left. This, in connection with the fact that General Burnside, with his corps, is ahead of us, and that we have heard heavy firing in that direction, induces me to believe that the enemy are leaving, and swinging around in the direction of Middletown, to take the valley between the Blue and Elk Ridges, and to recross the river above Harper's Ferry. At dark we encamped to the northwest of the Loaf, near its base, with our backs towards Frederick. It is surprising what a change has taken place in the feelings and appearance of the men.   The sallowness of face has given place to flush, the grumbling of dissatisfaction to joyous hilarity, the camp at night, even after our long marches, resounds with mirth and music.

The boys feel that we are now in active earnest, and McClellan stock is rapidly rising.

Saturday, 13th.—Môved this morning at 7, leaving Frederick behind us.   At 8, crossed the Monocacy, (a beautiful stream,) at Buckeytown, Maryland.   Here heavy firing in the direction of Frederick, but as the day advances, swinging around towards Harper's Ferry, from which we infer that Burnside is driving the enemy.   Burnside is one of our reliable men, and rarely fails in what he undertakes.   The enemy has been promised that if he will come in force into Maryland, he will get fifty thousand recruits from the State. He has come.   Will the promise be met?   A few days will tell.   We too bear more towards the Ferry; I hope to intercept the retreat.   But we move more slowly.   Why?   God forbid that our General, so rapidly rising, should, as he approaches danger, fall into his old habit, and disappoint all of our new born hopes.   We laid still a long time at Buckeytown, then moved slowly forward for two miles, having made only four miles march to-day.   At 9 P. M., as I write this, we are called to move, and the journal of to-morrow must tell the events of the night.

14th.—At 9 o'clock last night we took up our march across Catochtin Mountain.   At 9 1-2, as we climbed the mountain side, the moon rose beautifully lighting up hill and valley, and shrub, and tree.   'Twas all beautiful.   The mountain air was brisk and cool.   A march of four miles carried us over the mountain, and we bivouaced in Middletown Valley, one of the prettiest countries I ever saw, in the suburbs of the pleasant and flourishing little village of Jefferson. Here we got varied and various estimates of the strength of the enemy, who had passed through. We found here much evidence of loyalty, and were confirmed in the belief that Lee would be disappointed in his expectation of receiving fifty thousand recruits by his raid into Maryland.

Of all the States I have yet seen, Maryland bears off the palm. Its people, its hills, its valleys, its soil, its climate—all bespeak it one of the most favored States of the Union. The loyalty of its people, too, is intense, for whilst the sympathies of nine-tenths of them are with the people of the South, and opposed to our Administration, they positively refuse to join the insurgents in any illegal step. They would like to go out legally, but will fight for execution of the laws which confine them to the Union. The very limited success of Lee, in adding to his already large army in Maryland, is the strongest evidence of their sincerity. May God preserve this beautiful and loyal State from the ravages of actual war, and its people in their horror of treason and rebellion.

'Tis again Sunday, and again we are fighting all around. How strange that so many of our big fights should occur on Sunday. Six miles to our right, and in full view, Generals Burnside and Sumner are fighting, in an attempt to force a strongly defended mountain pass, one mile and a half in our front, the advance of our own corps are trying to force another pass, (Crampton's,) whilst seven miles to our left, the fight at Harper's Ferry is raging. How much hangs on this day.

4 P. M.—Hurrah! Burnside has forced the pass at South Mountain, has crossed and is following up the retreating

enemy.   He has had a severe fight, with heavy loss on both sides.   General Reno, I hear, is killed; another of our best men gone.   Some are so uncharitable as to accuse General McClellan of wilfully and unnecessarily ordering him to a position from which escape from death was almost impossible.   I will not believe it.

7 P. M.—Hurrah again!   General Slocum, from our corps, has forced Crampton's pass in our front, and is in pursuit. The enemy's loss is heavy; ours comparatively slight.   This is a terrible pass, and it seems wonderful that any army could force it against an opposing foe.   It is in the shape of a triangle, the base being at the top of the mountain, the apex at the bottom.   Into this narrow point our army had to crowd its way, up a mountain almost perpendicular, whilst musketry and artillery enfiladed our advancing lines at every point.   Yet our men, with the cool determination of veterans, forced their way steadily through the Gap, up the precipitous sides of the mountain, and drove the enemy from his stronghold.

Again am I separated from my regiment.   Sent for at 8 o'clock, to organize and take charge of another hospital for the wounded; but this time I do not complain.   My regiment was not in the fight, and will not suffer by my absence, although I leave it without an Assistant Surgeon.   How strange, that in no instance, since the battle of Williamsburg, have I had an assistant in the *time of battle.*   Always sick or out of the way.   Could I thus be absent without reproach?   Not without self-reproach, at least.

15th.—1 o'clock A. M.—I am now through dressing the wounds of those in my hospital.   The next house to me is also an hospital, (a large church in the village of Burkettsville.)   In it I hear the cries and moans of distress.   To me,

the sounds seem at this distance to be those of men neglected. God forbid that it be so, for they have plenty of Surgeons there.

Having, by the kind assistance of Doctor Garrett, a good
and excellent physician of the village, got through with my
dressings and seen my patients all asleep. I, in company
with Doctor G., visited the other hospitals to offer our services to the Surgeons there, but we found the Surgeons had
gone to bed, leaving the wounded to be cared for in the
morning! I then returned to my hospital, and to my great
gratification, found nearly every wounded man asleep, and
this, notwithstanding they were wounded in all parts of
the body—broken thighs, legs, feet, shot through the lungs,
back, bowels. After they were dressed, the free use of ano-
dynes and anasthæctics had relieved the pain, and after a
day of fatigue, danger and suffering, they were resting
quietly.   *   *   *   *   *   *

At 9 1-2 this morning, I was, at my earnest request, relieved from the care of hospital and permitted to return to
my regiment.

A little circumstance occurred last night, which, as it may
be important, I here journalize. A rebel Lieutenant was
brought into my hospital to take care of his Captain, who
was severely wounded. After I had got through my dressing, I fell into a conversation with him on the subject of
the war and its probable results. He was well informed, intelligent, and communicative. During the conversation he
quizzically asked me what I thought of the surrender of Harper's Ferry? I replied, laughingly, that it would be time for
me to think of it when it should take place. "But," said
he, "it has already taken place!" "When?" "About
sun-down." "How do you know?" "No matter; it is

sufficient for us that it took place about sun-down." His manner was assured and confident. What does it mean? Is there treason there, and has he had an inkling of it? This is a strange war, and a strange world. This noon we hear whispers that Harper's Ferry *is* surrendered. At 9 o'clock this A. M., the firing there ceased. It could not have been surrendered at sun-down last night, as the Lieutenant stated: but has it been this morning? And if yes, had he any knowledge that it was to be, and some circumstances have occurred to delay the act? We must wait and learn.

But why did we not go yesterday to the relief of Harper's Ferry, if it were in danger? We had whole divisions of men idle all day, and were within two hour's march of the place? Had we another rival there to kill off? Why did we permit a whole transportation train to pass under easy range of our batteries, and escape without a shot? God forgive my suspicions as to our leaders, but preserve the country from their machinations—if they have any.

16th.—The mystery is solved. At 8 o'clock yesterday morning, Harper's Ferry capitulated, (report says, with eight thousand men, forty cannon, and one thousand two hundred horses,) and we have been for two days in sight, and marching less than five miles a day, by a circuitous route. It looks as if the old game is to be re-enacted. Who is there at Harper's Ferry to be jealous of?

2 P. M.—Tremendous firing along the mountains to our right, some five miles distant. A rider has just arrived from that direction, and reports that Reno's forces, to the number of ten thousand or fifteen thousand, has surrendered. I do not credit it, but if true, it would indicate a larger force in our front than I supposed, and will explain the necessity of our lying here idle, instead of going to Harper's Ferry.

But it seems impossible that we could permit two surrenders in one day, in sight of us, and we lie all the while idle. Well, well; we are engaged with the enemy, and shall soon know the worst. Another arrival from Harper's Ferry. He confirms the story of the surrender there, and says that Colonel Miles capitulated, almost without a fight, and that he was instantly shot by one of his own men. This last story I doubt, though he is certainly shot and mortally wounded. At night, Colonel Miles is dead.

Wednesday, 17th.—A day of momentous events. The battle of Antietam is fought. I had before been near battles, at battles, in battles; but never till to-day was I *through* a battle. For miles around me, it has been one continuous battle field. Look where I would, and when I would, the battle was all around me. Since Friday last, this series of battles has been growing harder and harder. To-day, both parties were reinforced to about one hundred thousand men each, and the battle has been terrible, but there is nothing decisive. We hold most of the ground held by the enemy in the morning, but the parties lie on their arms in sight of each other, ready to renew the slaughter with the coming of light. So terrible has been the day; so rapid and confused the events, that I find it impossible to separate them, so as to give, or even to form for myself any clear idea of what I have seen. I hope it will be different when the mind has accustomed itself a little to thinking over the events and the horrors of the scene. Many illustrious dead will be counted to-night, and, oh! how many sad hearts to-morrow, and how many to-morrows of sadness. Amongst the sufferers, I hear that Generals Mansfield and Richardson are mortally wounded. Surgeon White, Medical Director of General Franklin's Corps, is killed. Poor fellow, the excitement of the battle upset his intellect. He applied to the General for a regiment to dislodge the rebels from a wood in our front. The General replied that his whole corps could not do it. Then said the Surgeon, " I must do it myself," and putting spurs to his horse, dashed off for the woods. Before reaching it, he of course was shot and killed.

As for myself, I feel that I have relieved much suffering to-day. I have shed many tears, too, over the distresses of both loyal and rebel men. As I approached one poor fellow, a Georgia rebel, lying wounded on the field, he was hiding something from me. I took it from him, and on unfolding it, found it to be a potograph of wife and children. I raised him up to look at it, and our tears mingled over the shadows of his loved ones, whose substance neither of us is ever like-ly to see. How easy the gradation from sympathy to affec-tion. I am getting to love these suffering rebels. * * I wish I could describe something of the scenes of to-day, but cannot. They are all indistinct to me. Perhaps some day I shall be able, from these notes, to give them shape in my journal.

At 9 o'clock to-night, an officer, a confidential friend of General McClellan, rode along the lines, and said that the General promises us an infantry fight to-morrow. This means a hand to hand fight, when the best army must pre-vail and *a decisive* result occur. There is great rejoicing thereat amongst our troops. They say, here we are, both armies in force. Let us now come together and settle this war. If they can whip us, why not let us die like soldiers, and end the war. If we are the stronger party, why delay? Let us destroy them, close the strife, and return to our homes. Loud huzzas and hosannas for McClellan resound along the lines to-night. Should he destroy this army to-morrow, he will be the biggest man in America, and will have merited the title of the Young Napoleon. How rejoiced I shall be to find that all my censures of him are unfounded!

Our wounded have suffered much to-day for want of chloroform. I think that not over three or four surgeons on the field had a supply. I saw but two who had. Why will surgeons permit themselves on a campaign like this to be without the necessary articles of comfort for the wounded? The few pounds on hand were exhausted in less than three hours. The men lay suffering from their wounds, and in many instances surgeons were operating without it. Government teams had not come up. What could we do? In this dilemna, at the very right moment, in stepped Mrs. Harris, of Philadelphia, with the announcement that she had just arrived with twenty pounds of chloroform from the U. S. Sanitary Commission. What an angel of mercy is this Mrs. Harris! What a source of ever present comfort and well directed effort is that Sanitary Commission! The soldiers of this army will have cause of prayer for it in their living and in their dying hours.

18*th*—7 A. M.—All night the litter-bearers were passing by and over me where I lay on the ground They were bearing off the wounded. I had worked from daylight till 11 at night, and was exhausted. Yet I could not but reproach myself for resting whilst these men were at work among the sufferers. I could not help it. My Assistant Surgeon left me on our arrival at the battle-field. I worked without his aid, and was worn out. From the General's promise last night, we expect to-day the great fight of the war.

9 *o'clock.*—No fighting yet. I have ridden over the battle-

field of yesterday, and what a scene!   The dead in rows—in in piles—in heaps—the dead of the brute and of the human race mingled in mass.   Here lies the boy of fifteen years, hugged in the death embrace of the veteran of fifty—the greasy blouse of the common soldier here pressing the starred shoulder of the Brigadier.   The moans of the wounded draw me further on, and whilst I administered to their wants, the bullets of the enemy's sharpshooters passing in unpleasant proximity admonished me that I was too far in advance.   I returned, and what a comfort to be *again amongst the dead !*   With the wounded I must speak consolation, but could feel none, at least in many instances; and whilst I was leaving dying strangers with their kisses on my hands, and their last prayers for me (because of the hopes I had revived) on their lips, I felt that I had deceived them.   But I am again amongst the dead, where no moans, no death struggles, no last prayers excite in me the painful consciousness of impotence to relieve, and with a deep feeling of relief I can say of those around me, that

"After life's fitful fever they sleep well."

At 10 A. M. the battle is not renewed. My regiment, though in line all yesterday and till now, has taken no part in the battle.   It will probably open the fight to-day, for which we are all growing impatient.   I have scarcely a hope that one half of it will ever return from the attack for which it is so impatient.   God preserve it.   I love this regiment, and I have now good reason to believe that all my affection is reciprocated.   For its sake I am willing to bear much—risk much.   I just learn that we had five Generals badly wounded in the fight yesterday—Mansfield and Richardson, mortally; Hook, Max Weber, (the other I have not learned.)

No fight yet. Little flags of truce, which none acknowledge, but all respect, are on all parts of the field to-day, and the day is being spent in caring for the wounded, and in burying the dead.

Night has come, but the day brought no fight. The army is disappointed and impatient, and here and there can be heard a complaint at the returning tardiness of McClellan. The universal prayer of the army is that we may be permitted to end this war, now and here. At 10 o'clock at night the flags of truce still wave, and are seen by the bright twinkling of the lanterns over the battle-field. The voice of war is still hushed in the solemnities of burying the dead.

19*th*.—At daylight this morning I was called up by an orderly with an order to repair to the battle-field at once and organize another hospital, and with the intelligence that during the night the enemy had been permitted to escape across the river, and had left some three hundred of our wounded, who had fallen into their hands, on the field. At the moment of my entering the building intended for the hospital, letters dated 6th, 7th and 9th inst., from wife and children, were put into my hands, but though I had so seldom heard from the loved ones at home, the scenes of suffering about me forbade the indulgence of a selfish inclination to read the highly prized missives, and I put them aside till the business of the day was over.   *   *   *   Oh the demoralization of an army. But I will not write a description of what I have witnessed of this, as I hope to forget this trait in human nature, as developed by this war.

Our army have given chase to the enemy, and the organization of my hospital being completed, I left it in other hands, and have followed on and overtaken our corps on the Potomac river, about two miles above Sharpsburg. The feeling against Gen. McClellan to-day is no longer expressed in muttered disaffection, but in loud and angry execration. The soldiers cannot be reconciled to their disappointment, and to our having permitted Gen. Lee to escape with his army. My own hopes that he would retrieve his lost character are all gone. I have lost all confidence in him. He can be nothing short of an imbecile, a coward, or a traitor.

The battle field this morning presented scenes, which, though horrible, were of deep interest to the physiologist. On a part of the field the dead had lain for forty-eight hours, the Northern and the Southern soldier side by side. Whilst the body of the Southern soldier was black and putrid, wholly decomposed, in the Northern decomposition had scarcely commenced. Why this difference?

A fight at Shepardstown took place this afternoon. The enemy were posted on the mountain, on the opposite side of the river. A division (Butterfield's, I think,) was sent over to reconnoitre. They encountered a murderous fire, and enough got back to tell the tale. Yet, we get despatches telling us of our victory there, and of the large amount of transportation we have captured. The old story over again.

I omitted to say in the proper place, that the report of the surrender of General Reno's command, last week, was a canard. I regret that of his death was too true.

20th.—11 o'clock A. M.—I worked too hard yesterday, and was so tired that I could not sleep last night. Fortunate for me that we have not moved to-day; I must have been left. I am feeling better now, however, and if we rest till evening I shall be able to go on. Terrible fighting ahead, within three or four miles, and in hearing of us. I do not know where, nor by what forces. I was stopped writing here by—

who comes to me, loaded with packages from home? How appropriate the contents, and what a relief. This morning, put on my last pair of socks, having worn ragged ones for a week, fearing to use the only ones left. The package contains some beautiful ones sent me by good friends, who seem never to forget my needs. I ought to be grateful and I am. A box of cigars, too, very fine ones, from my good friend B———. I fully appreciate the kindness which dictated this attention, and shall not forget it.

P. M.—I have kept my bed—no, my lie-down on the broad surface of mother earth, with her clean and fragrant spreads and quilts and counterpanes of clover, and now feel rested and refreshed. Was called an hour since, to have all ready for a move. I am packed, and hear that we are to march to-night.

11 P. M.—Called into line from our earthy beds and under the cover of the dark black night, through which peeps a few bright stars we take up our march. Passing Sharpsburg, and one or two log cabin villages, we halted at daylight about two miles southeast of Williamsport, a village on the Maryland side of the Potomac, with a population, I should judge, of five or six hundred.

Sunday, 21st.—The rebel army, reported at eighty thousand, but probably a small portion of it, numbering less than one quarter of that estimate, was encamped last night, within two miles of where we halted this morning. They left, however, on our approach, and we did not get sight of them. We moved again at 9 o'clock this morning, and having wandered through the fields for two hours, apparently without a definite object, we have again bivouaced almost in sight of Williamsport. We are in a beautiful grove, and here I hope we shall be permitted to spend the Sabbath in quiet.

The enemy has escaped our " bag," and why splutter on now, as if we meant to do something. *I am now satisfied that this army will win no decisive battle whilst under command of General George B. McClellan.* It is not a part of his programme.

Monday, 22nd.—A beautiful morning and all quiet, except that the officers are pitching tents and fixing up tables, as if for a stay. But that is no indication of what is in store for us; even before night we may be ordered to pull up and move again. But this would be very cruel. Our poor, worn out enemy, having fought and been driven for seven days, and now being entirely without provisions, must be exhausted and need rest. How cruel it would be to pursue him, under these circumstances. The kind heart of our Commander can entertain no such idea.

In the afternoon, I rode up to Williamsport and found the town full of soldiers. A little incident occurred, which I shall notice. Walking through the streets I encountered a young lady, fresh, rosy, plump and pretty. Her look told me that she would like to speak to me, but she was hesitating as to the propriety of doing so. I spoke, and she at once commenced a conversation on the war. She said that last night there were three thousand rebels encamped near by, and that we might easily have captured them. She pointed out to me with much military tact, how they might have been surrounded, and then said she could not get any one to come in the night and inform us, though only two miles away; that she got ready to come herself, but (with tears and sobs) that her father would not let her, *and only because it was night.* Poor child, I did want to kiss her.

Not for the sake of the kiss. Oh, no!
But only for sympathy, you know—you know.

I have suffered some to-day, from a most singular pain in my finger. It is peculiar, and runs up the lymphatics to the arm and shoulder. Ordered to move at 7 to-morrow morning.

23*d.*—Hung around, and did not get into motion till to 2 P. M. Marched four or five miles down the river and bivouaced. The pain in my finger grows more severe and extends to the scapula. It is a sickening pain and proves to be the result of a scratch by a spiculum of bone, whilst I was examining a gangreuous wound at Antietam (dissecting wound). I cannot say that I apprehend danger from it, but I wish it were well.

General Hancock has been removed from the command of our Brigade, and we have had a whole week of quiet, without the startling profanity to which we were becoming accustomed. For a whole week, I am not aware that a single officer of our Brigade has been ": d—m-d to h-ll."

24*th.*—All quiet this morning. The day is beautiful and bright. I am feeling badly, but as my wound has began to superate, I think I shall be better shortly. I have great confidence in the recuperative power of my constitution, and trust it will be sufficient to eliminate this poison.

We have now had time to look over the late battles and to reflect on the results. We have successfully fought the whole force of the enemy for five days. We drove them at every place, and on the sixth day we permitted them, worn out, discouraged, and out of rations, to depart unmolested. They admitted to our wounded, whose haversacks they robbed, that all they had to eat was what they had taken from our wounded. Gen. McClellan's aims were satisfied with clearing Maryland of the enemy, when destruction or capitulation should have been demanded. This I do not doubt will be the verdict of history. But how terrible was our loss! Nine Generals fell, killed or wounded, in their determined efforts to vindicate McClellan. All in vain.

We are again on the sea of uncertainty, in relation both to the character of our leaders, and the prospects of the country.

25*th*—Well, Gen. Lee is, safely to himself, out of Maryland, into which he came in the confident expectation of adding at least fifty thousand men to his army, but which he left with fifteen thousand less than he brought in.

My hand is excessively painful, though all constitutional symptoms have left. Suppuration has fairly set in, and I no longer feel any uneasiness as to results.

26*th.*—Another quiet day in camp. I applied to-day for a furlough, which I doubt not will be granted. I have worked hard and constantly for sixteen months, and as I am now for a time disabled, I can conceive of no reason why I may not be relieved for a few weeks. No attempted solution yet of the question "Why did not McClellan crush or capture the rebel army after the battle of Antietam?" This question is made peculiarly pertinent by the fact, now ascertained, that we had on the ground the morning after the battle, a force of men (not one of whom had been in the battle of the day before) nearly if not quite equal to Lee's entire army.

27*th.*—"All quiet on the Potomac," and no movement of troops to-day."

28*th.*—Rode to Sharpsburg to-day to procure some medicines, of which we are sadly deficient. Found a purveyor there, but he had no medicines except morphine and brandy. I passed over Antietam battle-field. The smell was horrible. The road was lined with carriages and wagons conveying coffins and boxes for the removal of dead bodies, and the whole battle-field was crowded with people from distant States exhuming and removing the bodies of their friends. 'Twas a sad, sad sight, and whilst the world is calculating the chances of war, and estimating its cost in dollars, I am dotting down in my memory the sad scenes I witness as small items in the long account of heart-aches.

29*th.*—To-day received the anxiously expected furlough, and now for my dear, dear home, from which I have been absent for nearly a year and a half. Now for a visit to my dear wife and children! I have ridden since night to Hagerstown, where I shall stop till morning, then hie me onward. My hand is very painful and much swollen, but I anticipate no results from it more serious than severe pain.

30*th.*—Left Hagerstown at 8 this forenoon. Stopped five hours at Harrisburg, Pennsylvania, and now again am on the way to ———, and I hope to meet with no more delays.

31*st.*—Reached home a little after midnight, found my *family* all *well*, and *I verily believe* are glad to see me.

[The month of October was spent away from camp, and I omit my private journal during the time.]

CHAPTER XVIII

November 1st.—At 12 o'clock, night, I reached camp, two miles north of Berlin, Maryland. Again I have left the pleasures of a cheerful, happy home, to encounter the hardships of camp life and to engage in the turmoil, the trials and the dangers of a war in which it is difficult to tell whether the hope of manufacturing political capital or of sustaining a government is the dominant motive.

Sunday, 2d.—All quiet to-day, preparatory to moving. Spent most of the day in calling on and receiving calls from the officers and soldiers of the regiment. All seemed glad to welcome me back. I hope and believe they were sincere Went to church in the afternoon, but heard no sermon.

3d.—Division left camp at 7 this A. M., crossed the Potomac at Berlin, on a pontoon bridge, and march in a southwestern direction through Lovettsville. The Blue Ridge loomed up all day, to our right, and separated us from the Shenandoah Valley. All day we hear heavy firing beyond the Ridge, at Snicker's Gap, through which the enemy was driven yesterday. General Pleasanton is after them.

4th.—We have marched about ten miles, and are encamped at Union, a dirty little worn out village.   It looks as if it was dying of dry gangrene, and was too weak to wash its face.   Cannonading heard all day, and although we are marching from ten to fourteen miles a day, we do not seem to get nearer to it.   We are now again over twenty miles into Virginia, and everything looks like a general movement which is " to be continued."

5th.—Broke camp at 2 in the afternoon; moved four or five miles in a southerly direction, still keeping a few miles to the east of the Blue Ridge.   No enemy encountered, and none found to-day by our advanced guard.   Troops in fine health and spirits.

6th.—Marched ten or twelve miles to-day. Crossed railroad below Manassas Gap, and encamped near the village of White Plains.   There has been no firing in hearing yesterday or to-day.

7th—Cold and blustery last night.   Ice half an inch thick, with driving snow storm this morning; very uncomfortable.   No move to-day

8th.—More pleasant than yesterday.   In camp all day. There is a rumor that the enemy have taken one hundred and fifty of our teams in the Shenandoah Valley, and that they are again at Harper's Ferry   The report is not credited here,* but it is certain that they have cut the railroad four milest east of us, stopping our supplies from Washington. Hard times ahead.

Sunday, 9th.—How little like Sunday the day has been; marching, whooping, hollering.   Few even know it is Sunday.   From present appearances, one would judge that—

> " The sound of the church going bells,
>   These valleys and rocks never heard."

* Proved to be false.

March to-day *with all teams in advance*. What does it mean? Are we again retreating with our two hundred thousand of the best troops the world ever saw? I will not believe it yet, though McClellan's friends claim that he is the best retreater known in modern warfare. We are encamped to-night near New Baltimore, a Virginia town, which once boasted a blacksmith shop and two houses.

11th.—Reconnoisance by our Brigade to-day. Marched over precisely the same road we came yesterday, to the same place, and returned to-night to the place whence we started the morning: distance going and returning, sixteen miles, over a tremendous mountain:

> " The King of France, with forty thousand men,
> Marched up the hill, and then marched down again!"

We have done that twice to-day. Why should we not figure in history as well as he? We discovered nothing. But there has been heavy firing again to-day, beyond the Ridge, in the direction of Waterloo.

11th—In camp all day. Beautiful and clear but windy. Heavy firing towards night some twelve or twenty miles to the southwest.

McClellan relieved, and to-day Burnside succeeds. Surely,

> " De kingdom's comin',
> And de day ob jubelo."

Some of the army depressed to-night in consequence of the change. Natural enough, but it will be all right in a few days, or I am no prophet.

To all the claims to greatness for Gen. McClellan, the question *will* obtrude: With the best army on the continent, of two hundred thousand men, what has he accomplished in the fifteen months during which he has been in command? Whilst on the other hand, another question comes up: Why, if he has accomplished nothing, and is not a great man, is he the most popular man, with his army, in the United States? My own solution is this: There is a tendency in armies, to love and venerate their Commander. General McClellan has been at the head of the armies. In addition, his friends hold him up as a political aspirant. *He, then, who shall accomplish most for Mc Clellan's popularity, stands first in the list of promotions!* Every Major and Brigadier General feels it to be his own personal interest to eulogise McClellan, and the struggle amongst his followers, is not for who shall distinguish himself most in the service of his country, but who shall stand highest on the list of friends to him who is soon to wield both the civil and military power of the country. The soldiers know nothing against him, because they know nothing of him. He is rarely seen by them, and the encomiums of his sycophantic eulogists, such as Porter, Franklin, Hancock, "et id omne genus conspiratorum," is taken as true, whilst such men as Kearney, Reno, Couch and Burnside, must be sacrificed for being in the way of others, who substitute intrigue for genius.

12*th.*—Quiet in camp all day. It seems hard that we must lose this beautiful weather, when winter is so near at hand; but I suppose it is necessary to allow the new Commander-in-Chief to perfect his plans. General Fitz-John Porter re-arrested to-day, and taken to Washington, on charge of disobedience of General Pope's orders, at the battle of Bull Run, on the 29th of August. That the defeat of Pope's army there, the slaughter of thousands of our true and loyal men, the escape of Lee's and Jackson's commands from capture or destruction, was the result of treason, there is not a shadow of doubt. If Porter is proven to be the traitor—hang him, hang him; for God's sake hang him; and if a traitor at the instigation of a higher in command, hang him too. We have had enough of this thing of staking the lives of our men, by whole brigades, on political chess games. Hang a few of the traitors to save the sacrifice of true and honest men.

13*th.*—Beautiful day; and all quiet. What a pity that we must lose this fine weather. Already, as I predicted, I can hear many of McClellan's friends, who were depressed yesterday, admitting that he had failed, and expressing their gratification at the change of Commanders. It will go hard only with the aspirants in high places, who have spent so much time and breath in inflating McClellan, that he became an unmanageable balloon, broke from his fastenings, and has "gone up." Can we trust that they will not betray Burnside, as some of them did Pope. I confess that I am apprehensive on this point.

14*th.*—Another day of sunshine and quiet. I rode to Warrenton to-day, a pretty little town five miles from us; but, oh, how desolate to those whose home it has been; every house and church a hospital or a barrack; dirty, squalid soldiers crowd the streets; the sick and wounded of both armies hang on every door step, whilst hundreds of mules, with their braying, and their drivers swearing, vie with each other in their efforts to Babelize the scene. All this, if not a necessity, is a concomitant of war.

I mixed freely with the prisoners, hoping to find some from Texas or from Georgia, who could tell me of my friends in those States, but without success.

15th.—Another beautiful day ; no move. Heavy cannonading this forenoon, in the direction of Warrenton. At 2 P. M. received orders to march to-morrow. Where to ?

Sunday, 16th.—What a Sunday ! What a day of rest ! Troops were called at 5 A. M. Carried heavy knapsacks, guns and ammunition, and march till 9 1-2 P. M. ; sixteen and a half hours, and no enemy near ! Truly, "Old Burney" begins vigorously ; but, if this is an earnest that he means business, let him push on. His men will not complain.

This morning I got up sick, with a painful diarrhœa. Have been feeble all day, and as 9 o'clock came, with its cold and piercing winds sighing through the pines and over the hills, how longingly I looked for that "little candle," which in times of peace was wont to "throw its beams so far" to greet me on my return to home, after a long night's ride ! How I yearned, in lonely thoughts, amidst this crowd, for the cheerful scenes and comforts which had often welcomed me on such a night. When shall I enjoy them again ? When will this thirst for blood, and unholy struggle for power, yield to the love of peace and happiness at home ? We passed Cattlett's Station in our march to-day, and encamped for the night near Weaversville, with orders to continue our march at 6 o'clock to-morrow morning.

17th.—I am feeble to-day, from my indisposition of yesterday. Army was astir at 4 A. M. Have had a fine day, and marched fifteen miles, towards Stafford Court House. Men in fine spirits. The prospect of work has reanimated them, and they are perfectly satisfied with the exchange of Commanders. At 8 P. M. it is raining hard, and I fear the good weather is over. Hard as we have worked for the last two days, and unfavorable as is the prospect of the weather, when the order came, a few minutes since, to continue the march at 6 A. M., to-morrow, there went up a long, loud "Hurrah for Old Burney!" The men want business. They wish to close this war; *and, if the officers only prove true to the country and to their Commander-in-Chief,* I predict for him, (based on the energy of his troops,) a brilliant campaign.

18*th.*—Nothing of moment to-day. We started early; it rained a little, and to-night we are encamped within three miles of Stafford Court House, six miles from the mouth of Acquia Creek, on one of its tributaries, and about twelve miles from Fredericksburg.

19*th.*—The army is reorganized. Instead of the former divisions of only brigades, divisions and corps, it is now brigades, divisions, corps, and grand divisions, of which last there are three, General Sumner, at present, commanding the right, General Hooker the centre, and General Franklin the left. I wish I had more confidence in General Franklin, but I cannot forget his conduct at West Point, Virginia, nor at Centreville, where he failed to reinforce General Pope.

This is a dark and rainy night; and a little sad, and a good deal home-sick; I sit unattended, (except by my faith_ ful "General,"*) reflecting, over my log fire, on the beauty of the opening stanza of the sixth canto of the "Lay of the Last Minstrel;" (what an expletive of possessives.) In my home-sickness, I have called up all my BACHELOR acquaintances, and even above the patriotic reflections stands forth each one—

"The wretch concentered in himself."

* A black servant.

How intensely this stanza reflects my feelings to-night. I have not only a country but a home, and, oh, how often, and how deeply have I prayed for the preservation of integrity to each—

> " Breathes there a man with soul so dead,
> That never to himself hath said—
> This is my home, my native land."

20th —A hard, cold rain all day. The regiment is out on picket. I wish those comfortably housed at home could realize what picket duty is, in such weather as this. To-day they stand from morning till night, on guard. Night comes, but with it no relief from the exposures of the day. In his thoroughly soaked clothes, with the snow flying and the wind whistling about him, without fire and without tents, he must stand; he must still stand and guard the lines till the coming of another day. However much nature may give way under the trial, however exhausted the man, should he be caught slumbering a single moment on his post—the penalty is death. The soldiers bear all this cheerfully, to the shame and disgrace of those disaffected, cowardly cavillers at home, who would sacrifice together these noble, self-denying men and the Government for which they fight. 'Tis said that we go into winter quarters here. I cannot believe it. General Burnside has not been pushing us forward at such a rate for a week past, to winter us in this most gloomy and desolate country. We are forty miles from "any where," in the midst of a pine forest, the roads in winter impassable, the people semi-civilized. Whugh! I shudder to think of it.

23rd.—'Tis too bad! For eight days, we have been without a mail, and to-day, when the big bag was opened, not a scratch for me!   I feel shut out from home; but this is only one of the discomforts of a soldier's life.   The soldier, when he enters the field, is presumed to sever all ties of home.   What an imagination it must require to presume that he can do any such thing!   However, that is the rule, and the theory.   But is it not bad, both as rule and theory?   True, a man cannot have a home without a country; but what is country without a home, that centre of all his hopes and his affections!   The soldier who enlists with the feeling that because he has a family, he has so much the more to fight for, is but poorly paid, when you remind him, that in entering the army he gave up his home and family for the good of his country.   Strike from his affections that of home and family, and how much of country will be left?   When I get back I'll ask some old bachelor to tell me.

Through this journal I have freely expressed opinions as to our leading men.   When I now look back at my entries, at and after the battle of Williamsburg, on my return from the Peninsula, on leaving Fort Monroe, and in reference to our trip to and from Centreville, in the latter part of August, relative to Generals McClellan, Franklin, Pope and Hancock, and of my fear of the jealousies amongst Generals, and when I compare these entries with revelations on investigation of the Harper's Ferry surrender, I think my friends must be willing to recall much of the harsh judgment they passed on me for entertaining such opinions "of these great and good men."

What are we going to do?   I am of opinion that we are waiting here for the repair of docks and bridges at Acquia Creek, so that we can land our rolling stock for railroad.   I hear some whispers that Burnside cannot advance, because of some disappointment in the arrival of pontoons.   Can it be that there are parties already playing false to him. I confess to fears. It will do no harm to venture a prediction as to our course. So soon as we get the railroad repaired, and are running on it, with our bridges across the Rappahannock, we *shall take* Fredericksburg, at all hazards, then push forward to Saxton's Junction, cutting off Richmond from all its northern connections, then rest for the winter. This can be done ; and if treason can only be kept out of our ranks, I verily believe it will be done, and that before the 20th of December, we shall be in winter quarters, around Saxton's.

1st.—To day I rode over a mile from camp, to see—right in the woods, with but a little settlement surrounding it—the most aristocratic pile I have yet seen in Virginia. 'Tis a large brick church, built in the form of a cross. As I approached it the first thing which attracted my attention, after I had wondered what it was doing there, was a black panel over the main entrance door, with this inscription :

"Built A. D., 1751; destroyed by fire, 1754,
and rebuilt
A. D., 1757, by Mourning Richards.
William Copen, Mason."

I entered, and found two broad aisles crossing each other at right angles. The pulpit is built after the fashion of Trinity Church, New York, or somewhat in the style of that in the large Cathedral in Milwaukee, Wisconsin; but the the work is more elaborate than either of them, the minister having to pass into the third story of his pulpit before he has approached near enough to the Divine presence to catch his inspiration. The two lower stories are occupied severally by the Register and the Parish Clerk. The floor is of fine marble; the pews are square, with seats on all sides, and large enough to have seated, before the advent of crinoline, about twenty persons to each pew. At the end of one of the main aisles is a semi-circular enclosure, a resting place for the dead. On the beautiful marble floor which covers the mortal relics is deeply inscribed, and inlaid with gold:

"In

Memory

Of the race of the House

of

Monclure."

Ah! and must the "memory of the race of the House of Monclure" be preserved only in gold? Could not he, the Vice-gerent of God—have written on hearts stony enough to retain the impression, the memory which he would have to live forever? Could he not have inscribed on tablets of memory, to pass as an heir-loom from generation to generation, an appreciation of that great precept which he professed—"Peace on Earth, and good will to man?" Then he might have gone, triumphantly exclaiming—

"Exegi monumentum perennius auro."

But having entrusted the preservation of his memory more to gold than to Godliness, he is likely to be remembered in a manner which he little expected, for our soldiers have broken in, have torn up this marble floor, and are carrying away this golden momento "of the race of the house of Monclure," as trophies of this unholy war. "The house," at least, will be remembered. I have asked permission tonight, to occupy this church as a hospital, my chief object being to protect it from further vandalism.

In the wall, over this little enclosure which I have described, are four large black panels, the first and second containing part of the XXth Chap. of Exodus, the third, the Creed of the Church of England, and the fourth, the Lord's Prayer, all in silvered letters—bright silvered letters on a black ground! How fitly emblematic of the spirit of the inscriptions to the darkness of the minds on which the living principles were to be impressed.

At the other end of this aisle is a high gallery. Another large black panel in this gallery bears the names of the
i ng actors here, more than a hundred years ago. Let me help to imortalize those names:

"Iohn Monclure, Minister;

Peter Hageman,	Benjamin Strother,
Iohn Mercer,	Thomas Fitzhugh,
Iohn Lee,	Peter Daniel, ⎫ Church
William Mountjoy,	Francis Cook, ⎭ Wardens
Iohn Fitzhugh,	Iohn Peyton.

Vestrymen.
1757 "

May their names be recorded as plainly, and more durably, in a house not built with hands, as in the ephemeral pile now threatened with destruction.

2nd.—I have just written a long letter to my wife, and as this has been a day without incidents, I insert a copy of the letter as my "journal of to-day":

CAMP IN THE WOODS, NEAR STAFFORD C. H., VA.⎱
December 2, 1862. ⎰

Here we still lie in the woods, four miles from Stafford Court House, about ten from the mouth of Acquia Creek, and fifteen from Fredericksburg, and here we have lain for the last ten days, and for all we can now see, like old Massachusetts, here we shall lie forever. But why we lie here, the Lord and the General only know, and as neither think it good policy to be communicative on military matters, we poor subordinates must be content with the knowledge that "great is the mystery of ———" Generalship. This much, however, we do know:—that we are on a hill "Among the Pines," surrounded by mud and amidst a net-work of roads, almost impassable, since the late heavy rains,—that we are drawing our rations from Acquia Creek, when there is a good railroad, with cars running to within about one-third of the distance from us; that we every night send out a heavy picket guard *to our rear*, perhaps, on the principle of a certain railroad company in our State, which attaches its cow-catcher to the rear of its train, "for reasons perfectly satisfactory to themselves."

When our new Commander started off, the wind whistled about our ears, under the great impetus which he gave his army, and so rapid was our progress that many expressed the hope that he would not prove only a quarter horse, instead of a thorough bred turfster, with wind and bottom. The first heat was certainly run with great speed, but the length of rest between heats is out of all proportion to the length of the race. The army, however, has great faith in the mettle of "Old Burney," and express no fears that, when the tap of the drum calls him again to the stand, he will be found either to have "let down," or be broken-winded.

Amidst all the gloom which our partial want of success has cast around us, amidst the trying and discouraging circumstances in which our lot is cast, a bright star shines forth from the darkness and gives warrant of redemption from the errors of the past. The evil spirit of party, which like the wily snake had inserted itself amongst the flowers and fruits of true loyalty—which was mingling its slimy poisons in every dish of the patriot, has been detected and cast from the garden. The army feels that it was being seduced by the charms of the serpent, and now rises above the temptations. When McClellan was removed, much feeling of bitterness and disapproval was manifested, but since we have had time for reflection, and asked ourselves, why did not McClellan surround and destroy the rebel army at Manassas last winter, as he weekly promised us? Why did he not destroy him when he found him weak and divided at Yorktown? Why he staid ten miles behind the army and was not in time to support the gallant Hooker at Williamsburg? Why he waited on the Chickahominy till he buried in the ditches more faithful men than there were in Richmond, to oppose his entry at the time of his arrival there? Why in his statements of the results of battles he either ignorantly or perversely mis-stated the facts? Why, when the rebel army at the battle of Malvern Hills, was *utterly routed* and demoralized, when one-third of our army had not fired a gun, but had been at rest all day, was our Commander, instead of following that routed army into Richmond, like Pompey, dallying away his time on one of his galleys, if not with a Cleopatra, with a charmer not less seductive? Why on our march from Alexandria to Manassas to succor Pope, did he compel us to lie by the road side for hours, in sight of the battle's smoke, where we knew that our brave fellow men were struggling and sinking by thousands before a superior enemy; aye, struggling against every hope of success, except the coming of McClellan? Why did his parasites, refuse even the aid of his Surgeons to the wounded and dying of that noble army, when they sent imploring messages for aid ? Why did he lie still and permit a retreating enemy, penned in betwixt the river and the mountains at Antietam, to move quietly off, when he himself says officially, that over that enemy he had just gained a great victory ? Why, under those circumstances, and with all these faults, we loved him still ? We discover that the poisons of party had so perverted our vision, that we could not see things in their true light, and almost every man when he looks back on what he has been made to suffer *by* McClellan *for* McClellan, restrains his curses, simply because of his sense of inability "to do the subject justice." We have gloriously exchanged the army of partisans, for that of patriots, and a bright star beckons us "*onward !*"

4th.—This afternoon I procured signatures of Surgeons to certificates, that in consequence of my long continued labors, I was breaking down. I immediately drew up my letter of resignation and started to present it in person, and to ask the approval of the Colonel. Before reaching his quarters I was met by a courier with an order to march at daylight tomorrow morning. I, of course, withheld the paper till the march, perhaps to battle, was over.

5th.—Broke camp this morning, marched southerly through the village of Stafford, the most miserable and dilapidated looking place the imagination can picture, unless it should take for its pattern some other Virginia village. About a mile and a half south of Stafford Court House we crossed, at Brooks' Station, the railroad leading from Fredericksburg to the mouth of Acquia Creek, and, after marching about one mile further, in the night, we bivouaced in a most woe-begone, hilly, pine-covered, tobacco-eaten country.

Shortly after passing Stafford Court House, I rode up to some "negro quarters," to see if I could get a canteen of milk, or something "fresh" for my supper. An old black woman came to the door, expressed gratification at our arrival, and fears that we should not be able to retain our hold in the country. She seemed about seventy years old. I asked her if she cared anything for her freedom, or whether she would rather continue a slave, and be taken care of by her master?

" Ah, massa, my freedom ain't wuf much to me now, but if it please de Laud, I would love to live to see dis a Free State; seem like 't would be so good to die in a free country, and den when I sings praises in hebben, it would be so nice to tell de Laud to his face, how I lub him for *dat* goodness."

The slave may be "satisfied with his condition," but it strikes me that this expresses a strange yearning for change in a mind already satisfied.

6th.—This morning, during a rain, we moved our bivouac about a quarter of a mile, and encamped. To get settled, we have worked most of the day in the rain, and to-night I feel about as miserably as the most miserable wife on earth could wish a more miserable husband, and this, I presume, is as miserable a condition as a miserable nostalgia can well imagine.

Letters from home to-day, but they are from twelve to twenty days old. The comfort of a regular mail, the Government, with a very little well directed effort, might easily afford to the soldier, and it would be, even as a sanitary measure, a great stroke of economy. How many a poor fellow would be saved by regular cheering letters from home, from a depressing nostalgia, lapsing rapidly into typhoid fever, and death.   But it is folly to think of a reform in this, when the families of so many of our soldiers are in a state of destitution, simply because the pay due to them is withheld for five, six, and even, in some instances, for eight or nine months.   One of my hospital nurses has just come to me, with tears on his face, showing me a letter from his wife, in which she says that her little home has been sold under the hammer, because she could not pay a debt of fifty dollars! and this when the government is in arrears to them over a hundred dollars.   This seems unjust, and ought to be remedied.

CHAPTER XIX.

The following letter, though not a part of my journal, is occasionally referred to in it, and I therefore have it inserted here :—

CAMP NEAR BELLE PLAINES, VIRGINIA,
December, 10, 1862.

MY DEAR C—— :

* * * * Our whereabouts is four miles from Falmouth, three and a half from the mouth of the Potomac Creek, and about three to the nearest point of the Rappahannock River. As we may be ordered to leave here within an hour, that is sufficiently explicit. Although I have not hesitated at times to express my opinion, confidentially, of the conduct and merits of men, I rarely venture one prospectively, of military matters and strategy. As, however, you express so great a wish for *my* opinion on the prospects and plans of the war, I will tell you what I know of the present, and guess of the future state of things, reminding you that I am not a military man, and give but little of my attention to military affairs. The Medical Department occupies al my time.

One month ago to-day, our forward movements were arrested by General Burnside superceding McClellan, in the command of the army. We supposed that it would require at least a week or two for him to mature a plan of operations, and have the army mobilized; we were mistaken. Five days sufficed, and we were off like a quarter horse; but just as we arrived at the seat of operations, we were suddenly brought to a stand by the failure of somebody to furnish the supplies to enable us safely to cross the Rappahannock, and to take possession of the heights before the arrival of the enemy. We were consequently stationary, and he got possession of the ground we meant to occupy. Did we do right to stop? My partiality for and confidence in the opinions of General Burnside strongly incline me to think we did, whilst my own reasoning questions it. *It seems to me*, that we had at Falmouth, before the arrival of the enemy, a force sufficient to have taken the ground and held it till we should get the railroad from Acquia Creek, in order to transport supplies for the whole army, and then, for an object so important, we might have put our men on half rations, for a few days. The enemy, in all his campaigns, runs a heavier risk than that. Indeed, in one of his reports he speaks sneeringly of " the immense transportation trains, without which it seems impossible for the Yankees to move." But there are doubtless many reasons which I cannot see. But the position is lost. What next?

We must advance.—Public pressure will compel us to, against any odds. Yet we cannot advance without crossing the river. The enemy occupies all the heights, both front and enfilading, and with a force at least equal to our own, commands the crossings. Shall we risk it against such odds? In my opinion we *must*. But is this the only place to cross? Our pontoons are already in the river, some above, some below. An hour's time will suffice to throw them into bridges, *where we choose.* Have we not ingenuity enough to draw attention by a feint at one point, whilst we bridge and cross at another. Should we cross either above or below, we shall occupy a flanking position with decided advantage. I think we shall cross, and I shall not be surprised if even before this letter is finished, we are summoned to attempt it. I think, too, that we shall cross without much resistance. What then ? Will the enemy withdraw ? *Not an inch.* He cannot fall back without disaster, and every foot of ground hence to Richmond, will be contested. For, give us Saxton's Junction, twenty-five miles south of us, and Petersburg, which we can take when we want it, and Richmond is cut off from supplies, and must fall. I stop here to say that my prediction is already verified. Major B. has this moment left me an order to move at 2 in the morning. He says that in a council of war just held, it is decided to cross at three points at daylight. Shall we do this ? I doubt it ; and simpliy *because it is the result of a council.* It is too public. Burnside is not the man to send word to the enemy when he is coming. This, however, is all conjecture. The morning will tell how well grounded.

*   *   *

Yours, &c.

11*th.*—At 5 o'clock, A. M., as clear and calm a morning as ever a bright and beautiful moon shone on. We struck tents and took up our line of march in the direction of Fredericksburg, only five miles distant. At a quarter before 6, precisely, the heavy reports of two large guns came booming through the woods, telling us that the ball was opened. The sound came from Falmouth. Frequent and more frequent came the peals, and in half an hour, so constant was the roar that the intervals between the reports was undistinguishable. At 11 o'clock, A. M., we are in line of battle along the north bank of the Rappahannock, about two miles below Fredericksburg. A pontoon bridge is nearly completed just in front of us. The artillery fight at Falmouth continues; our troops are pouring into the plain along the river. Will the enemy contest our passage? Doubtful.

At 11 1-2 o'clock, I sit on my horse, on a high ridge overlooking Fredericksburg, Falmouth, the river, and the vast plains on either side, where the hosts of both armies are marshalling for the great trial. How beautiful the plains, the cities, the river! How grand the *tout ensemble!* How different may be the scene on which the rising moon of tomorrow morning may shed her silver light.

> " On Linden, when the sun was low,
> All bloodless lay the untrodden snow,
>   *   *   *   *   *   *
> But Linden saw another sight
> When the drums beat at dead of night,
> Commanding fires of death to light
>   The darkness of her scenery."

Oh, beautiful Rappahannock! are you on this most beautiful day to take the dark rolling Yser for your type? And must this bloodless and untrodden snow, e'er another rising sun, be stained by the blood of valiant hearts, struggling in the cause of government and humanity, against anarchy and oppression? I am at this moment notified of my appointment as a "Chief operator" for General Howe's division, during the approaching battle, and am ordered to duty. This is a most flattering distinction, but I rather regret it, as it takes me from the scenes of the field.

3 P. M.—Having prepared my hospital, and the fight not

having commenced in our division, I have ridden to Fredericksburg, two and a half miles, and, for the first time, witnessing the bombarding of a city. Rebel sharpshooters are concealed in the houses, and have been shooting our pontooniers. The city is already on fire, and thus ends this ancient town, where children, and childien's children, have lived and died in the same house. for generations. Alas! their homes are destroyed and they homeless. To them the seat of their acutest joys and sorrows. of their hopes and their fears, their histories. and their traditions will be known no more forever. But how strange that I should sit here writing on horseback. almost in the midst of their sharpshooters, without being able to reason myself into a sense of my danger! Have I a life charmed against such exposure, that I should be thus insensible to it? However, if some were here, who have an interest in this matter. co-ordinate with myself, they would say "Go!" and I will do it. Come, Joseph,* yours is not a charmed life. and you at least must be taken away.

Night has come, and we have not crossed the river. Rumors are rife, that the enemy has evacuated. I do not credit them.

12*th* —At 9 o'clock, A. M.. troops are crossing, and again has commenced *our* cannonading, but there is no response. I sit in the building prepared for hospital, out of sight and out of danger. Are we to have a fight to-day? Doubtful. I find myself indulging in some feelings of pride on the distinction which was conferred on me, unasked, yesterday, though I do not doubt it will excite some of my brother Surgeons to jealousy against me. I almost wish it were otherwise; for, after the long personal battles I have had to

* My faithful and affectionate horse.

fight, to maintain my proper position in the regiment, I was getting at peace with all, and I should have liked a little quiet. God grant that I may prove adequate to the responsible duties imposed by my new position. I deeply realize the fact that it places in my hands the limbs and lives of many poor fellows who are to be brought under my care. Ambulances and litter-bearers are passing to the expected battle field, and I too, must prepare, though I much doubt our having a fight to-day.

11 *o'clock.*—We have "crossed the Rubicon," and I now sit on the south bank of the Rappahannock, watching the crossing of our left wing, about fifty thousand strong. I hear that our centre and right wing are crossing on bridges from two to four miles above us. Not a shot of resistance yet this morning, except from a few sharpshooters, and they are now silenced. The smoke of the burning city, and of the heavy cannonading of yesterday, have settled, casting a thick pall over all the country, and we cannot see more than a few rods around us. We know not, therefore, whether the enemy is before us, but the general impression is, that he has fallen back, to draw us on. I am of the opinion that it will require but little suction to draw our Commander on to destruction or to victory. He evidently means business; But will McClellan's friends, who now hold most important commands under General Burnside, betray him as they did Pope? or will they prove true to the country in this hour of its greatest trial. When I see General Franklin in charge of the most important position, my recollection will revert to his conduct at West Point and at Centreville, and whilst I hope, I fear. From what I have seen of that man, I have lost all confidence in him. How I hope that he may now retrieve

imself in the estimation of those who feel towards him as I

do. The developments being made in the trial of Porter may make some Generals cautious. God grant it may.

It has been a matter of wonder to me, how the rebel army lives in its marches through this country, without transportation. We have now marched over one hundred miles in this State, and on the line of our march for a width of six miles, (making an area of six hundred square miles.) I am satisfied that there are not provisions enough, if all were taken, to subsist Lee's army one day.

At 1 o'clock I take possession, for a hospital, of the house of Arthur Bernard, on the south bank of the river, two miles below Fredericksburg. This is one of the most magnificent places I ever saw. I shall not undertake to journalize a description of it. It is owned by one of the old bachelor F. F. V's. He is now trying to compromise with us, so as to be permitted to retain a part of it. He is very ridiculous in his demands, and it will not surprise me if it results in his arrest. Weather still beautiful, but I fear that the great smoke hanging over us will bring heavy rains, and embarrass our locomotion. Night has come, but brings no fight. There has been an exchange of a few random shots, killing and wounding some twenty or thirty.

13*th*.—At a quarter past 9 o'clock, picket firing commenced, and at 9 1-2 o'clock the enemy opened with artillery, on our left wing. In a few minutes the engagement was general. The smoke hangs thick and heavy, making it impossible to tell, this morning, whether the enemy is in force here, or whether his opening the fight is a ruse to cover his falling back. My own opinion is, that he means fight. If he had intended to fall back, he would have taken advantage of our crossing, then have opened on us and have fallen back under the fire. Large fires were seen all night in the rear of his lines, which many inferred were from the burning of his stores, preparatory to a retreat.   I entertain no such thought. His position is too strong, and should there fall a heavy rain during the battle, it would, by inundating the large flats on which we are posted, render the situation of our army an exceedingly perilous one.   I have not a doubt that the enemy has seen this, and *permitted us* to cross.   I saw some very bad surgery yesterday, and I here enter the remark, that I have witnessed but four amputations by other surgeons since I came to the army, and two of those *had to be amputated a second time,* before they could be dressed. This speaks very badly for our Surgeons.

Night has come, and the firing has ceased.   It has been a terrible day.   The wounded have been sent in to us in great numbers.   I have been amputating and otherwise operating all day.   The result of the battle I do not know.   It certainly has not been decisive on either side, and although the wounded brought to us talk freely of "our victory," I am strongly inclined to the opinion that we have had the worst of it.   Gen. Vinton is wounded, and now lies in the hospital. Gen. Bayard, Chief of our artillery, and Gen. Campbell, also lie near me, the former mortally, the latter badly wounded.

The enemy is very strongly posted, and I exceedingly doubt our ability to dislodge him.   I hear hints of the want of hearty co-operation of our subordinate Generals.   I have feared this from the start, but I will not yet credit it.

Whatever is the result it has been a terrible day, and I now write amidst the groans of the wounded, just dressed, but not yet had time to be relieved of pain.

In my letter of the 10th inst., to C——, I prophesied that we should cross without much fighting; that when we should cross, the enemy would contest every inch of ground, but that if Burnside was heartily sustained by his officers he would drive the enemy. The two first have been fulfilled to the letter. He has not yet driven the enemy, but the fight is not over, and has he had hearty co-operation? On this last point we are not informed. I hope he has, for I would rather suffer defeat honorably, than gain success amidst the treachery of our trusted officers.

14th.—Sunday is again ushered in with a fight. At 7 this morning our batteries opened with a few guns, but the firing is not active. Our long line of battle extends across the vast plain, and is now (8 A. M.) rapidly advancing, apparently to renew the combat in earnest. The enemy is posted in a wood, on a chain of high hills, each one of which is a Gibraltar. Our Generals seem determined to take the position at whatever cost. God send them success, but I have misgivings. With an army of as good fighting men as are in the world opposed to us, with numbers greater than our own, and in much stronger position, my misgivings are not culpable.

9½.—All has been quiet for an hour—probably the lull before a storm. I have just left, lying in one room, Generals Bayard, Campbell and Vinton—the two first mortally, the last severely wounded. Gen. Gibbons is, I hear, in another part of the house, and I am told must lose an arm.

1 P. M.—The battle is not renewed. What does it mean? A telegram is said to have been just received, stating that our gunboats have taken Fort Darling, and are at Richmond. This may, if true, account for our not renewing the attack. In that event the capture or dispersing of Lee's army here will be only a question of time, and a short time at that, for if Richmond is taken they are cut off from their supplies, and must give way. But suppose it is not true, what then? And why stand we here all the day idle? My construction

of the whole matter is simply this : that yesterday's experience taught us the impracticability of dislodging the enemy by direct force, or that there is a want of co-operation amongst our officers, and that they are in council, devising some strategic plan, to either advance or get back.

5 o'clock.—A rumor is afloat, seeming authentic, (a General has just told me that it is positively so,) that Gen. Sigel has crossed the river with his corps some miles above, and will to-night be in position in rear of the enemy. If true, we shall have lively times to-morrow.

The estimated loss of our left wing in yesterday's fight is 3,500 in killed and wounded. From the center I have not heard. The loss on the right is said to have been somewhere from twelve hundred to three thousand. I am inclined to believe that the largest figure is much nearest the truth.

The day has closed without a renewal of the fight, and now everything looks as if the morrow was to be the day of days in the attempt to take the Heights. There is only one thing which leads me to doubt it, and that is the publicity which is given to the statements to that effect. In my letter of the 10th inst. I stated my disbelief of the statement that we should cross the river next morning at 2 o'clock, *because* of the publicity given to the decision of the council of war which decided that we should. We did not cross. I now doubt the statement that we are to renew the fight in the morning, only because everybody knows it. Even Major-Generals have been here and said that our wounded Generals must be taken from the hospital, " because they will be too much exposed in the fight to take place to-morrow." When an army is to make an important move its Generals do not publish it the day before. Yet our troops are buoyant in the expectation of driving the enemy to-morrow. They love Gen. Burnside, and their confidence in him is already more uniform than it ever was in McClellan, and it is of a different kind—no party feeling mingled with it. It is a confidence in him as a man and a General. Much stir and activity of some kind is discoverable in the enemy's camp to-night, and a report has just come in that they are retreating. I do not believe it. The record of the hospital for the last two days is just made up. Two hundred and four operated on, amputated, and dressed in the two wards of this hospital yesterday after 12 o'clock, and all laid away comfortably before 10 at night—a pretty good half day's work. Seventy have been operated on and dressed to-day.

15th.—"How brightly breaks the morning" clear and beautiful. What of the passions and ambitions of the hosts marshalled in hostile array to each other? Oh that they were calm and unspotted as the bright sun which shines on them and lights their way to this wholesale and legitimate murder. I have been a backwoodsman; have lain concealed, and by false calls have lured the wary turkey within range of the deadly rifle. I have climbed the forest tree, and from this ambush have watched the cautious deer as he came at hot summer eve to lave his sides and slake his thirst at the bubbling spring, and have slaughtered him in the midst of his enjoyment. I have lain behind the precipice to surprise the wily wolf as in hot pursuit of his intended victim he became rash and incautious, and by a shot I have arrested his life current and his chase. But never have I planned with half the care with which man here decoys and plans against the life of his fellow man, or felt half the pleasure at my success as do our men of God, when, at their nightly prayers, they in the same breath thank that God for the murders we have been permitted to perpetrate—the misery to inflict—and ask for peace on earth, and good will to man.

'Tis 10 o'clock, and no action has commenced. Has there been some change in the rebel positions since yesterday to delay us, or did I judge rightly when I supposed that the public promises of a fight to-day were made to deceive the enemy, not doubting that some traitor or deserter would manage to get the word into their lines?

Orders have come to send our wounded to the other side of the river, and now at 12 o'clock a city of hospital tents is being built up on the plain about a mile further back, but in full view, because we are too near to the expected scene of action. But why, if we expected a fight to-day, was this not done yesterday? It looks very like a ruse of some kind. I do not quite understand it, but something's in the wind. I have been gratified to find, in my rounds to-day, that my patients seem to be doing so well.

Having sent all the wounded to the rear, at half-past 2 o'clock the surgeons received orders to evacuate immediately the premises we had so busily and so bloodily occupied, and to "re-cross the river." This order being rather indefinite, I took occasion when across to select my whereabouts, so I rode up to a point opposite to Fredericksburg, which I found that our troops had saved from entire destruction by extinguishing the fire when the enemy evacuated it. I there found General Sumner's troops in full possession, and heard that General Lee had this morning given us notice to leave it in six hours, (improbable.) Whether true or not, he had just commenced shelling the city, but, during the half hour that I watched proceedings, with very little effect. I then hunted up the new locality of our hospital, where I now sit, and where I wait for "our misguided brothers" on the other side to send me work to do.

9 p. m.—Night has come, without any important action during the day. I have just received intelligence that our troops are recrossing the river in force! Can it be that we are retreating? Is this the key to the apparent indiscretion of our Commanders, in proclaiming from the house tops, preparations for a battle? If so, it is a shrewd move. I do not like the idea of falling back. However, if we have become satisfied that we cannot force the enemy's position, nor draw them on to the plain, 'tis better to withdraw and try some other plan, than to sacrifice our men in a struggle where it is evident we must lose. The whispers of two days ago, that there is disaffection, or defection amongst the officers, is swelling into murmurs, and I confess my fear that it is not without reason. At two points, to my knowledge, during the hard day's fight, the enemy was dislodged from his entrenchments, yet we almost immediately withdrew and permitted him to repossess them. Why? But there is a story current, that General Jackson (Stonewall) made an attempt to cross to our side to-day, and that it is only General Smith's corps of our army that is recrossing, to guard against any possibility of his success, should he attempt it again.

16th.—I am too stupid, to-night, to write intelligibly even a journal of the day. After we had shaken the broken and grating bones of our wounded, by moving them in ambulances, yesterday, we had scarcely got the poor fellows lifted out and placed quietly on a coating of straw on the ground, when we received orders to reload them for a move farther to the rear; so we worked nearly all night, and by daylight, were thoroughly rain-soaked. This morning, having reloaded them all, we moved about two miles further to the rear, repitched our tents, dumped the men into them, and, for the first time since Friday morning, commenced dressing their wounds. But what was my surprise, on rising the hill on this side of the river, to find all of our great army encamped as quietly as if they had been settled there for a month, and that our pontooniers had taken up the bridges? *We are all back!* What next? I am hardly in condition to reason much about it to-night, but, taking it all together, and admitting the necessity of a withdrawal, from whatever cause, I must think it one of the most brilliant achievements of the war. The great preparatians of two days in the face of the enemy, as if for a decisive battle, the giving out, on the authority of the Generals themselves, that it would certainly be fought, the mannei of moving the wounded, and the pitching of the hospital tents, and filling them with patients, in full view of the enemy; the story got up of Jackson's attempting to cross, and the necessity of *one* corps of our army recrossing to prevent him, thus so thoroughly deceiving our own troops, that each corps supposed that it was the only one recrossing; and the strengthening of our pickets and videttes that night, all so completely deceived the enemy, as well as our own army, that not a gun was fired or a suspicion entertained of our retreat.

17th.—To this day I have lived fifty four years—cui bono? With all my defects in moral, mental and physical organization, I believe that in the aggregate of these powers, God has favored me, up to the average of men. Have I used those capabilities up to their power, for good? If asked positively, I do not hesitate to say, No! There have been many opportunities for me to do good, which I have not embraced; but if asked comparatively, I as unhesitatingly answer, Yes? No man is perfect, and few, I think, have struggled harder or more unselfishly to be useful and to alleviate the sufferings of others than I have. As, then, I have failed, by my own admission, to do all I could, but have satisfied my conscience, by striving to do better than others, shall I continue to be satisfied with this measure of my efforts? Can any man, with that alone as his guide, say and feel that he wholly divests himself of the motives of public approbation, and that there is not, after all, something of selfishness in his efforts. I fear that a close examination of this question, would, to my conscience, be less pleasant than profitable. Rivalry is a motive necessary to advancement, but unsupported, it is a weak staff on a long journey through a life of temptations. Support it, however, by a desire to live for other's good, and the lame and the halt may lean on it with confidence and with comfort. God grant that for the short time remaining to me, I may have all these for my support, and that I may live more usefully than I have done.

> " Teach me to feel another's woe,
> To hide the faults I see."

Well, I am at a loss to judge what will be the next move in the great game now being played. I am two to three miles from the army, and being shut up in my hospital, I have less means of judging than if I were in Washington or Wisconsin. But how little, oh, how little, do our people at a distance from the seat of war realize of the sufferings it inflicts, say nothing of the abandonment of homes, where only the joys of childhood can be recalled in all their freshness, where the whole history of the family is written on the very walls and trees, to which we bid farewell forever, where little " tracks in the sand" constantly remind us of our deep but joyous responsibilities of directing little footsteps to good, to high, to holy walks, or where the little empty arm-chair chains us, through sad memories by a tie stronger even than that of our joys. Say nothing of the thousands of larger chairs made vacant, and the deep heart aches which they cause, still the sufferings, little, when compared with these, would strike terror to the minds of those who have not witnessed these scenes of distress.

At a farm house. in the yard of which we have our medi-cal headquarters, I met this morning a young lady of gen-teel appearance. I soon learned that she was from Freder-icksburg. It was a cold morning. Rude soldiers, and officers not much more polite, regardless of the comforts of the household, had filled every space and had crowded her, with the rest, into the open air. Her teeth chattered from the cold. I invited her to my tent, in which was a good, warm stove. With a look of surprise, a little hesitation and a pleasant laugh at the novelty of the situation, she accepted my invitation. Having remained with her a few minutes, and obtained her promise to dine with me, I left her in the enjoyment of the warm stove. I found her highly educated, and a lady. Her father had died, leaving a handsome pro-perty in the city of Fredericksburg, the rents of which sup-ported the family aristocratically. During the dinner, I made a laughing apology for offering her some sweet meats on a tin plate, with an iron spoon. The cord which she had held tense and tightly, now gave way. Dropping knife and fork, she exclaimed: "Oh, sir! excuse me. Two days ago this would have been palatable, though eaten on the trodden road, but now I cannot eat; five days of fasting and anxiety have destroyed even my power to hunger, and here I am a starving beggar, dependent even for shelter on the charity of the poor paralytic owner of this house, who has not a mouthful to feed himself, his wife and children. Oh! my poor, poor mother!" "May I know what of your mother, Miss G———?" "Four days ago I stood near you, as you watched from the river bank the shelling of our city, I witnessed the pleasure with which you noted the precision of the shot which fired the veranda of my mother's house.* In that house I last saw her, ten days ago. Oh, my God, where is she to-day? Old and feeble, she could not get away!"

"But did you abandon her there?"

"When you ordered the evacuation of the city, within six hours, I was from home. I did not hear of it till the time had expired, and since I have been denied admittance to the city, and have had no means of learning how or where she is. Can not you, sir, procure me a pass through your lines?"

She told me, too, of her sister, whose husband, a Colonel in the rebel army, was killed in battle two months ago. Three days after, her sister died of a broken heart, leaving in her charge an orphan child of two years; and this child, too, was left in the city, with its grandmother. How many years of civil life would it require to accumulate the misery historied in these dozen lines, intended only as an apology for a lady's want of appetite? The misery of herself, the starvation of the paralytic and his large family, the deaths of the heart-broken sister and her husband, the orphanage of the child, and the destitution of the poor decriped mother! and not a tear did I shed at her distress. Did my benevolence owe a single tear to each case as bad as this, my whole

---

* I remember it well, and a beautiful house it was.

life-current converted into tears, would never pay the debt; yet it is well to record a case, occasionally, that when I feel inclined to complain of my lot, it may serve to remind me of how much worse it might be.

After dinner, Surgeons and attendants were collected to dress the wounded, who were operated on four days ago. As I halted at the door of the tents containing the two hundred mangled men, I thought of the three-fifths of the amputations which had proved fatal, after the battle of Hanover. I pictured to my mind the two-fifths who had died within five days after the battle of Antietam, and I rallied all my fortitude to meet with composure the anxious dying looks of the poor fellows who had been jostled and dragged from place to place, for four days, and whose dependence on me had won for them my affections. Oh! who would be a Surgeon?

Before sun-down, all were dressed, and every man deposited in ambulances for general hospital, and except some four or five, wounded in organs which rendered them necessarily mortal, to our surprise, we found every wound doing well, every patient apparently recovering, and as we left them with a farewell, and heard the muttered prayers and benedictions of the poor sufferers, I found a tear to spare. Who would *not* be a Surgeon?

18*th*.—To-day has been spent in clearing up, as if in preparation for a move or a battle. We have given our surplus "hard talk," with some tea, coffee, sugar and other necessaries of life to the poor, paralytic old man, whose premises we have occupied. He is an uncompromising rebel, but humanity forbids that we should permit him to starve.

What will be the effect of this repulse on the spirits of the army? I shall watch with much solicitude. For the Commander-in-Chief, it has happened at a most inauspicious moment. He had just superceded General McClellan, who had many warm friends, who stood ready to take advantage of every misstep, or misfortune of the new Commander, and to turn it to the credit of their friend, now in disgrace. Though the army was rapidly growing into an affection for General Burnside, the feeling was of new growth, and not yet confirmed by long acquaintance, by trials, or by successes. The friends of McClellan, true to the instincts of human nature, will magnify the reverses, whilst they will withhold credit for the merits of the manœuvre. Already General Burnside's friends are finding it necessary to defend him against the attacks of the croakers, by following the example set by the friends of McClellan on the Peninsula, in attributing the failures to the interference of the President, to General Halleck, or to Mr. Secretary Stanton. For my own part, I feel that defence is unnecessary, for when I consider the fact, that public opinion compelled the crossing and the attack on Fredericksburg; that no commander could have withstood the outside pressure, however great the danger of advance; when I recollect the successful crossing in the face of so large a force, the successful attack and capture of part of the heights, the falling back, made necessary by the tardiness of some of his Generals to support him, the ruse of clearing the decks for action, the removal of the hospitals and wounded to a point out of reach of fire, yet in full view of the enemy, the withdrawal of the army so quietly and so adroitly that even his own divisions were deceived into the belief by each, that it was the only division recrossing, altogether mark it as one of the most adroitly managed military manœuvres since the crossing of the Delaware by General Washington.

19th.—To-day we have fallen back on to the same camping ground which we left on the 11th to advance to the capture of Fredericksburg. How different the feelings of the soldiery on that beautiful moonlight morning, whilst they struck and loaded their tents amid their cheering huzzas, and bidding farewell to the ground which they supposed they were placing in their rear forever, from what they are to-night. Whilst beaten and repulsed, they are this moment re-pitching their tents on the identical spot where they cherished such bright visions of glory. 'Tis unfortunate that we did not find some other place to fall back on.

20th.—A deep gloom hangs over the army to-day. I have at no time seen it so depressed—depressed not only at its new defeat, but at its own halting between opinions. Though the affection of the soldiers for Gen. Burnside was warm and active, it had not been confirmed by trials and experience, and the "expectant friends of Gen. McClellan" are still busy in taking advantage of this defeat to depreciate Gen. Burnside in the confidence of the army. This causes halting in opinions, and fears that our new Commander-in-Chief may not prove competent to the charge entrusted to him. It is of a piece with the McClellan tactics. Rule or ruin has been the motto of many of his friends.

21st.—Oh the glorious letter of Gen. Burnside! He asks no subterfuge to hide him from what others might deem the disgrace of defeat. His honor overrules his reticence, and he comes nobly to the rescue of his commander, of the Secretary of War, of the President, of the Government. Right or wrong, he assumes the responsibility of the late battle, with all the odium. I feel that he may safely do so, and await the verdict of history, which in my opinion will place this in the list of the most brilliant military manœuvres. But how different his course from that of some others whose reticence prevailed, and whose high sense of honor could permit them to listen to abuses heaped on the Government for their acts, without the manliness to come boldly to the rescue. How plain the line between the patriot and the partisan! We feel joyous to-night. This letter is a strike. We have an honest man to lead us, and we will follow his lead.

22nd.—This morning I tendered my resignation ; it is approved by the Colonel, and has gone forward. I am worn out by the labor of the last year and a half, and feel the necessity of withdrawing from the army. I trust that it will be accepted, and that I may be permitted to retire and rest for a time. I shall leave the regiment with regret. for I have grown to love it, both individually and in mass. But it is necessary.

We probably go into winter quarters now.

23d.—"More trouble in the wigwam." Charges are preferred against the Colonel of the regiment with view to a court martial and dismissal from the service. 'Twill amount to nothing more than to hurry his resignation, which he has for some time had in contemplation.

24th.—My resignation is accepted. I am no longer a surgeon in the army, and to-morrow I leave the camp for a home.

Go now, little book, and tell the world you have a mission. Tell it you have been entrusted with secret thoughts which to divulge would be dishonorable, but for the hope that they may assist in rescuing from disgrace or from opprobrium an army of as noble patriots as ever went to battle; that the half a million of their sons, sent to Maryland and Virginia by New England and New York, by Pennsylvania, Ohio, Indiana, Illinois, Michigan, Iowa and Wisconsin, were not their effete children, but their very bone and sinew—their pride and their hope. If the world reply that your secrets are sad ones, ask it to lay aside all prejudices and prepossessions, and to answer frankly if the scenes of wrong and abuse of that noble army in which you have had your existence, are not enough to preclude from the head or heart of the philanthropist all ideas or feelings other than sad ones. Whilst the world claims that the army of the Potomac, during the dates of this diary, was a failure, does it, or even the party politician, claim that its material was of either cowards or effeminates? Let its quiet submission and discipline, under eight months of inaction, at Washington, or its unflinching gallantry and endurance, under the seven days fight before Richmond, shame the traducer. Come Maine and Massachusetts, Connecticut and Rhode Island, New Hampshire and Vermont, say Western and Middle States, did you send cowards to the army of the Potomac? Why then has it been a failure?

Go, little book, and if the world charge that you are effeminate or puerile, tell it that you, no more than it, were the artificer of your own power or weakness. Tell it of the adverse circumstances through which you have struggled, and challenge its wonder that you even exist. Tell it that whilst you struggled through eight months of infancy, in an atmosphere stagnant of all but political breezes, your lot might have been cast in the invigorating blasts of Donelson or Pea Ridge; that whilst you struggled under the crushing misfortune of Ball's Bluff, you might have been expanding in the successes of Springfield, or of Romney; that whilst you waited and watched the stove pipes at Munson's Hill, and

the wooden guns at Manassas, you might have been cheered
by the tonic thunders of columbiads and howitzers at Win-
chester and Shiloh ; that you were dwarfed in witnessing the
tremendous antics of poor Hancock playing "hide and go
seek" behind the walls of Williamsburg, whilst fate might
have changed the whole current of your existence by casting
your lot in the midst of foray with the gallant and daring
Garfield ; that in depressing shame you were gallopading
with a handful of horsemen around the entire army under
McClellan asleep, whilst you might have proudly witnessed
the capture of a whole rebel fleet on the Mississippi, or by
waiting a little might have made a daring dash into the pure
mountain air of Tennessee, with the bold and gallant Carter,
always awake; that whilst you languished under the apathy and
"starvation policy" which buried so many thousands in the
sickly swamps of Warwick and Chickahominy, you might have
been winning vitality under Foote and Grant in active campaigns among the sicklier bayous and lagoons of the Mississippi ; that whilst you might have been with Pope, as like
the lofy spire he invited the lightning's stroke, and led away
the destroying bolt, you were cooped and confined in the endangered edifice till after the storm had passed, when the
structure fell on the rod which saved, twisting, warping,
bending, but not destroying it ; but tell it boldly, and draw
vigor from your boldness, that time and history will straighten
every angle in that rod, will brighten every point, and raise
it, that like Israel's emblem in the wilderness, it may carry
encouragement to good works for all who look upon it; tell
the censorious world that you sickened in sympathy with that
noble army at Antietam, baptised in its own tears of disappointment and chagrin when it was denied the golden opportunity to retrieve its honor which had been sacrificed, or to

win the glory for which it pined, and this at the moment when you might have been buoyed and toned up by taking part in the inspiring chase at Iuka; tell it that that army, which it has called a failure, and loaded with degrading epithets, *though it was never whipped in battle, was never* PERMITTED *to win a victory !** that even in its retreats, in obedience to orders, no enemy, however large, ever trod upon its heels without paying dearly for its rashness. But "thus far shalt thou go and no farther." 'Twas never permitted to win a victory. Why? I do not believe that "the incompetency of the Commanding General" is so great as to disqualify him from answering this question, nor that "his reticence" should forbid his telling why this army, which could never be whipped, became under his command a by-word and a reproach? Why during the year and a quarter it gained no honors, won no glory, suffered no defeats, and achieved no victory? If he will not answer, then go on little book, and be in turn the catechist; ask if these results may not have been in some measure dependant on the commander's great faculty of "destroying his enemies by making them his friends?" Ask how it is that, all rebeldom having been his enemy, not a rebel throat can now be found, from the Aroostook to the Gulf of Mexico, which is not always ready to enlarge and elongate to sing hosannas to McClellan—but not

---

*Never whipped after its reorganization in the fall of 1861. The cavilling reader may claim that this army was whipped on the 27th June, at the Chickahominy. He would make a mistake, the whole force of Lee was precipitated on its right wing under Porter, and after a day of as severe fighting as any of the war, stopped only by the darkness. Porter being flanked, crossed the river in order, and formed on the center. Early in the morning the enemy renewed the attack, and was repulsed with severe loss. As well might the enemy claim that he whipped Gen. Rosecrans at Stone River, because for a time his right wing was driven back, and he had to change his order of battle.

always "for the Union." He left his army in disgrace. It had never won a victory, whilst he had "destroyed most of his enemies by making them HIS friends. Ask if *his* semi-Warwickian faculty had anything to do with the disgrace which hovered over his noble army? Did ever rocket rush up from signal hands with such rapidity as Lee and Longstreet, Jackson, Hill and Ewell, mounted from obscurity to greatness in the presence of McClellan? What a pity it would be if some successor should prick the bubble of this semi-decemvirate, and bring it down to the same plane on which Beauregard, Pemberton, Price, Magruder and Bragg, are now made to dance to the fiddling of Grant, and Foote, and Rosecrans, and teach it how easy for men of ordinary stature to become giants amongst Lilliputians! Ask if the waning of the phosphoric lights received from contact with their great prototype by Porter and Franklin, is in consequence of the rising sun of Burnside, and of the true fire which Hamilton has lighted at Iuka?*

Go forth, little book, fearless of critics; you will never suffer from their censoriousness, and should now and then a "galled jade wince," dodge the heels, and be sure you have "touched the raw." Tell all the world that for the sufferings which your author shared with the army of the Potomac, he loves it and its reputation with a deep affection, and that if

---

*It may not be generally known that whilst the army of the Potomac was waiting before Yorktown, and sickening by hundreds daily, Gen. Hamilton, of Wisconsin, having acquainted himself with the strength of the enemy, begged of the Commander-in-Chief permission to take the town with his brigade alone, giving his opinion that he could do it, or at least that he could open the enemy's lines, so as to permit our army to pass, with less loss of life than he was now suffering in the ditches. For this he was arrested and disgraced. He appealed to Congress, was reinstated, ordered to the Mississippi, and distinguished himself in the several battles in which he fought there.

your advent shall relieve that army of one undeserved reproach, and lay the blame where it properly belongs, he will excuse you for this betrayal of his secret thoughts, and feel more than doubly paid for all the labor he has bestowed on you.

June, 1863.

APPENDIX.

As an appropriate Appendix to this book, I feel it incumb-
bent on me, as a Surgeon in the army, to make full acknowledgment tó the United States Sanitary Commission for
the immense benefit it has conferred on the sick and wounded soldiers under my care, and for the consolations it has
afforded, through me, to anxious and enquiring friends. I
know of no manner in whicfl I can better perform this duty
than in giving a simple epitomised history of the acts of that
Commission. Should it speak in terms of commendation of
the institution, I beg the reader to bear in mind that he 's
reading, not my eulogy, but its history.

The immense benefits resulting to the armies of the Crimea,
from the organization of a Sanitary Commission, early suggested to benevolent men in this country, the advantages to
be derived from a similar organization for our armies, and at
their suggestion, the President, the Secretary of War, and
the Surgeon General of the United States, granted to them,
as a United States Sanitary Commission, certain privileges,
and required of them the performance of certain duties. At
the same time Congress appointed a Committee to confer
with them, and to tender them not only the facilities for carrying relief to the soldiers, but money for its expenses and

authority to carry out its designs. The Commission declined all pecuniary aid from the Government, preferring to be untrammelled by those forms characterized as "red tape," which cause so much vexatious delay at the very times when promptness of relief is imperatively demanded, and threw itself confidingly on the humanity, the liberality and the patriotism of the people, asking that the suffering soldier should receive aid through the voluntary contributions of friends at home, rather than by compulsory taxation. How nobly that confidence has been met, let the following statements attest :

It declined, also, all authority to enforce its designs, confiding rather in the soldier's sense of appreciation of the kindness to be tendered, and in the interest of commanding officers in the health and efficiency of their men, for that welcome to the army which would enable it to carry to the battle fields and hospitals the thousands of supplementary comforts which the heavy machinery of Government could never furnish ; and thus it stepped boldly into the strife with no authority but its reliance on the respect of the soldier, with no means save its trust in Providence, and its dependence on the broad benevolence of a mighty people, battling for a mighty cause.

The Commission, thus organized, started on its mission of mercy, proposing but few methods of carrying relief to the army, but so liberal have been the contributions, that it has been enabled greatly to multiply those methods. It now supports—

1st.—Its system of General Inspectors. These are medical men, who constantly accompany the army, pointing out and superintending the removal of all the exciting causes of sickness about camps and hospitals, suggesting improvements for the health and comfort of the troops, investigating the wants of the sick and wounded, and keeping the Government and the heads of the Commission advised of the needed supplementary supplies. The immense labor of these inspectors in the armies of the Mississippi are of such world-wide notoriety as to need no proof here, that their duties have been well and faithfully performed. Those in the army of the Potomac have been so immediately under the eye of the Government, and of the head of the Commission, that neglect of duty there would be almost impossible. Of the army of the Cumberland, Professor Frank H. Hamilton, a United States Government Inspector, and a gentleman of extensive information in such matters, in writing officially of its police, says : " It is better *than I have ever seen in any volunteer army !*" The testimonials of Generals Rosecrans, Sheridan and Negley, on this subject. have been so extensively published, that it is necessary only to refer to them in this Appendix, to prove how highly they prize the labors of this branch of the Sanitary Commission.

That the contributors to this Commission may form some idea of the value of their contributions, I offer a few statistics. The British Sanitary Commission, which suggested this branch of duties to the United States Commission, was organized under these circumstances: " In the Crimea, during the two years ending with March, 1856, 16,224 died of diseases of which 14,476 were of the zymotic or preventable class," that is, more than four-fifths of all who died might have been saved by proper Sanitary Inspections, and the British Commission was organized to arrest such seemingly unnecessary loss of life. Did it succeed ?

Mr. Elliott, in his report on the mortality and sickness of the United States Volunteer forces says : " During the win-

ter of 1854–5, embracing seven months, from September to
March, inclusive, the annual death rate from diseases (in the
army of the Crimea,) was 665 per 1,000. During the cor-
responding seven *months of* 1855–6, *the rate was reduced to*
48 *per* 1,000 (!)* For January, 1855, the *annual* death rate
was 1,174 per 1,000. For the same month in 1856, it was
but twenty-five per 1,000. For February, 1855, the rate was
979 per 1,000; whilst for February, 1856, the annual rate
in the same army was but 12 per 1,000. Now, these changes
as resulting from the system of inspections and removal of
the causes of disease, by the British Commission, are most
wonderful, nor is it less surprising, that under the supervision and inspection of the United States Commission, the
death rates in our army have been constantly kept to about
the lowest figures gained in the Crimean army, under the inspection of the British Commission. It is fair to infer then,
that had the British Commission been organized at the commencement of the Crimean war, ninety per cent of the deaths
occurring during the first year, would have been prevented,
or, that had not the United States Commission been organized, the death rate would have been multiplied in this, in
about the same proportion that it was decreased in that army,
and the friends of the soldier then would have had more
cause for anxiety at the close of each day of quiet in the
army, than they now need have during the most destructive
battles of the war. How well have their contributions to
sustain this system of general inspections been repaid ?

2nd.—A system of Special Inspectors of Hospitals: "Emi-
nent medical men, temporarily employed to make rounds of
inspection of the military hospitals." Amongst those who
have been employed for this purpose, I mention the names

---

* Between these two periods, the British Sanitary Commission was instituted.

of Professors Alfred Post, of New York, Gunn, of Ann Arbor, Goldsmith, of Louisville, Bigelow, of Boston, as sufficient guarantees that in this department of the Commission the contributions have been judiciously applied.

3rd.—A system of General Relief: "For the production, transmission and distribution of needed supplies not furnished by the Government." When I consider the vastness of the work being performed under this department, and the good resulting from it, I painfully realize my inability to present the subject in a manner to give the reader the least idea of it. The little child who has but strength to tear a bandage, the Octogenarian who totters up with his bundle of dressing rags, the poverty-stricken patriot who must deny his comfort to contribute even a quart of beans, the millionare who gives by thousands, the seamstress, the tailor, the merchant, the manufacturer, the chemist, the farmer—all pay tribute through this department to the demands of their own hearts, in the name of humanity, and of their own heads, in the cause of loyalty. The highways, the railroads, the rivers and the oceans are pressed into the service of transporting their contributions. For nearly two years this department has been in operation, during which time it has paid out in cash, over half a milion of dollars, and in different articles of produce, an average of over twenty thousand dollars a day. Yet, for all this, there is no taxation. It is the result solely of the offerings of generous hearts. So extensive and varied has been the relief afforded by this department, that I can barely more than allude to it, and make one instance suffice as an illustration of the good it is accomplishing: Early in April, 1863, the Inspectors discovered that the scurvey was rapidly on the increase in the army of the Cumberland. By the middle of the same month one half of the army was afflicted with scorbutic symptoms. Even slight wounds would have proved fatal to the men in this condition. The army had no issues of vegetables for eight months. The Government could not supply them. The Commission came promptly to its relief, and from its abundance sent forward large quantities of potatoes, onions, pickles and vegetable acids. During the succeeding weeks, one little store house at Murfreesboro, issued to the army, sick and well, three hundred and sixty thousand rations of those articles. The scourge was arrested, and at the end of the three weeks, scarcely a scorbutic taint could be found in the army of the Cumberland. Shortly after the army went to battle, many were wounded, and in all my experience, I never saw the wounded do better, if as well as at this time.

4th.—A system of Soldiers' Homes: In this I include Special Relief Agents engaged "in the distribution of stores, in procuring discharges, pay transportation and pensions for the disabled."

It is unnecessary to remind the reader that around the pay offices there has always hovered a flock of harpies, watching for opportunities to fatten on the misfortunes of even the crippled soldiers. The soldier, disabled in battle, procures his discharge and starts for his home, without money or a knowledge of the liberal means provided by Government for his transportation. He reaches the first Paymaster on the route, twenty, or, perhaps one hundred miles from his regiment. He presents his discharge papers to collect his pay. An error is discovered in them. By the carelessness or ignorance of some one of the many officers under whose pens they had to pass, a word is omitted, or the form not exactly complied with, and he cannot collect his pay till his papers go back to the regiment for correction. He has no money, either to go forward or to return. He is perfectly at the mercy of the harpies. The whole flock light on him; omnibus, boarding house harpies, the lawyer, the broker—each sends his harpy, till, in despair he assigns his papers to any one who will have them corrected, and when they get back, will pay him over the money. But before that is done, not a cent is left to help him on his way. Mother, your son lies crippled and in want, robbed of the little means he had. He is dying in despair in the street, among strangers. He finds—

"No heart to pity, nor a hand to save."

Such was the case. But now, on all the routes travelled by soldiers, wherever you find a stationed paymaster, beside him is "a soldier's home." On the stopping of a train or a boat, the kind voice of the sanitary agent cheers your crippled boy. "Will you let me see your papers? Ah! here is a mistake in them, you cannot get your pay till they are returned and corrected." But before he has time to be depressed by this sad statement, he is ushered into a cheerful, comfortable "home," where, without money and without price, he is taken care of till the papers can be returned and the error corrected. They are sent back where agents of the commission receive them, and as soon as steam and rail can return them, your boy is again on his homeward way. Perhaps, kind mother, when the error in the papers is discovered, the disappointment of your boy may reveal the sad fact that *time* is an essential with him; that the oil in his lamp may be nearly exhausted, and that he may by the delay be shut out from the sweet privilege of dying at his home, or perhaps he may be hurrying on in the hope of receiving the last caresses of a dying mother. He is not allowed to wait. The Sanitary Commission becomes his paymaster, breaks the barriers of "red tape," advances him his pay, and hurries him on to family and friends. But who does this charity? The Government? The Commission? Neither, madam. 'Twas yourself. Oh could every woman, as she spends an hour in lively talk over her sewing, in her own little meetings for the benefit of the soldiers, could each hale and happy farmer, as he sends forward his barrel of potatoes, or each millionaire, as he empties his purse at the call of the little committees at home, realize—fully realize—the misery he relieves—the power for good which he or she is creating, what a source of home happiness it would add to the great relief it affords abroad.

Over eighty thousand disabled soldiers have been thus taken care of since the organization of this commission. How many hours of pain and anxiety have been relieved! How few are made poorer by what they have done!

5th.—Closely allied to this last is the establishment of hospital cars and boats, on all important routes connected with the army. An average of one hundred soldiers, unable to travel without help, is daily transported in beds on railroads or boats, through the aid of this system of relief. The cars and boats are furnished with physicians, nurses, agents, and all things needed to insure the comfort of the soldier.

6th.—Hospital Directories—The soldier is often in hospital too sick to write home; often moved from one hospital to another so frequently that friends cannot find him. The Commission keeps a directory, in which is recorded from day to day the names of all soldiers admitted to or removed from the general hospitals, in all parts of the United States. Through this system any one can, by writing or telegraphing to the Commission, ascertain the situation of his friend, also his condition, whether sick, wounded, discharged or dead.

The above are but a small part of the duties of the Commission, but a desire to do it justice has induced me to extend this appendix far beyond my original design. I close it with the remark that in all my experience with the army of the Potomac, the Commission was an inestimable power in the relief of the sick and wounded, and that in my observations with the army of the Cumberland, its beneficence has been even more marked than on the Potomac. If this statement of the object and of the workings of the Commission will not suggest a duty to every patriot, my own suggestions would fall on them, as they would on those who refuse to hear Moses and the Prophets.

THE NEW WISCONSIN FORM BOOK.

A Compendium of Legal and Practical Forms, with principles of law, adapted to the Statutes of Wisconsin, including a digest of amendments and judicial decisions, designed for the use of Business Men, County and town officers, the Legal Profession, and all classes in the community, to which are added complete official forms and instructions, under the recent Bounty and Pension Acts; by Joseph F McMullen, Attorney at Law, Milwaukee, Wisconsin.

THE NEW WISCONSIN FORM BOOK, which we are now printing, will be ready in August, 1863. The price of it will be THREE DOLLARS; at which price we will sent it by mail, *free of expense*, to the purchaser.

We wish to procure Agents to sell the work in every part of the State. The discount we allow, will enable any active Agent to make good wages. Persons who wish to act as Agents, can learn terms, &c., &c., by addressing us by mail, enclosing a stamp to pay postage on our reply.

We are now printing a new edition of

ALL ABOUT THE TAX LAW,

Ten Cents Each—75 Cents per Dozen. Postage twelve cents per dozen.

THE TAX LAW COMPLETE,

As amended by the Act which passed finally March 4, 1863, with all the rates imposed, including the New License Taxes, together with a Complete Stamp Directory.

Full Directions for every class of Business, and all kinds of property subject to Excise Duties; especially important to Mechanics, Manufacturers, Professional and Business Men, and all who have to pay taxes; alphabetically arranged, embracing every pursuit and every article taxed:

To which is added the complete

CONSCRIPT ACT, OR NATIONAL MILITIA LAW,

STRICKLAND & CO., Milwaukee, Wisconsin.

We offer at less than Manufacturers' prices

Two Superior Seven Octave Pianos,

Rosewood Case, Iron Frame, Overstrung Bass, and all modern improvements.

THE CRAIG MICROSCOPE.

We cannot interest the curious, inventive, and knowledge-loving portion of the community more than by giving them a decription of a new miscroscope, lately patented and introduced into public notice. It is, indeed, a new revelation to the natural vision, and opens up and extends indefinitely the field of observation and investigation. It is thus described by one who has used it and who knows its merits:

"This beautiful and useful instrument was patented on the 18th day of February last. The microscope, as the reader is aware, is an instrument used to magnify minute objects; it reveals whole races of living beings which the unaided eye has never seen, and enables us to behold the wonderful beauty and adaptation to the purposes for which they were intended, of the most minute parts of animal and vegetable organizations. No field of inquiry is more inviting and promises a richer harvest than that which is opened by the microscope, and few departments of education are more important and interesting than this.

"There are two kinds of microscopes, denominated simple and compound. In a simple microscope we look directly at an object through a single lens, whereas in a compound microscope there are two glasses—one near the object and the other near the eye—and the focus is adjusted by changing the position of one of the glasses. So much time, skill, and patience are required to use a compound microscope, that it has never come into popular use, notwithstanding the wonderful interest which attaches to microscope investigations.

The simple microscope, if of a high power, can be used with but very little satisfaction and comfort, owing to the fact that both the object and the eye must be very near the lens, and it is difficult to get and retain the focus during the examination, as every one is aware who has attempted to use the little lens set in a plate of silver or other metal. But we have now in the "Craig Microscope," an instrument which requires neither skill nor experience, and but little time and patience, to make numerous examinations of microscopic objects. The lens is neatly mounted in hard rubber, at the summit of the instrument; the stand is either of brass or rubber, about five inches high; the focus is on the under or flat surface of the lens, the object glass is placed immediately beneath the lens, and, two or three inches below this, there is a mirror to reflect the light on the under surface of the object and lens. The magnifying power of this instrument is greater than that of the cheapest compound microscope, and in fact is just about the power most frequently required in making microscopic examinations, and the inventor has had the good sense to offer it to the public at a very low price—simply two dollars.

" There is no end to the objects suitable for a microscopic examination—they are innumerable. Take, for illustration, a common house fly. Now, the reader must not expect to place a whole fly in the focus of a microscope which magnifies one hundred diameters, for the field is not large enough —the higher the power the smaller the field of vision—if a whole fly could be magnified one hundred diameters, a full-grown turkey could apparently stand in his shadow, but this is impossible. To examine large opaque objects a simple magnifying glass should be used; of course this has but a limited power. In order that a microscope may be used for this purpose, it must be a compound instrument, and have a separate glass to condense the rays of light on the upper surface of the opaque object, so as to render it visible, and then only a minute portion of the object can be seen at once. To be able to use such an instrument, with any satisfaction, requires an amount of skill, patience, and experience possessed by but few scientific men. The microscope, then, as an instrument for popular use, is intended to examine either very minute objects, or such as are at least sufficiently transparent for the light to shine through them. But to return to the fly: First, we find his feet; we have all noticed the ease with which he walks on the ceiling with his feet up, and we, perhaps, have wondered at this, but the microscope reveals two small sharp claws. But how can he walk on the under surface of smooth glass? surely his claws can be of little service to him here; but on examination we find that he has two pads, or spongy bodies, between the claws, which enable him to adhere to smooth surfaces. Remove his proboscis, and place it beneath the lens, and it will be found to be a wonderful and beautiful object. Shave off the front part of one of the eyes, wash it in a drop of water, and then examine it, and you will find a multitude of small eyes through which the insect looks in different directions, for his eyes are stationary. Examine his wings, for they are worth looking at, although not as beautiful as those of the black wasp and many other insects Next, shave off his face and examine it, and you will find it a beautiful object. Beneath his wing you will find a small scale, or wing, which will pay for the trouble of an examination. So we may examine every part of the fly, which is either very minute or sufficiently transparent for the light to shine through it, and discover new wonders and new beauties. Every insect may be examined in the same way, for no two are alike even in the same parts, and some have additional organs. The bee has his sting, the roach and cricket their antennæ, or feelers; all very beautiful objects when viewed through the microscope. Hair, wool, fur, feathers, silk, linen, scales from a butterfly's wing, small seeds, thin slices of orange, lemon, or apple peel, or of the surface of a strawberry, are only a few of the multitude of interesting objects. Liquids are very readily examined by the aid of this microscope. The globules of the blood, milk, and pus may be seen; also, the animaculæ of stagnant water, and the eels in vinegar. Sugar or salt, partially dissolved, or dissolving, presents a beautiful appearance; and when dissolved and the water allowed to evaporate on the lens, the wonderful manner in which crystals form may be witnessed.

"A fine assortment of microscopic objects, with a microscope, furnishes a chaste and elegant entertainment for friends and neighbors, young and old, far more interesting and instructive than stereoscopic views, and at a less expense. The stereoscope can only be used with a given set of pictures or views, but this microscope can be used to view innumerable objects, of the most beautiful form and color, which the unaided eye can never see, and which cost nothing. In this microscope, then, we have a scientific instrument adapted to popular use, and so simple that a child can use it, and so cheap as to be within the reach of all.

"The microscope, like a book, spy-glass, telescope, &c., should be found in every school house and college, as one of the means and facilities for thorough and complete education. But the microscope likewise makes one of the best, most interesting, and instructive means of entertainment in the family at home."

The farmer who often wishes to examine the insects which infest his crops, will derive great pleasure from the use of it; while the younger members of the family will find it an unfailing source of amusement and instruction.

The price of the microscope is two dollars. It can be sent by mail, at an additional cost of twenty-five cents.

For sale by Strickland & Co., Booksellers, Milwaukee, Wisconsin.